MEATWORKS

MeatWorks

JORDAN CASTILLO PRICE

jcpbooks.com

First published in print in the United States
in 2014 by JCP Books
www.jcpbooks.com

Meatworks. Copyright © 2014 Jordan Castillo Price. All rights reserved. No part of this book may be used or reproduced in any manner whatsoever without written permission except in the case of brief quotations embodied in critical articles and reviews.

This book is a work of fiction. The characters, incidents, and dialogue are drawn from the author's imagination or are used fictitiously.

First Edition

ISBN 978-1-935540-68-7

*For Celia, who found poetry
in the darkness.*

CHAPTER 1

"You're here for the meeting? It's supposed to start at seven. And you are?"

"Me? I'm Desmond Poole."

"Hi, Desmond. I'm Pam Steiner. Come in, make sure you close the door behind you."

Nah, I figured I'd just let it rain in. I forced a smile. Baring my teeth probably wouldn't fool anyone, but I couldn't afford to make a new enemy.

My hostess Pam, a thirtyish chick with sandy, blunt-cut hair and a painfully earnest face, smiled in return. Her smile looked as forced as mine felt.

"I can take your coat. Shoes go there." She took my wet jacket and pointed to a pile of shoes beside the door. Most of the shoes were in pairs. But a few of them were single.

Gah. I knew the support group was a shitty idea. "I'm gonna leave my shoes on."

"Oh, is it an issue with your prosthetic? I thought it was your arm, not your leg."

How she could say the P-word without gagging on it was beyond me. My arm felt like it was full of lead weights. Even though the thing stuck to the end of it supposedly weighed less than my original arm had.

"No, it's an issue with my...socks."

"I'm sorry. I just had the hardwood floors waxed last week, is all."

Pam stood, blocking the doorway from me and effectively trapping me in the front hall until I relinquished my shoes, which would mean being stuck in my socks—and *that* meant no quick getaway. I considered grabbing my jacket away from her and sprinting out the door. But this was my last chance to prove I'd done the mandatory "sharing" that would help me "heal."

Like I'd ever heal.

Unfortunately, my *social worker* said if I kept cutting class, Social Services would stop cutting checks.

Pam clutched my jacket harder. I could wrestle her for it, but half a foot shorter, thirty pounds lighter or not, it was a good possibility that she had a robo-arm too. I didn't know that for a fact, since one of her hands was currently hidden, with my leather jacket draped over it. But come on, why else was Gimp Group being held at her house? If she did have a robo-arm, it'd be just as strong as mine. Plus, she'd probably have a lot better control over hers than I did, given that for the past three months, I'd been doing my best to pretend the hunk of junk on the end of my stump didn't exist. Meanwhile, she'd been hanging balloons off her porch light, dusting off the folding chairs, and laying out a spread of stale cookies and decaf.

I bent, untied my combat boots with my real hand, and slipped them off. Pam was smiling harder when I straightened up. "Okay, then. You're the last one on the list. Shake hands with the housebot and we can get started."

"I'll take a pass."

Pam looked at me like I was nuts. If I didn't "shake" with the housebot, how would it be able to add my temperature preferences to those of the group and adjust the HVAC system accordingly? And the lighting system? And the music mix? While my own preference for old school punk usually resulted in some bizarre selections when I mingled with a group of more conservative folk, and the housebot averaged our musical taste into something that all of us could snigger at...I'd been less than enthused lately about baring my soul to just any old piece of machinery. "If you don't scan in," Pam said, "your social worker won't know you made it to the meeting." She gave a little nervous chuckle. "Besides, if you don't scan in, you could be anybody, and I wouldn't know the difference."

Did I even know anyone who'd be willing to pretend to be me? Maybe someone from the gin mill who wouldn't mind an easy twenty bucks. Too bad none of 'em were gimps. "I'll show you my I.D."

"Theoretically, I mean. I don't actually think you're lying about who you—"

"Couldn't you just call him or something?"

"Call your social worker? On the telephone? I don't think I even have his number." I did, but I was busy convincing myself I'd forgotten it. Pam hugged my jacket to her chest as if by doing so, she could vicariously comfort me. She lowered her voice so that she sounded very confidential and concerned, and said, "Is it some sort of phobia?"

"Something like that."

A muscle twitched in my neck, and my robo-arm flung its fingers wide, like it was so happy to meet Pam it wanted to slip her an exuberant wave whether or not my shoulder chose to get into the act. I ignored it.

"Don't worry," she said, "it's totally safe. There are no moving parts in the scanner. Not one. And I just upgraded a few months ago. It's very fast. You'll have your hand back before you know it."

I would not have my hand back before I knew it. I would not have my hand back, ever. It was an effort not to say as much. Hell, it was an effort not to scream it at the top of my lungs. But I couldn't take the chance that Pam might decide to actually figure out how to use her phone and tattle on me to my *social worker* if I started acting like a prick, so I kept my mouth shut and let the fucking housebot scan my remaining hand.

It wasn't that I was afraid of the dumb thing—I'd repaired enough of them to know there were no moving parts—it was the principle. Can't a guy go somewhere without being read? What if I want to sweat for a change—or shiver? What if I'm in the mood for some country and western? What if I want to tell my *social worker* where I've been and have him take my word for it?

"And here's the group," Pam chirped, leading me into a living room the size of my entire apartment. She introduced me around. There was a young black soldier who'd had his leg blown off in Afghanistan, an older woman who left a foot behind in a car accident, and a paunchy mathematician named Ken Roman. She didn't say what happened to Ken's arm.

"My husband Hugh is on the couch. He won't be staying for the meeting. He's got a project in the garage." Hugh was hovering over a bowl of party mix, the good stuff with only a few pretzels and lots of peanuts, when a slightly younger Hugh lookalike in an English Beat T-shirt and stovepipe jeans came around the corner and plunked down on the couch next to him, knee brushing knee, and jammed a robo-hand into the bowl. "And there's my brother-in-law, Corey."

Corey spared a quick glance in my direction, then did a double-take that told me which way he swung. His eyes went to the chain and padlock around my neck, then up to my hair, down to my package, lingered briefly, and finally wended back up to my eyes. "I didn't catch your name."

"Desmond."

"Des-mond," he repeated, lilting the first syllable. "Well, Desmond, I guess it's time for show-and-tell." He pulled his prosthetic out of the bowl. A few crunchy squares of rice and corn cereal fell from between the actuators as he lifted it and rotated it to look at his palm, phalanges curled toward his wrist as if he had fingernails to check.

Some of 'em do, robo-hands. Have fingernails. The kind of pseudo-skin robo-hands that chicks get. And people who want to keep up the pretense of being whole.

Not Corey, though. He had a clear sleeve of grippy silicone that covered the palm and the circuitry. That was all.

"It was three years ago. On the assembly line. You've probably heard of the company—hint, second-largest manufacturer of robotics in not only Buffalo, but all of Western New York—but their lawyer tells my lawyer that part of the settlement says I can't go around telling people—"

"Corey," Pam said, and her voice was nowhere near as kind, or patient—or nervous—when she was talking to her brother-in-law as it had been when she'd spoken to the other gimps. "Don't monopolize the group."

He silently parroted the words "monopolize the group" with an eye-roll and thrust his prosthetic back into the party mix.

"Corey hurt his hand in a work-related accident that he's not supposed to talk about. Three years ago already? I guess it must have been."

Three years. Corey had been practically a kid when it happened. Probably fresh out of high school. At least I'd been able to cross the thirty-year mark with two hands to my name.

"Okay then," Pam said, with her fake brightness firmly in place again. "Come on, Desmond, let's sit you down." She pulled up a chair next to the soldier, and I sat in it. The sooner we started, the sooner we'd finish...and the sooner I could go home and have a drink.

The husband Hugh stood, and as he climbed over Corey's knees, murmured, "You comin' over for the game Sunday?" and Corey shrugged and said, "I dunno, maybe." Once Hugh cleared his lap, I saw Corey's soulful eyes were fixed on the padlock that hung against the base of my throat like he wanted to tongue the keyhole. Hugh said, "Bring some ice, if you come. Always run out."

Once Hugh escaped, Pam said, "Okay, then. Let's begin the meeting with a moment of silent prayer."

Prayer? I didn't blurt it out loud or anything, but come on. The time for praying was long past. The veteran bowed his head, as did Pam, and the car crash lady. Ken Roman glanced at me briefly, half-smirked, then dutifully lowered his head so his silver-whiskered double chin bulged, and shut his eyes. I glanced at Corey—who'd been watching me. He raised his eyebrows playfully.

I hadn't known what, exactly, to expect at my social-services-mandated support group. Talking. Exercises. Some psychobabble attempt to screw my head on straight again. Never in a million years would I have thought I'd be cruised by one of the other gimps.

But never, ever, *ever* would I have expected to be turned on by it.

Corey had the dark-haired, dark-eyed look of a guy who'd had some racial mingling in his family tree, far enough back that the only ones who knew about it for sure were the genealogy buffs. His brother was handsome, in a typical and middle-class kind of way. Corey, though, was devastating.

He didn't have bigger eyes or better bones or any of those things that might make one guy register as an 8 and another one a damn near 10. If anything, he should have been a notch more homely. He had a crooked eyetooth, just one, on the right side, that he bared whenever he smirked—which evidently was a lot. His eyebrows weren't quite the same, and his nose was too big. It didn't matter. He looked at me, smiled that naughty-boy smile, and I was putty in his hands.

I think he knew it, too.

"All right, then," Pam said. "Desmond, since you're new to the group, would you like to tell us a little something about why you're here?"

"Not really." I blurted it out before I realized what a dick I sounded like...but then I decided I didn't care.

Corey bared his eyetooth and rustled through the snack bowl with his prosthetic.

Pam waited, as if surely I would turn what I'd just said into a joke. When I didn't she said, "It's understandable, your first time here, you'd be nervous."

Ken Roman began picking at the silicone sleeves of his linear activators, the thin, bone-like parts that connected the fingers to the wrist. The sheaths were all tattered around the wrist, which I had probably assumed was due to age and use, but then I saw the sprinkling of vinyl all around him on the carpet and realized he'd picked apart the prosthetic himself. Just now.

"How long have you had your device?" Pam asked me.

Device. As if it was a clock radio or a can opener. "Four months."

"Were you in another group that didn't work out, or...?"

I stared at my knee. "This is my first one."

"But the past four months...." She trailed off as if she couldn't imagine what I'd been doing with myself all this time. (Drinking. Obviously.) Four months with a hunk of metal on the end of my arm, and three months before that waiting for the aching stump to heal. Seven months since the maws of hell opened up and I staggered inside.

But who's counting?

"I can tell the story about how my hand got caught in a conveyor belt," Corey said. Way too cheerfully.

"Corey..." Pam warned.

"The belt carried these filaments past—robotics, you know all the crap they use doesn't look like much of anything. This shit looked just like steel wool. And it was full of this other stuff, this slag, looked like BBs. My job was to sit there next to the conveyor belt with a pair of tweezers and pick BBs out of the steel wool. That's not what it really was. It was graphine robofilament. But it might as well have been Brillo pads."

Pam said, "Actually, if Desmond feels he can't talk about his situation yet, there's a trust-building exercise we're supposed to—"

"Only a certain percentage of BBs could slip by me, otherwise I'd get a warning. And three warnings could mean anything from getting my bonus docked or a day of suspension without pay. So even though it was about the dullest thing you'd ever see in your life—steel wool rolling past, hour after hour, day after day—I couldn't zone out. I had to watch. And I had to be quick."

"Corey...."

"I can't tell you how hard it is to sit there hunched over the conveyor belt five hours a day. You feel it in your back, your neck. You get up and your hands and feet are numb from sitting in that one position. And you can't even daydream, 'cause God forbid you let too many BBs get by. God forbid."

"Corey had an industrial accident," Pam said, as if beating him to the punchline would allow us to move on to whatever bullshit was next on the schedule.

Corey looked right at me—nailed me with his eyes—while the peanuts and bagel chips sifted through his prosthetic. "One day I was so numb—not just my ass and my fingers and toes, but my brain. My spirit. So numb that my tweezers just slipped out of my hand." He raised his prosthetic and spread its fingers, and a pretzel stick dropped back into the bowl with a dry clack.

"If I was gonna be docked for a few BBs slipping by, I could only imagine the stink they'd raise if I lost my tweezers in the robofilament. So I made a grab for 'em. Only there was a frayed edge on the conveyor belt, like a loop of string, and it caught on the button of my cuff. If I'd given it a good yank, I probably wouldn't have lost anything more than a button. But the thought that flashed through my mind right at that moment?" He said it with a smile, but he was anything but happy. "The goddamn fucking insane idea that cost me my fucking arm? It was this: I can't drop a plastic button in the steel wool. That'll get me fired for sure."

I heard a whooshing sound in my ears and my throat worked like I was gonna puke.

"You got to learn from your mistakes," the soldier said. I jumped. He'd been sitting there so quietly, and then, boom. His voice sounded like it had been groomed for a much harder space. It rang through the north-side-yuppie living room like a pistol shot. "You got to follow your gut. You seen your hand getting sucked in, you wanted to react, then you didn't. Don't second guess yourself. That's the lesson you got to take away from it."

Corey's prosthetic closed around a few squares of party mix that had stuck in the activators. They crunched, loud.

The soldier looked him over in disgust—and I had no idea if they'd been butting heads for months (maybe long ago Corey had done his flirty thing with a homophobic straight guy and was now paying the price), or if they'd met recently and it was simply a case of instant dislike.

"Don't second guess myself?" Corey said. "Come on, that sounds like something you read at a gift shop. So I lost my arm, and all I got was this lousy T-shirt?"

The soldier looked at Corey, cool and level, like he'd seen so many things during his tour of duty, he had no need to fill the silence, and he'd be damned if a mouthy queer was gonna get the better of him.

"Okay," Pam said, "I'm going to pass around a list of resources for augmenting your prosthetics, some software, some hardware, some accessories—"

"You can't wait to get back," Corey said to the soldier, "can you?"

"That's right. I've got another year and I plan to serve it, soon as the docs say I'm ready. Most likely re-enlist when I'm done."

"A land mine in Afghanistan blows off your leg and you can't wait to go back for more. What kind of sense does that make?"

The soldier considered Corey for a moment, then said, "There should have been a bot on that line you were working, not a person. A couple grand in machinery and a few hours of programming, and they would've had themselves an employee that could work 24-7 for years without so much as a lunch break. You lost your arm doing a mindless government-subsidized job that cost that company big money to delegate to a human being—and now you gotta deal with a bot-arm for the rest of your life. What kind of sense does *that* make?"

Corey's prosthetic phalanges closed around a single peanut, as precisely as if they'd been his real flesh-and-blood fingertips, and he flicked the nut into the air and caught it on his tongue. "Believe me," he said, chewing. "I'm well aware of the irony."

The soldier crossed his arms as if he was disgusted that Corey had ended the skirmish by agreeing with him, and Ken Roman gave a weird harrumph that could have been discomfort or amusement.

"So," Corey said, swinging his gaze around to me. "You change your mind about letting us in on your gruesome details? Because really, your social worker might tell you otherwise, but the whole focus of these support groups is this—who lost what, and how painful and bloody and fucked-up it was when it happened."

"I feel sorry for you," the car crash lady said.

Corey went on as if he didn't hear her. "C'mon, Des-mond." He drew out the syllables of my name. His eyes sparkled. "I showed you mine. Now you show me yours."

Oh, I wanted to show him something, all right. Or I would have wanted to, if we were anywhere else but there. Talking about anything else but that. As it was, the sight of that ground-up peanut coating his tongue was enough to make my TV dinner repeat, and I wondered if maybe the housebot had seriously misread my preferences, because the room felt so stifling I could hardly breathe.

Corey dropped his voice low and said, "Well, Desmond? What happened to your hand?"

"I-I don't remember," I stammered. It probably sounded like the world's biggest cop-out. Unfortunately, it was the truth.

CHAPTER 2

Either the bus down the block from the meeting was way behind schedule when I finally caught it, or so far ahead that I'd actually snagged the next one in line. It stunk of bleach that was attempting to cover up old beer puke. Even so, I was more comfortable sitting in that molded fiberglass bus seat than I'd been in Pam Steiner's ritzy North Buffalo living room, where the only things we'd been allowed to talk about were gimp things.

Normally, soaking up the ambience, I'd start thinking I needed to get my old beater of a Gremlin back on the road. But not now. Not when I'd need to take my road test again to prove I had the hunk of junk on the end of my stump under control...which I didn't. And I doubted I ever would.

Besides, my gimpy bus pass was only ten bucks. Owning a car would mean registration and inspection and insurance. Think of how much money I'd be throwing away that I could be spending on liquor.

From the diner between the bus stop and my place, I grabbed a leathery burger that'd been forgotten under the heat lamp, wolfed it down in the rain, finished it before I got to my driveway, and chucked the wrapper over the neighbor's chain link fence. My Riverside apartment was on the second floor of an old Colonial, typical of the neighborhood, that'd been split into four units decades ago in an ambitiously haphazard way. The guy who'd done the construction had possessed either a great sense of humor or an overinflated opinion of his own carpentry skills. The hall was narrow, the floor sloped down, and the number 3 on my front door had been hung crooked and then sealed tight with about ten coats of yellowed shellac.

The housebot thumb-press panel beside my front door was dark. I'd be surprised if it had ever worked, even when it was newly installed. Now and then I would make a token complaint about it—followed up by a lengthy bitch session about something a lot easier and cheaper to fix. Not that I actually wanted the bot replaced. Acting dissatisfied just kept the landlady from raising the rent. Awkwardly, with my left hand, I dug a key out of my pocket and unlocked the front door with the manual lock.

The hand scanner in my vestibule was dark, too. The scanner slot was filled with a plastic container of Sea-Monkeys—my poor-man's version of a wall-mounted aquarium. I slipped off my leather jacket, let it hit the hardwood with a wet splat, and stopped to feed the critters their tiny scoop of granules. In terms of sentience, I knew they were the aquatic equivalent of an ant farm. Still, taking my twisted need to nurture something and turning it loose on a cup of brine shrimp held me more accountable than buying one of those pet pocketbots you see everywhere these days. Real, living creatures don't come with an off-switch to keep them nice and convenient.

I watched the Sea-Monkeys glide through the crusty plastic container in their pint of salt water, with their limbs rippling like the wings of tiny little manta rays. I wasn't sure how many arms they had, exactly. Too small to count, plus they were always undulating. Lots, though. Enough that they probably wouldn't notice if they were to lose one.

My TV set was thirty years old and my couch was even older than that. The couch was old because I was too lazy to find another one. The TV was old by design—it had a functioning remote but it predated the graphite chip of the early 90's, when suddenly graphite was not just for pencils anymore. The availability of fast, cheap memory spiraled into a robotics craze, and suddenly everything from a garbage disposal to an electric razor started talking back to you. The set might've been missing a volume button and its tube made the people on Channel 12 seem a little green, but at least it didn't try to dictate what I could watch—supposedly by way of being "helpful."

My last boyfriend was like that. Bossy, and oh-so-helpful. But at least he would buy me a new pack of smokes when he finished mine, and he gave good head. A TV set would need to work pretty hard to top that.

I grabbed the vodka from the freezer and parked my ass in the groove I'd worn into the couch. There wouldn't be anything on, but I moved to pick up the remote anyway. Right-left. That's how I grabbed for things. Right—because I'd been a righty my whole life. And then, even seven months later, I'd regard the fucking robo-hand with a certain amount of surprise, and switch to my left hand. Which was still clumsy. All these months later.

Tonight, though, instead of the ol' right-left, something different happened. Something that was more like a right-left-right. This image stuck in my mind, an image of Corey—and I didn't want to dwell on him, since I wanted to think of him sliding his hand down my pants, but then I'd remember he only had one hand (and was I really remembering which hand was meatworks and which was robotic, or had my recall gone faulty?) Then all I could remember was what that soldier had said about him losing a hand in the world's most stupid and worthless way. And then the fantasy died before it was even born.

One thing I remembered about Corey for sure, though, was the way he raked that damn mess of metal through the bowl of party mix. The way he could pick something out—a bagel chip, or a pretzel—as if he'd been doing it with an actual hand. Me? I'd be lucky if my hand even landed in the bowl without knocking it on the floor.

Robotic limbs aren't hardwired into the nervous system, like the general public seems to think. Graphite chips might be fast, but they're not bionic. The prosthetic responds to fine movement of the surrounding muscles, detected with sensors. Nothing more high-tech than that. A gimp's prosthetic sleeve extended a few inches up his stump, and the cuff not only held it on, but it was practically made of sensors, so that if the software's programming was successful, all the little gestures that began in a gimp's brain and ended at the tip of his stump could carry through, with some semblance of accuracy, into his robo-limb.

In theory. I've never been able to so much as give someone the finger. And I've wanted to. Believe me.

With Corey, his hand really did work that way. It moved just like a natural hand. That ugly bundle of hinged titanium rods and wires was capable of picking up a single peanut and tossing it into the air. How, though? How could Corey tell a peanut from a pretzel without looking at it? Because it wasn't as if the prosthetic had sensation in it. Sensors, sure. But that can't replace the nerve endings of a guy's meatworks.

I feel plenty in the place where my hand used to be, but all of it is pain.

Left-right.

My robo-hand swung toward the remote, but I pulled it back, horrified, as if I'd just betrayed my meatworks by even considering it. I picked it up with my left hand. My only hand. Mustard from my hamburger had stained the side of my left pointer finger yellow. Even though I'd relied on that clumsy non-dominant hand for the past seven months, sometimes it seemed like it would never get any more accurate than the fucking prosthetic.

How much of a betrayal would it really be if I were to start using the robo-hand? It wasn't as if Ol' Lefty had really stepped up to the plate in these past seven months. Dedication goes both ways. Right?

I switched the remote from the meat hand to the robotic.

It didn't register as *I'm holding a remote*, but it felt weighty. Supposedly the brain, the paragon of all meatworks, can re-route its circuitry to begin interpreting that sensation of heaviness as "I'm holding something." But that would take practice. Lots of it. Unlike Corey, I would need to actually look at that hand to try and figure out what it was doing.

I imagined myself hitting the on-button like I would have with my real hand, and I tried to move the robo-thumb. The whole hand twitched. Thumbs didn't move independently, I supposed. I took the remote out of my robo-hand. Using Lefty, I mimicked the gesture I wanted my prosthetic to perform. Christ, it was a hell of a lot more complicated than I realized. The fingers curled around to support the remote, the wrist gave a little twist, and I lifted the whole thing to aim the business end toward the TV set. And the only thing I'd been consciously thinking was to hit the on-button.

Would it ever become automatic? Or would I stand there like a dumbass for the rest of my life trying to figure out the ten thousand things that needed to happen before I could perform even the simplest gesture?

I knew going to that support group would be a shitty idea. I should've listened to my gut and stayed home.

Okay, first things first. Curl the fingers. I could do that. It was the only thing the prosthetics training team had successfully taught me. I slapped the remote into the robo-hand and curled the fingers. It registered nothing but the weight. Not the temperature or the texture or whatever else I expected to feel. I raised my arm—that was controlled by higher muscles, and yeah, they still worked. The twist of the wrist? That was harder. Way harder. I was sweating by the time I managed the twist.

One more thing, I told myself. The thumb. Push that button in, and you're golden.

I'd never imagined moving a thumb could be so brutal. I tried. I strained. My jaw started to ache, and I realized I'd been clenching my teeth together, and every muscle in my neck was taut with effort. I was holding my breath. The veins on the back of Lefty were bulging. And just when I thought, *screw it, I might not be left-handed but it's a hell of a lot easier than this bullshit,* the thumb moved.

It moved.

I got so excited that the robo-pinkie detached itself from the others and made a circular gesture. What the fuck kind of programming was that? Really fucking useful. Not.

Once I calmed down with a few deep breaths, I focused again on executing the wrist twist while I attempted the thumb push, and felt the thumb begin to move again. It was easier, too, as if repeating the gesture only one time had caused a few neurons to get the hang of what I needed them to do.

One time. Not hours and weeks of practice. Just once.

I was so ecstatic with the notion that maybe it was doable, to achieve some kind of utility without spending every waking hour repeating stupid gestures that would only make me feel like it'd be easier to go walk in front of a bus, that I hadn't realized I'd overshot until it was too late.

The sensors took my rusty enthusiasm for a call to arms, and the thumb came down on the button hard.

Plastic shattered.

The remote broke into five parts: the top, cracked in half; the bottom, cracked in half; and the door that covered the battery compartment, flying free. A pair of batteries rolled under the couch, and the old circuit board hung, swaying from a pair of red and black wires.

I stared at it for a moment while the failure sunk in...and then I decided I'd fucking well give that fucking remote a fucking reason to break, and I slammed it against the fucking coffee table until five plastic parts became ten or twenty plastic fragments, and the fucking circuit board split apart like a puzzle.

And then I was sweating for sure. And breathing hard.

And that was when the intercom crackled.

Bzzzt...does this thing seriously work?

Corey.

What a throwback. Oh, Des-mond. Des-mond Poole...bzzzt...you'd better not tell me I came all the way down to this nasty white ghetto and you're not even home.

And then I looked down at the wreck of my remote—did my temper realize I'd be lucky if I could even replace it?—and I was ashamed. I jumped up, kicked the parts under my ancient couch, and pressed the "talk" button with my left thumb. "Yeah, I'm here." I glanced at my living room. I hadn't hooked up with anyone new in forever—and it showed. "Just a second." Even though I suspected Corey could deal with the mess, I ran through and picked up the worst of it, the dirty socks and underwear, and crammed them into the already-full hamper. I looked around again. Everything was dusty. He'd need to deal with that, too. I hit the "talk" button again, said, "Come on up," and buzzed the lock.

Then I looked down at the stack of mail beneath the intercom that had piled up so high it fell over and became more of a mound, and I saw it: a notice from Social Services. Suddenly it seemed like they were everywhere, with their innocuous yellow envelopes and their tired dot-matrix printing on the front. No doubt Corey received his fair share of yellow envelopes. But I'd bet he didn't have little personal notes scrawled on his—on the outside, no less, since my *social worker* was so familiar with me, he'd know I would avoid opening them for all I was worth.

Read this, Des. It's important.

—and another yellow envelope on the coffee table—

Des, are you okay? I worry about you.

—and another one on the floor by the bedroom—

Call me, when you feel you're ready. My number is the same. Love, Jim

Yeah, like every other gimp, Corey might get those stupid yellow envelopes in the mail. But I doubted his social worker signed them "love."

I grabbed as many yellow envelopes as I could see and stuffed them under the couch cushion just as Corey knocked on my front door. I opened it, and there he was. Same T-shirt, same stovepipe jeans. But he'd swapped his ratty high-tops out for a pair of mod brogues, and his face was baby-smooth like he'd just shaved. He was hoping to get laid.

Weirdly enough, I couldn't say if I was hoping the same.

Look at him, I thought. Hot rudeboy like that, what's not to want? But I needed to keep my eyes from dropping to his prosthetic, and I knew. I might not be able to handle it. His robo-arm wasn't the problem. He seemed perfectly at ease with his.

With mine.

"What's crack-a-lackin'?" he asked as he slipped between me and my doorjamb, and dropped his plaid Harrington jacket on top of my leather. "Are you alone?"

"Yeah. Just me."

He planted his feet in the middle of the vestibule, put his hands on his hips, surveyed the apartment with one sweeping glance, and said, "So, I was thinking you might want some company."

I paused—marveling at the fact that I'd forgotten how to get picked up—and then said, "Company's good."

"Good."

We stared at each other for a nice, awkward pause, and finally I said, "C'mon in," and gestured toward the living room. He nodded at the Sea-Monkeys as he went past, and a shard of remote control crackled under the sole of his brogue.

"I got your address from Pam." He drew out his sister-in-law's name like it contained two or three syllables. "Well, not exactly from Pam. From her filing cabinet. She keeps hard copies of everything. Like your Function Report form."

"She has my Function Report form?"

"So I knew you lived alone—your form said so—and I figured maybe you wanted some company. But you never know. Those things can be months out of date."

That form was like eight pages long. I'd filled it out as minimally as possible, but still. "I live alone."

"You sure about that?" His gaze dropped to the padlock at my throat. When I didn't let on that it was anything more than a nickel-coated fashion statement that made the skin of my neck turn a little green, he shrugged and picked up the vodka I'd been working on earlier. A coating of frost had formed on the bottle up to the level of the liquor, then small beads of sweat misted above that. He took a long drink and set the bottle down, right on top of a yellow envelope. His thumb left a clear spot in the frost. He'd picked up the bottle with his meatworks hand, though I had no doubt he could've done it almost as easily with his prosthetic. "You don't seem like the type to live alone," he said.

"How's that?"

"I just figured you'd be taken."

I reached for the vodka. Right-left. Hoped he didn't notice. Drank. Hardly felt the frozen burn going down. "Nah. The necklace is just my ode to Sid Vicious. I'm not seeing anybody." And if he just wanted a hook-up, hell, what did he even care? Wasn't it enough that I said I was home alone? I put the bottle back down and his meatworks hand brushed mine when he grabbed the vodka for another pull.

"If you say so."

"What's the deal with Pam? Why does she host Gimp Group at her house if she's still got all her arms and legs?"

Corey smirked around the lip of the bottle, took another swallow, then said, "She was stuck carting me around to rehab, to robotics, all that crap after my accident. Decided it was her 'calling.' Whatever."

I noted that he could say "my accident" like it was nothing. Then again, his accident had occurred three years ago.

More importantly, he knew for sure what had happened to him actually was an accident.

Corey was no dope. He must've guessed that while he could say "my accident" without batting an eyelash, those two words took a hefty toll on me.

"Do you want me to go?" he said softly, without a trace of playfulness. "I'll leave."

"No." I grabbed the bottle from him and took a swig. It burned less now as it flowed down my throat, and my fingertips were tingly. My brain thought the places where my right fingertips used to be were tingly, too. "Stay."

I put the bottle down and reached for him, cupping my hand around the back of his neck. He leaned into the kiss with his eyes closed. For all that he was bold enough to steal my address and show up on my doorstep with no more than a few longing looks as an invitation, he was a cautious kisser. Only lips at first, cool from the mouth of the bottle, like mine. Tongue, a hint. A clean vodka taste. More lips then, gentle, urging me to lead.

I reached for him—right-left—and nearly pulled away when I realized what I'd done. But he'd slid his meatworks hand around my shoulders and he held me there, as if he felt a flinch that had filled in any gaps that might have been left after he analyzed my Function Report.

He stopped kissing me and said, "You haven't been with anyone since...?"

"Nope." I tried to act casual about it but I doubted I was fooling anybody.

"I hope you didn't lose a boyfriend and a hand all in one fell swoop."

"No. I was a free agent when it happened." And the only one

willing to handle all the aftercare was my know-it-all ex.

"Seven months." Corey leaned in closer and pressed his mouth to my ear. In a whisper so quiet I felt it sizzling against my ear more than I heard it, he said, "I can't wait to see how far you shoot."

CHAPTER 3

I wear long-sleeved T-shirts—that goes without saying. The hand of the robo-arm isn't covered, though. I don't wear a glove. And I don't have one of those creepy rubber hands, the kind with fake fingernails. The dishonesty of those pseudo-skin hands, the way they just imitate meat, seems worse, way worse, than an in-your-face piece of robotics. I was okay with the part of the prosthetic that hung out of my sleeve, at least as okay as I was ever going to be.

But when Corey led me to the bedroom, lifted up the hem of my T-shirt and started kissing his way from my stomach to my chest, I got real uneasy at the thought of taking that shirt the rest of the way off and letting him see the spot where the sensor cuff covered my forearm. It was the splice where man met machine that filled me with shame, and left me as mortified as the time in second grade I'd had an extra orange juice with breakfast and ended up pissing myself during the Pledge of Allegiance.

Maybe there was no logic to me being embarrassed about the coupling. But it didn't seem like there was much logic to anything else in my life, either.

Corey kissed his way over to my nipple. Seven months ago my nipples had been pierced, plus both my ears and my left eyebrow. Medical staff had ignored the grungy padlocked chain around my neck, but removed all my surgical steel for "sanitary" reasons. That's a government-run institution for you. I woke up in the hospital with all my barbells on the nightstand in a County Hospital envelope, the kind they use for sending out bills.

I tossed 'em in the trash when I was discharged. Guys like me pretty themselves up to get laid. I'd figured I was a lost cause from there on out.

Seemed like Corey was dead set on proving me wrong.

I stared down at his shoulders, stretching the fabric of his thin white T-shirt. A tattoo started at his hairline on the back of his neck, worked its way down until it was almost hidden by the white cotton, though the general shape of it, a string of music notes, showed through.

Every time I passed a tattoo shop I considered getting a tat myself, even went as far as flipping through the books. But I never went through with it. Couldn't figure out what to get that I'd still be able to look at ten, twenty, fifty years from now.

Too permanent. And that freaked me out.

Corey cradled my ass with his meatworks hand while he sucked my nipple, but his robo-hand hung at his side without getting in on the action. I thought about the peanut, hovering there on the edge of his robotic thumb, waiting for the flip. There was no doubt in my mind he could have mirrored the ass-grab with such accuracy that if I hadn't been looking, I wouldn't be able to discern meat from machine—at least, not through my jeans. But he didn't do it. Like I said, Corey's no dope.

He teased the center seam of my jeans with his middle finger, stroking, and that sent a signal surging down to my cock to stand up and take notice. I hadn't thought he could put me in the mood to take it up the ass. Corey, though, he was such a good-looking kid. And careful. Controlled. Like he wouldn't just bang away at you so it hurt. Like he'd finesse himself in and find that spot that'd really make your dick sing, and he'd work it for all he was worth.

When he pulled his head out from under my T-shirt, he nailed me with a look, and said, "It's not any different, being with someone after you get your robotics. It's just a hand. It's not like we've got robo-puds or anything."

"If you expect me to get it up, you'll need to change the subject."

"Come on, don't be a puss." He stepped back and undid his fly with his robo-hand. His dark eyes were sparkling—because he really was as easygoing as he came across, or because he enjoyed taunting me? Maybe that was for the best. Maybe, if I could tell he felt sorry for me, I would've bailed. "You make too big a deal out of it," he said. "I can tell, just by looking at you."

I stood, frozen, with the backs of my knees pressed against my mattress. "You can, huh?"

"Sure. You don't say much. And you smirk a lot. You stick your chin out, too. I keep expecting you to cross your arms and really shut everyone out. But I figure you don't want to touch your robotics any more than you absolutely have to."

Eerie. Jim always said the same thing about me, that I shut people out. And he'd had a couple of years to come to that conclusion.

"You should join the carnival," I said. Up by the ceiling, a remnant speaker from the old housebot system began squalling—no rhyme or reason as to why it would happen, but I kept an old broom handle by the nightstand to poke it with. I gave it a prod and it shut up. "You could guess people's weight and birthdate."

He stepped out of his brogues and pushed down his tight jeans. He had briefs on. His cock rested sideways beneath the clingy fabric, partially erect. He ran his meatworks fingers along the length of it, absently, while he looked me up and down. "Can I undress you?" he said.

No. That's what I wanted to tell him. But I could hardly expect to get fucked with all my clothes on. Plus, the weird part was, I did want him to undress me. All these years I'd taken it for granted, the thrill of having someone pull my shirt over my head or shove my pants down to my knees. And now, here it was, a chance to have it again. New, like everything lately seemed new. But unlike much of anything lately, new and good.

I gave him a look—hell, he was right, I did stick my chin out at people—and I raised my arms up. Both of them. Corey ran his tongue over his lower lip and smiled, and he sauntered up against me and took the hem of my shirt between his fingers, meat and metal, and raised it slowly. My stomach was exposed. Then my chest. Then I needed to duck my head through the neck of the shirt. Then my arms.

Corey tugged the shirt...and it caught on my prosthetic.

Patiently, he said, "Park your thumb." That's Gimp 101, but I'd been too busy gaping at the sight of him undressing me, watching his eyelashes flicker as he took in my chest, my shoulders, and yeah, my robo-arm, too. And waiting for the pause of disgust.

I parked my thumb, he gave the shirt another pull, and there I was. Exposed.

Meat...and metal.

Corey peeled off his shirt, too. He'd lost more of his arm than I had. His metal sleeve was up to his elbow. I looked away as I realized I'd been staring—and he'd damn well caught me doing it. "It's okay," he said. "Look. Go ahead, it's fine. Doesn't bother me. Aren't you curious?"

I shrugged.

"The more you dwell on it, the longer it's gonna take you to get back to normal."

I gave a bitter little laugh at the thought of ever being normal again.

"I'm serious," he said. He caught my robo-hand between both of his, and our metal clattered, and our silicone bumped. He guided it to his cock, and caressed the back of the fake hand, where the silicone wasn't so grippy, up and down the length of his shaft. He was as hard as he was before, and getting harder. I couldn't feel it, exactly—not like I could have felt it with my fingers. But I could still tell. "Plenty of people out there think robotics are no big deal," he said. "And some people kinda get off on it."

"Like you?"

"Not me. Sadly, I was born without any interesting kinks. Unless you count the gay thing." He rubbed himself on my prosthetic. "But I've met some guys who were into robotics. Really into it. If you know what I mean."

Ugh.

He pressed his mouth to mine before I could embark down the

road to Smartass-ville and ruin the moment. Firm with the lips but teasing with the tongue. And all the while, he flexed his hips so that his cock rubbed my actuators. Maybe he was lying to himself about his lack of robo-kink. Because it seemed to me that he was getting harder.

He let go of my prosthetic and grabbed my waistband. I could've jerked my metal arm away, but it hardly seemed fair, given the way he was grinding himself into it. He worked my fly as surely as he had his own, then hooked his thumbs in my boxers and shoved them down along with my jeans, so fast I didn't have enough time to remember which thumb was which, not without looking. And I couldn't look while his tongue was dancing along the bottom edge of my top teeth and keeping my face busy.

Until something touched my cock, and I did pull away, then. But it was only his meatworks hand. "I'll warn you before I touch you with it," he said.

"How 'bout you don't touch me with it at all?"

"That would be a serious handicap." He tilted his head to kiss my neck. Then he dragged his tongue downward, over the heavy chain, along my collarbone, and down to my nipple. He tongued it a few times and then sucked. Same one he'd sucked on before. The nerve endings that led there must've been like the ones that controlled my thumb push—quick memory. Because now a jolt sizzled down to my crotch and my dick got that hot and heavy feeling that comes over it just before it gets shiny-hard. He blew on my nipple then, and the cool air tickled. And then he said, "I'm touching you with it."

"Wait."

But he was quick, and the phalanges of his prosthetic clamped onto my other nipple with a quietly audible whir. It was freakish, the speed. And the precision.

And it felt good.

My cock rose and nudged him in the hip.

That was okay, I decided. It wasn't as if I'd never fooled around with a set of nipple clamps. That's all it was. A very big and expensive robotic nipple clamp.

"Harder?" he asked, between flicks of his tongue on my other nipple.

I didn't answer. Which he took for a "yes"...and pinched harder.

"Uhn." My knees wanted to buckle, but I locked them so I only swayed. He pinched and sucked, while his meat hand traveled down my side and back up again, warm and tender, learning the curve of my ass, my pelvis, my ribs. My cock bobbed there, untouched, grazing his side, vulnerable now that it was just jutting out there, super-hard.

A whir, a release, and the blood came flooding back into my pinched nipple. "Lay down," he said against the other one, wet with spit and tingling from getting sucked.

"Whatever you do, don't touch me...there. With that."

"Okay. That's cool. I can fuck you regular, though. Right?"

My ass clenched itself in anticipation. "You'd better."

He kissed his way up my shoulder, neck and jaw, and laid another wet one on my mouth. Bolder now. More tongue. More spit. And then he stepped back and shucked off his briefs.

His body was hot. Lean, and smooth-chested. He had another music note tat down the side of his left thigh—almost enough to distract me from his prosthetic. Which was hanging there, fingers slightly spread, waiting for the twitch of his muscles that would tell it to touch me.

"Don't make me take it off," he said quietly, when he saw I'd finally got up the courage to look. "I think it's worse that way. With the arm totally missing."

"No. I wouldn't."

"Okay." He nudged me onto the bed and climbed between my knees, and then he was kissing my chest again, lavish with his tongue, generous with his mouth, pausing to lick and suck every place that made my breath catch. Not just my nipples but the swell of my ribs, and the veins down below my navel, and the bend of my thighs. As he worked me, I wondered how I'd managed to miss that maybe he wasn't so blasé about his accident after all. And I figured I'd probably been complaining too loud to pick up on the fact that maybe Corey could use a little stroking, too.

"You look amazing," I told him, and man, was I ever out of practice at sweet-talking a guy. "All through that fucking meeting, I couldn't stop watching you."

He ran his fingertips through the drying trail of spit he'd left down my stomach, and smiled to himself. "Yeah?"

I touched his cheek with my knuckles. "Great eyes."

He preened a little.

I dragged my thumb down to his mouth and ran it across his lower lip, and said, "Hot mouth."

He turned and took my thumb into that mouth. It was hot. And wet. And my cock was aching now to introduce itself and get acquainted. I gave his shoulder a nudge and he got the idea, sinking down between my legs, kissing all the way. This constant-kissing thing was new for me. He ran his cheek along the side of my shaft, and then opened wide and took it halfway down. "So hot." I touched his hair as he did it. It didn't feel like Jim's short-cropped hair.

What a stupid thing to notice.

I got my elbows under me and watched, so I could see how perfectly obvious it was that this was not Jim going down on me. It was Corey Steiner, the kid from the meeting. He gave pretty good head, too. And while he was nearly as full of "helpful" advice as Jim, it didn't sound quite as patronizing coming from Corey. Probably because he didn't learn his amputee-coaching from a textbook. Like Jim.

Corey gulped his way down to the base of my dick so it prodded the back of his throat. His right hand stroked my thigh. His robohand clutched the blankets. Just like a meat hand would have.

"Hey," I said, "I'll bet you fuck real pretty."

"Yeah?" He plunged down again and met my eyes with his mouth wrapped around my dick, and he smiled around the shaft at me. No, he didn't look at all like Jim. Jim was way too serious to look at me like that. Corey sucked his way back off with a smack and said, "You need lube?"

"Yeah, I need lube. Look in the cigar box, under the bed."

He stuck his real hand under there—because as much as it seemed like he could feel things through his prosthetic, of course he couldn't—and he came out with the box. "Ooh. Poppers." He offered the bottle to me, but I shook my head. Not yet. He set it on the nightstand, broke out the lube and greased himself up. Then he bent one of my knees and stroked his slick fingers over my hole. "I'm gonna keep you on your back, so I can watch your face when you get off."

I forced myself to look at his eyes. Not his prosthetic. And not mine.

He worked a finger inside me. My breath hissed. It had been a while since anyone had rooted around in my ass, a long while, and maybe it'd be a good idea to relax with some rush. But I didn't ask for it. Maybe I wanted it to hurt.

"Ready?" he said. I wasn't, but I nodded anyway, because I figured I'd never be ready. He lined himself up and started stroking my hole with the greased head of his cock. Every time I steeled myself to take it, he just kept on stroking.

Finally, I said, "You're being a tease."

"I told you, man. I wanna make you shoot like a Roman candle." Finally, he started to push. Just the tip, and then he stopped, waited. Watched.

Then I changed my mind about the rush, since I was practically seeing stars. I reached toward it and he grabbed it for me, held it for me, and with a fruity chemical whiff suddenly it was all good. I felt good, actually good, for a few seconds—and if I didn't have a dick up my ass I might have actually laughed. He pushed in, slow a few times, then faster, steady, while I rode the rush and reveled in the not-caring I'd be allowed to experience, if only for a few seconds. When he started jacking me, it felt even better. He still had the poppers there, next to my face, and I turned for another whiff as soon as the first one ebbed.

I was flying when I realized that if he was holding the poppers in his meatworks, he must be jacking me with the metal.

I dug my heels into the mattress and tried to push away from him, but Corey took it for a simple shift in position. He angled his hips so his crown glided across my prostate with each and every thrust, and he started pounding my ass. And his grasp on my dick was perfect. He'd greased the silicone grip surface while he was lubing my hole, and it felt like a hand. Only I knew it wasn't.

"Hey," I said, but between the vodka and the rush I didn't follow it up with anything sensible.

"Are you close? Because I've got a trick that'll really blow your mind."

Don't. Except I didn't say no, and I didn't even shake my head, and he'd encouraged me to take another whiff—which I did. Another headrush, and then I felt a subtle vibration.

"Oh my God," I said. I think I meant, *what the fuck do you think you're doing?* But, you know. It didn't come out that way.

"Ride it," he said, and he was huffing and puffing over me, veins bulging at his neck and temples, breathing in that stuttery way guys do when the dam's ready to burst. "Mm, yeah, I'm gonna make you nut so hard."

"Wait—"

"Do it—I can't hold back. Come with my dick up your ass. Come hard."

I saw it before I felt it, a weird flick of his shoulder. Not only did he have the fine control over his prosthetic to do all the things I wished I could do. He'd hotwired his software to make it do things it had never even been designed to do. The vibration grew strong—fast and fine—and it sent me hurtling toward that brink before I even knew what hit me.

My back arched, and I drew breath to scream—'cause poppers'll do that to me, get me going, good and loud—but it was so intense I couldn't even do that. I made a choked noise and just went rigid all over. And when I shot, finally shot, it felt more like I'd turned myself inside out.

It was so intense I couldn't say for sure it even felt good. Maybe it did. Maybe it was more of a sickening surge of relief.

Once I slid back down to earth, reality came back to me. The little brown bottle on the windowsill. The fitted sheet pulled right off the mattress—that must've been me, since Corey'd had his hands busy. His softening dick in my ass, squelching that sloppy juice inside my hole for a few final, self-satisfied thrusts. The spunk dripping down the wall. His robo-hand hanging at his side, still, and shiny with grease. My robo-hand, wadded in the bedding, thumb parked, pinky circling uselessly with the motor whir muffled by the blanket.

"What the fuck was that?" I said, once I could talk.

"Cool, huh? You know that cleaning routine? You're supposed to do it once a month in a solution soak when you take it off? When I realized it was all vibrations—"

"I told you not to touch me with it."

"You told me not to fuck you with it." His eyebrows screwed up in bewilderment as he fished a bandanna out of his jeans pocket and wiped off his dick. "And I didn't."

The idea that he'd even considered pushing those metal fingers up my ass made something in my head break. I rolled over and faced the wall, and said, "You need to go."

"Desmond...."

"Now."

He dressed without saying anything else. I listened to his stovepipe jeans rustling as he stepped into them, and the zip of his fly. And I wondered which hand he'd zipped up with. Both, I guess.

His footfalls crossed the room, then he paused in the doorway and said, "I thought..." and didn't finish the sentence. "Can I call you?"

I sort-of shrugged. As freaked out as I was that some kid had just dragged my load out of me with a vibrating robo-hand, there was something in his voice that made me wonder if he seriously didn't realize how fucked-up this thing was he'd just done.

When I didn't answer, he gathered his jacket from the hallway floor and left, closing the door gently behind him.

CHAPTER 4

Des?

I swallowed back the urge to puke. Pain lanced through my head. It was like I'd fallen asleep wearing a hat two sizes too small. And someone had stuffed a used jock in my mouth while I was out.

Des, are you home? Buzz me in. It's important.

Jesus Christ. That was Jim on the intercom.

I sat up and pulled a shirt on. The sleeve glided easily over my stump. My robo-arm...where the fuck was it? The end of the night was a blur. I staggered out of the bedroom with one long sleeve flapping at the wrist and tried to retrace my steps—but those steps ended somewhere around me finishing the last of the vodka, warm and straight-up.

Three long buzzes—once Jim made his mind up there was no stopping him—and then his voice again. *I can do this a lot longer than you can ignore it.*

I slumped against the wall, hit the talk-button and said, "Yeah, okay, gimme a sec."

If I was a prosthetic, where would I be?

Buzz me in—it's pouring out here.

I buzzed, and then tried to retrace my steps. I'd told Corey to take a hike, then what? Wallowed in bed. Pried myself out, drank, went to the shower. Rinsed the good time out of my ass, drank. Tried to turn on the TV, remembered my remote was trashed...then thought about what could've happened to my dick just as easily in Corey's robotic grasp.

Drank.

A tap on the door. "Des?"

"Hold on." I looked around again, saw no sign of the arm, and then decided, screw it. It wasn't as if Jim had never seen me without a hand. He'd seen the damn stump plenty, right after my first surgery, when it had looked like something you'd find in a butcher shop display case. He'd changed the bandages on the fucking thing.

So gently, so carefully. Like he didn't realize how numb I'd become.

I stepped over a pizza box on the entryway floor—evidently I'd ordered out—and toed the greasy cardboard behind the front door before I opened it a few inches. "There he is—good ol' Jim. All growed up. Looks just like a real professional."

He didn't, actually. He looked more like a barely-tamed rebel who'd slapped on a shirt and tie to appease a parole board. He was just as burly as ever—his clothes still fit like they'd split a seam if he moved wrong, and the tie was strangling him in an attempt to keep the ink on his neck covered. But his hair was longer now than the burr of a buzz cut that used to tickle the insides of my thighs while he ate out my ass, and he didn't have his septum ring in. Maybe he'd even let the piercing heal shut. I couldn't fault him for that—and he looked pretty good with hair, especially when the rain had shaped it into dark, wet points that framed his blue eyes. He squinted at me, and said, "Are you okay?"

"Fabulous."

"Aren't you gonna let me in?"

"The place is a mess."

He laughed—and when he smiled, he looked just like Jim. Probably because he actually *was* Jim. "Yeah, I'm shocked. C'mon, I need to check in with you."

Check in? It took me a second to register what he meant, and then the disappointment rocked me—and then surprise over the idea that I was disappointed that he'd come on a professional call, not personal. "Here I am. Fine and dandy. Is that good enough? If there's anything that needs my signature, go ahead and sign it for me. Isn't that what you did to get me into the support group?"

"Let me come in," he said. "I've got to verify you're not covered in bedsores and living in your own filth."

"No one told me I'd need to do something about the filth."

"Yeah, well. Be thankful I know what your apartment looked like before."

There was no getting rid of him since he had his heart set on seeing the place, so I stepped back and let him in to the entryway. I could have offered him a slice of pizza, but I didn't know if there was any left—and if there was, who knew what I'd done to it while I was blacked out? He didn't mention the box, so I didn't either.

"I went to that dumb meeting, so...."

"I know." He set down his briefcase beside the door. "Pam Steiner's house. Her housebot faxed my office this morning."

I looked at the clock. Fuck. It was almost eleven. He'd been at work for two and a half hours already—and since when did he carry a briefcase? My head throbbed. "You got a smoke for me?"

He pulled a Camel soft pack from his pocket, tapped out a cigarette and gave it to me, then cupped his hand around mine as he lit it. It wasn't the gesture of a social worker coddling a gimp, either. He'd always lit my smokes for me. Even when I had two hands.

I'd always liked that.

"I tried to call," he said. "Is your ringer turned off?"

"I don't know. Maybe." Me hating the phone was also nothing new.

"You know you need to go once a week. If you miss a meeting, you'll need to find another group, an alternate group that meets in between to make up the days. They're really strict about it. You have to go to at least ten in the next twelve weeks, since you waited this long to start going."

"Okay. I know."

"There isn't much wiggle room. Call me if you miss one so I can find you another."

"Okay." I walked into the kitchen, put the cigarette in an ash tray and started making coffee one-handed. He followed, and leaned against the sink. I said, "Do you want any?"

"Where's your prosthetic?"

"Why?"

"You need to wear it. Do you want it to stop fitting you? Is that what you want?"

I swung around with the open coffee can in my hand, and ground coffee scattered everywhere. "I fucking wear it." Who'd started yelling first, him or me?

"Because that's what'll happen, you don't wear it and it won't fit you anymore—and they're not gonna keep paying to have it re-seated."

"I was sleeping, okay? I wear it. When I'm awake, I wear it."

"Then answer me. Where is it?"

Since I had no good answer, I resorted to saying, "Fuck off." That was my pattern. Nastiness.

He turned and walked out while I scooped coffee into the filter. That was his pattern—leaving in disgust. All these months and there they were, just waiting for us to fit ourselves into them as if we'd never managed to break free.

I tried to tell myself he was just doing his job, but that seemed to piss me off even more. How had he ended up with my case? Yeah, they were overworked at his office—but shouldn't that mean that one more gimp-file could be slipped into *anybody's* teetering in-basket? It couldn't have been coincidence that my file ended up on his desk.

Then I thought about the way he looked when he asked me if I was okay, and that knocked the anger down a few notches to a stinging kind of sadness. And it made me feel like an ass for yelling at him. Any other social worker would have recommended to have my benefits yanked by now and let me slip off the system's radar since I was so shitty about following their protocol. Not Jim. He was worried for me—genuinely worried. I could see that the minute I looked into his eyes. "You're right," I called out to the entryway. That was as close as I ever came to *I'm sorry*. "When the arm shifts and the prosthetic sleeve starts fitting wrong, it's a bitch."

I turned on the coffee pot and went to join him—because while Jim might start yelling just as quick as I do, he's also just as quick to calm down, and he never was much for holding a grudge. Well, until our last official night as a couple, when I'd ditched him at a party because I ran into my old gang and somehow ended up leaving with them. And yet, weeks later when I woke up in the hospital, even that well-justified grudge had been forgotten. Or at least set aside.

I expected to find him poking through the pizza box, or maybe saying hello to the Sea-Monkeys. They weren't the same Sea-Monkeys that he'd known, back in the day. Those particular shrimp died off. Like their box said, once they'd all gone to Sea-Monkey heaven, I let their water evaporate down to a bunch of dried crystals, and then I added water. The crystals were mostly salt and dried Sea-Monkey shit—but there were some eggs in there, too. Eggs that needed to go through a dry spell before they could hatch. A day later, maybe two, I'd been able to see those telltale movements in the water, jerky little motions from tiny creatures so small at that newborn stage they were almost invisible. From the barren salt, life.

Maybe some things only seemed like they were dead. But a little patience, and a little time....

I found Jim standing in the doorway to my room. He was very still.

Oh, fuck.

I glanced into the bedroom even though I knew damn well what I'd see. Fitted sheet with the corner torn off the mattress. The cigar box out and a tube of lube lying beside it, still open, drooling its contents onto an abandoned sock. A little brown bottle on the windowsill. And when the light hit it just right, a strand of dried jiz gleaming on the wall.

On second thought, it was nothing like I'd imagined. It was worse.

He said, "When I saw you were still wearing the chain, I thought...." but he couldn't bring himself to say any more.

"Listen," I told him, but he was already halfway to the door. "Wait." Shit, what could I even say? That I thought I might feel like less of a freak show with another gimp—but when everything was all said and done, it was just as bad?

That I felt crappy for doing it?

That I wished it was him?

Jim picked up his briefcase by the door, and without looking at me, said, "I hope you at least used a condom."

I couldn't answer. It felt like a punch in the gut. Jim took my non-answer for a "no." He's no dope, either.

He couldn't quite look me in the eye when he turned back around, but he did face me when he said, "Sometimes I wonder how you're even still alive."

He closed the door behind him as gently as Corey had.

I slumped against the wall, raised my eyes wearily—and spotted my prosthetic through the bathroom door, sticking out of the puke-spattered toilet bowl.

Yeah. Sometimes I wondered, too.

CHAPTER 5

The week leading up to the next Gimp Group stretched long. I'd thought weeks were long after the surgery, but back then I'd had more drugs to help me pass the hours. Now I only had my TV, always at the same volume, slightly too loud. Pretty soon I got tired of getting up to change the channel, and left it on a shopping channel once the local news got too depressing to watch.

And then one day I woke up on the couch to "Ro-bo-nanza," with everything from can openers to cat feeders whirring like the actuators in the hunk of metal on the end of my stump, all for eight easy low payments of $19.99, and I barely stopped myself from putting a shoe through the damn screen.

I hauled my ass off the couch and turned the set off.

Empty vodka bottles clattered under my feet as I cleared the coffee table on my way to the bedroom to try to figure out what to wear that wouldn't make me look jaundiced—then decided on black, which was what I wore every day, anyway. Showered, considered shaving, didn't bother. I've heard I carry off the "rugged" look pretty well.

When I thought about eating, the sight of food turned my stomach. I managed a slice of white bread washed down with cranberry juice, and belatedly realized it wouldn't be pretty if I puked up a pink ball of dough at Pam Steiner's house. But it might be pretty funny.

The mathematician Ken Roman was enthroned in the living room's only recliner when I got there, cradling his tattered prosthetic in his opposite hand, and smiling like royalty at the other members of the group. Car crash lady was there, and Pam, and her husband, Hugh, poaching the Cheetos. The soldier wasn't there yet. Neither was Corey. A new kid named Felipe who'd lost half his fingers to some fireworks showed up, looking as stunned as if the M-80 had just misfired out in the driveway on his way in.

"Okay," Pam said. "We can get started."

"What about Corey?" I said. My voice sounded a lot louder than I'd realized it would, since I'd never really used it much in the Steiners' house. Their newly-refinished hardwood floors made for some interesting acoustics.

Pam gave me a look that could frost a bottle of vodka, and said, "Corey's found another group." She stared at me for an extra moment, as if I was supposed to understand why that was my fault, and then said, "And Private Ball is on his way to Fort Drum; he's been cleared for duty."

Who gave a rat's ass about the soldier? All week long, I'd been thinking about that thing that happened, and not knowing how I felt about it, and wondering what I would say to Corey when I saw him. And now I wouldn't. "Oh."

"We'll start with a moment of silent prayer," Pam said, and lowered her head.

Beyond her, Ken Roman caught my eye and smiled his knowing smile, then dropped his double chin to his chest as he pretended to say a little prayer of his own. Hugh took off with a handful of Cheetos.

"All right," Pam said when she was done praying. She sounded nowhere near as friendly as she had the first week. "You first, Desmond, since you were unable to share with us the last time."

"Share."

"What happened to your hand?"

Did she need to be so blunt about it? Fuck. The New Pam made the soldier look warm and fuzzy in comparison. "I told you already." I started stammering again. "I d-don't remember."

"That's not atypical, with trauma. Tell us what you do remember."

"W-well, it...I was...."

Flashback. The smell of rain. Not rain on grass, like you'd smell near the Steiners' Park District Victorian. Rain on asphalt, oily and rank. Downtown, by the titty bars. By the black neighborhoods and the Polish market. By the abandoned factories that used to make things, back when people worked in big factories, and not just a few techs who kept the bots running in cramped spaces that needed no light, no air conditioning, no coffee breaks.

The smell of rain on asphalt and the sound of sirens.

And then I was in Pam Steiner's living room, staring at a piece of silicone sheathing as it dropped to the floor beside Ken Roman's recliner. I looked up at him. He was watching me with great interest as he picked at his prosthetic. His eyes were brown, and sharp. His eyebrows were salt-and-pepper, like his five o'clock shadow and his wild hair. Those brows were drawn down over his sharp brown eyes like he could see through whatever I couldn't manage to say.

And that scared me. Because I was telling God's honest truth—I really didn't remember.

"You're lucky you qualify for Disability at all," Pam said. "Recent reforms or not, if you don't participate, that's the same as not attending, in the eyes of Social Services. I reported that you participated during the first meeting because it was your first time. But I wouldn't be doing you any favors if I kept letting you slide."

No meeting, no check. No vodka. No apartment. "I...um...I was out with some friends." Rain on asphalt. "We were fucking around. Um, sorry. Fooling around. Downtown." Sirens. "We found this abandoned factory. It was dark."

Sure, it sounded pretty far-fetched that we'd just stumbled on this factory as we were rolling balls down Ferry—maybe "found" wasn't the most accurate word. We'd all been drifting in and out of there for months. Mostly, we partied. Sometimes bands set up and played. A couple of guys even lived there, even though there was no working plumbing. They just kept on shitting in the toilets anyway.

"It was dark," I said again, reaching for something to say. Sometimes the place had juice, sometimes it didn't. Those workbots you find inside the front door of a factory aren't just bigger than housebots.

They run on multiple telecom lines. It's one thing to re-scan your family and tweak your house's preferences when a graphite circuit goes, but another to lose a whole morning of production to get a burnt-out workbot up and running again. They've got redundancies built in as backups in case something fails.

"I must have been trying to light up the workbot. That's all they can figure." Rain beating on glass block windows. The shit smell of the toilets. "I don't remember opening the casing. They found it next to me. The paramedics." Sirens.

"And your hand?" Pam said.

"Housebots don't have moving parts. Workbots do. You probably wouldn't know, if you work in an office, since officebots are more like glorified housebots. Factory workbots are different. The scanners rotate, depending on which mode you access on the control panel. Human resources. Shift change. Production tweaks. Depends on the factory. There's a safety shutoff that's supposed to keep them stationary when something's in there. Maybe someone overrode it at some point." Someone like those dumbasses who took dumps in the overflowing toilets. "Maybe it was just old."

The kid with missing fingers groaned. I didn't need to spell it out to him. Not only had my hand been crushed in a rotating scanner... it'd happened good and slow.

That's what I figured, anyhow. Everything feels more intense when you're rolling, and I'd just dropped a triple-stack. Hopefully I'd felt it so intensely I blacked out fast.

Pam said, "What did your friends say you were trying to do?"

"I dunno."

"You didn't tell them? Or they didn't understand?"

Rain on windows. The shit smell. Laughter. "I don't know."

"Were you trying to rob the place? I read the report. It doesn't sound like there was anything to steal."

Sirens. "No. There wasn't."

"Then why were you playing with the wiring?" *Fire it up, Desmond. We'll crank the tunes. There's a bottle of Stoli in it for you if you get us powered up.* "Your file says you're an HVAC technician. You must've been doing something to the electronics that was beyond your friends."

Those guys Jim always hated. He said they were lowlifes. I said he was jealous. I didn't fuck any of those assholes who were with me. But when Jim was on his high horse, I let him wonder if maybe I did. Even though Jim had already split from me by then, hanging with the old crew still made me feel phenomenally smug. *Sirens.* "There's no one to ask. In the ambulance, the paramedic told me I was the only one there." I could still remember his face. A black guy, young and wiry, dark skin, shiny from the rain. "Those other guys bailed. I haven't seen them since."

The fireworks kid groaned again.

Pam watched me for a few seconds, and I thought maybe she had it in for me enough to force me to keep going, no matter how much I insisted there wasn't anything else to tell. But then the fireworks kid said, "I don't feel so good," and Pam went over and had him put his head between his knees and take a few deep breaths, and then I was off the hook for the rest of the stupid meeting.

On my way out, as I was struggling into my boots one-handed, I looked up and found Ken Roman hadn't moved from where he'd stepped into his loafers. He was still smiling at me.

"What?" I said.

He glanced over his shoulder to make sure no one was close enough to hear, and he said, "Is it true?"

"Is what true?"

"That they caught you fraternizing with young Steiner."

"Listen, perv. Go get your rocks off somewhere else."

The insult flew right over his head. "I have no interest in *those* kinds of details. That's not why I'm asking."

I tightened my laces as well as I could with one hand, and tucked the tips into the top of my boot to keep them from dragging behind me as I walked. Fraternizing. What, now there was some kind of law against gimp on gimp action? And though I did my best to staunch my curiosity, I couldn't help but wonder. If Roman didn't have a prurient interest in what went on between Corey and me, then what did he care? "Who told you that?"

"My own two ears. It's amazing what you can learn if you show up early and sit somewhere quietly...and learn to tune out the husband's moronic chatter while the wife makes her phone calls."

"You heard her on the phone?"

"With your social worker—that Murphy fellow, same one as me. And he dropped you. Same as me. Got me to wondering..." he glanced at my prosthetic. "Maybe we have a few things in common. Maybe we can help each other out."

"*Jim* dropped me?"

"Mr. Roman," Pam snapped.

I flinched at the sound of her voice, but Roman just turned around, still smiling, and looked down at her from his heavily lidded eyes beneath his bushy salt-and-pepper eyebrows with no concern at all.

"Ms. Steiner. Thank you for a truly delightful and informative evening. As always." He pulled on his coat, drew a business card from the pocket, and presented it to me with his meatworks hand. I took it numbly. Kenneth Roman, PhD, professor of mathematics, UB State. The edges were worn, and a few round spots on the cardstock were translucent with grease. "Don't worry," he told Pam on his way out the door. "My interest in Mr. Poole is strictly platonic."

She glared at him until he'd waddled down her front steps and climbed into his car, then she turned to me and said, "You have some nerve."

"Me?"

"Thanks to you, now Corey has to start over with a group of total strangers." Her color was high—she was angry more than anything—but tears gleamed from her lower lashes.

"I didn't mean to...I had no idea it would make any difference."

"It says in at least three different spots on your contract that there will be no fraternization among group members—*three* places—unless they happen to be married or living together, which only happens in rare cases where they've both lost a limb and they can't find separate support groups."

"Then that's fucked up," I said, because I hadn't said anything to anybody, and I couldn't imagine why Corey would have—but he was the one who'd shown up at my place and thrown himself at me, so how dare that little shit leave me holding the bag? "Maybe he told you because he just wanted an excuse to get into a different group—a group where his sister-in-law wasn't always breathing down his neck and telling him not to talk. You ever think of that?"

Pam rocked back as if I'd slapped her. She pressed her lips together so hard they went white around the edges, then said, "He didn't tell me."

Then it was my turn to reel. If I had no housebot to scan Corey in, and I hadn't said anything, and he hadn't either, then the only person who might have pieced it together was... "Jim Murphy. He's Corey's social worker, too?"

"He *was*."

Gah.

"The last thing he did, before he had both of you reassigned to a new caseworker, was to make sure your indiscretion didn't bump you out of the program altogether. He made me promise to let you stay in the group—since your injury is newer, I presume. And so you can stay."

Peachy.

"I suggest you check your mail," she said. "The information about your reassignment should be there by now. And this time, try reading it...unless you want to screw up again and make Social Services withdraw their support of you altogether."

I was half out of my head as I stumbled down the Steiners' front steps. Sure, Jim was pissed off at me—but to fuck me over like that by writing me up and dropping my case? And Corey's too? That was a side of him I'd never expected to see. What the fuck was he thinking?

Did he realize I only had one fucking hand?

I was so pissed off that when I rounded the shrubs at the end of the walkway, I almost knocked Hugh Steiner right on his ass. "Jesus Christ," I spluttered at him, when what I really wanted to do was give him a good shove. Because who knew what my prosthetic would actually do? It might shove him, or it might wave at him, or give him an A-okay gesture—or it might put his eye out. And then every night at the Steiner house would be Gimp Night. "Why'd you fucking sneak up on me like that?"

"Look," he said. Had I even heard him speak before? "Their rules are stupid." He worked his mouth as if he hadn't quite figured out what he'd say to me beyond that. But his voice was so much like Corey's I calmed down a few notches at the sound of it...and then guilt started creeping in where my anger had pulled back.

"Totally fucking useless," I said, a bit more calmly.

Me answering without biting his head off seemed to help him get back on track. "I talked to my brother—he said what happened wasn't anything, uh...you know. Sleazy. He said he likes you."

It had seemed pretty damn sleazy to me, but now I was so numb with anger and confusion I didn't know what to think. "He said that?"

"He said to tell you it's no big deal for him to find another group. There's one that meets on the Elmwood Strip that's closer to his apartment, anyway."

"Okay."

"And he said...you should call him." He passed me a folded slip of paper. It was soft, as if he'd been working it between his fingers while he waited for his wife to finish handing my ass to me.

I turned to go, and he said, "I hope you do. Call him, I mean. Seems to me no one can really understand what he's been through unless it's happened to them, too. And you'd be a lot better for him than the other guys he's been seeing since his accident."

"Yeah, well, you don't really know me," I said. "Do you?"

I walked to the bus stop, waited in the drizzling rain for almost half an hour, rode back to Riverside, then grabbed a burger on my way home. It was dry, as usual. I chucked the wrapper over my neighbor's fence, as usual. And I grabbed my mail, as usual—because the landlady bitched if I didn't. Said having mail all over the entryway made the place look bad. As if there was a single place within five miles that didn't look bad.

The mailbox was pretty full. It seemed like half the envelopes were yellow.

I turned on the TV and the shopping channel was running a cultured pearl showcase. I let the lady drone on about the ring that would look stunning anywhere from a picnic to a wedding, fetched a bottle of vodka from the freezer, and sat down with my mail. Phone bill. Credit card applications. Charities begging for donations from the guy who lived there before me.

Three letters from Jim. Or rather, three letters from Social Services. Just because he'd printed out the letter, folded it into the envelope and walked it to the mailroom, it wasn't the same thing as an actual letter from him to me.

The first one confirmed that I'd been at Pam Steiner's meeting last week. The second one said my latest psychiatric exam had been postponed for the fourth or fifth time—I'd lost count—and the third one was the mother lode of bureaucratic bullshit, full of bold red lettering, and the word "fraternization" and the word "warning" and the phrase "potential suspension of benefits." Also the phrases, "your reassignment is pending," and, "will be notified upon the selection of a new caseworker."

Not one of the envelopes contained a personal message signed, "Love, Jim." Imagine that.

The vodka burned cold going down my throat, and it stung my meatworks hand to hold the frosted bottle. I glanced down at my robo-hand—but I sure as hell didn't have the piss-poor judgment that would lead me to risk a perfectly good fifth of vodka to see whether I could handle drinking with the prosthetic or not. Whatever Jim might think of my recklessness.

I sagged into my couch as the cultured pearl showcase made way for the kitchen-bot extravaganza, and I wondered if I might be able to hit the TV's off-switch by lobbing empty vodka bottles at it...and I realized I might be a little drunk. And that probably my judgment really wasn't all that fantastic.

Although it couldn't have weighed much of anything, the business card from Ken Roman felt heavy in my pocket. I pulled it out to consider what the hell he might want with me, and a slip of softer paper, folded in half, fluttered onto my lap. I put Roman's card on the coffee table and picked up Corey's phone number instead. There was no special message written on it. Just seven digits. But I reminded myself I couldn't read anything into the lack of words. His straight brother had jotted it down for me. Not him.

I considered calling. He wouldn't care if I was drunk. Maybe he liked me better when I was drunk. He had a car—maybe he'd even come over. Maybe I could mention that it'd be a good idea to roll on one of those condoms in the cigar box before we swapped fluids. And maybe we could set some ground rules about what the prosthetics could and couldn't touch.

I sighed. Maybe that was all more trouble than it was worth.

In the couch that was at least as old as I was, a spring prodded me in the ass. I'd felt it brewing all week, this new discomfort-zone, but I'd tippled away my awareness of it. I could drink faster, or I could move. I shifted, and the spring poked hard. I supposed I should move.

When I shifted to the opposite end of the couch, a loud rustle greeted me—and then I remembered stashing my mail there when Corey came over the week before, so he wouldn't spot any Social Services communiques signed "Love, Jim."

Which I inexplicably wanted to look at. Just to see. And maybe to remember how it might feel, to have another person say they loved me.

I reached under the cushion and pulled out a handful of yellow envelopes. Some were pristine. Some were dog-eared and coffee-stained. I turned them over, one by one, and read the backs. "Did you ever meet with your physical therapist?" Pretty utilitarian. And, "This one's important." I'd never opened it. And, "Thinking of you. Love, Jim."

Love. What did that even mean?

I flipped through them, and inebriated as I was, the words became a blur. But the thing that did pierce the vodka-fog was the weight, the heft, of one of the envelopes. Then the big red stamp on it that read, "Check Enclosed." Fuck me, I'd almost missed a check? I didn't know what it would be for, since all my monthly checks had been cashed and spent long ago. But money's money. I turned it to the front and read the postmark. It was recent, just two weeks old. Then I set about opening it.

They make little bots that will open your envelopes for you. I'd never bought one, on principle, of course. The less robotics in my apartment, the better. Besides, it was so much easier to shove everything under the couch cushions and pretend it didn't exist. Being faced with something I actually did want to open was a new challenge, especially two and a half sheets to the wind. I held it down clumsily with my robo-hand while I worked my meat finger into the gap between the flap and the envelope, and I wondered if Jim had sealed the damn thing so tightly on purpose, just to give me yet another activity to be useless at.

I finally managed, though, realizing what was weighing the envelope down as I struggled the sheet of paper out and unfolded it. Jim had written me a note, and beneath the writing, he'd taped a key.

Dear Desmond,

Well, there's no check in here. Sorry. You don't answer my letters. I try calling you and get your answering machine. So I resorted to the check-stamp. The older caseworkers tell me it works like a charm.

The other night I put on a jacket I haven't worn since last spring, and I found this in the pocket. By now you've probably figured out some other way to lose that old chain, but it seemed like I should send it back to you anyway. I wanted to do it in person, so you could see that I wasn't being a jerk about it, but it would be too weird to give it to you on my next wellness-check visit. So I'm sending it now.

Having me in your life should have been a positive thing, but somehow, it never was. It was too hard to see what you were doing to yourself and feel like nothing I did mattered. I'm sorry for that.

Love, Jim

I peeled the key off the letter, held it up in front of my nose, and let my eyes cross a little. Jim had never owned a key to my apartment—never wanted one—but this was too small for a door key, anyway. As soon as I saw that bit about the old chain, I realized I was looking at a padlock key.

The padlock key.

No wonder Jim was being all sappy about the fact that I still had the chain on. He'd mailed this out a few days before he stopped by. Fuck. Everything I did hurt him—and everything I neglected to do hurt him just as bad.

I covered the padlock at my throat with my left hand, still holding that key pinched between thumb and forefinger. All those tiny motions—the forefinger-thumb pinch, the spread of the other three fingers to cup the warm metal, the rotation, the velocity, the aim.

Unlike my robotic arm, which was a struggle to even move, every nuance of the meatworks gesture happened without a conscious thought.

As I cradled the padlock in my left palm, the room swayed around me, and the TV pitch lady explained how the diet scale came with five different personalities pre-installed to best help me achieve my health and weight-loss goals. And I remembered how Jim had looked, standing there in my doorway, the last time I'd seen him. Crushed. Defeated.

I'm not sure if I actually expected to unlock the padlock with my left hand and no mirror. In my vodka-haze, though, it seemed perfectly logical to try. Mostly I jabbed uselessly at the lock, which kept shifting around. And so I went to steady it with my other hand—and ended up smacking myself in the head with my robo-arm. Knocked my damn self right off the couch, and even blacked out for a couple of seconds. I came to wedged between the couch and the coffee table with an empty vodka bottle attempting to sodomize me.

Holy fuck. It was a good thing I hadn't given Hugh Steiner a shove, back there on his driveway. I might have killed the guy.

Remembering that conversation with Hugh made me think of Corey, and I forgot about the key, wherever it fell, as I sifted through the old mail and empty packs of smokes on the coffee table until I found that folded slip of paper. It took me three tries to get the number right. But I managed to do it before I lost my nerve.

"Hello?"

"Corey. It's Desmond."

A pause. Had Hugh steered me wrong? Maybe he'd been downplaying his brother's reaction to getting fired from the group since he'd decided, however fallaciously, that I was the top pick for Boyfriend of the Month. But then Corey said, with that devastating lilt in his voice, "Des-mond Poole. I was just thinking about you."

"Liar."

"No, I was. This guy I've been seeing off and on just called to get me to meet him at the bar—but I thought of him, and how bo-o-ring he is. And I thought of you. Good thing you called. It'd be a real shame if I had to settle for boring."

Knees clinking through empty vodka bottles, I crawled to the TV set and turned it off. "God forbid."

"Have you been drinking?"

"You're pretty quick."

"Heh. That's what they tell me. So, to what do I owe this pleasure?"

I was sorry, that's what. Sorry I'd managed to ruin the group for him and make him start all over again at some stranger's house. Sorry I didn't know we'd need to be discreet about our hookup because I hadn't read any of the paperwork. Sorry that Jim took it so personally—and that he was smart enough to figure out who had done the deed with me based on the last place I'd scanned in. And once I'd ruminated on the situation by my lonesome for a week, sorry that I'd chased Corey out of bed to begin with. "I...I just thought I'd see if you were in the mood for some...company."

"It sounds like I'll need to catch up to you. Lucky for us I've got a fresh bottle of Absolut taking up space in my freezer."

"Then you'd better get a move on." I cast around for the key, which had probably slid down into the layer of trash, and decided I didn't have time to mess around with it just then anyway. If Corey lived near Allentown, he'd be over before I knew it. "That booze isn't gonna drink itself."

CHAPTER 6

I'm not sure Corey could have caught up to me without giving himself alcohol poisoning. Even so, our second time around was a hell of a lot better than the first, at least in terms of keeping the slag out of the graphine robofilament. Not that I remember much...but it must've been good, because the next day he swung by again. That night I was damn near sober, and between the two of us we soaked the mattress so thoroughly, I had to flip it before I could get to sleep.

It wasn't that I was merely grateful to trip someone's trigger again, either. It was him. I actually liked the kid. Liked him enough to start thinking beyond the next page in the Kama Sutra we'd need to try out. By the time the weekend was over, it occurred to me that in the interest of not coming off too *sleazy*, I should probably treat Corey to some kind of actual date.

And that's when I realized that I'd been so busy shaking the sheets, I hadn't noticed that my monthly condolence prize from Social Services had never materialized. I searched my house—really searched, since envelopes divide and multiply at an astonishing rate in my living room. No luck. No check.

The mailman nearly had a heart attack when he found me lurking around the vestibule. If I knew how to work my arm, I could've added a few dramatic gestures when I demanded to know what the fuck had happened to my check, although I'm not sure if that would have made any difference. Despite the fact that the arm was just riding along with me like a sleeping hitchhiker, the mailman did notice it. He noticed, and he kept his distance. But he couldn't have been all that freaked out, since in the end he told me I wouldn't find out anything more from him. No, he insisted I check at the post office.

I liked the post office better when it was in the squat brick building by my house. Yeah, you'd stand there forever if you showed up while there was any kind of line. And the heat was always blasting, winter or summer. And the clerk always acted like I'd written my address in Chinese or something. But at least it wasn't full of fucking robots.

This new place up on Hertel is crawling with 'em. The front door won't even open for you unless you stick your hand in a slot. "Scan in, please," it says, in this British accent. Why British? I have no idea. I guess they think it sounds classy. One of the automated kiosks says, "How would you like to send that? Press 1 for first-class, press 2 for economy..." while the guy who just wants to mail his mail and get the fuck outta there is jamming his thumb into his choice repeatedly, and it's beeping away at him, and still talking.

No kiosk for me, though. I needed to see a person.

I smoked a cigarette and watched a couple of people with packages shake with the officebot while the door slid open for them. I supposed I could've slipped in behind one of those guys, but chances were they'd think I was mugging them and have a hissy fit over it. That's what happened the last time I tried it, anyway.

I considered smoking another cigarette, but shook the pack and saw there were only three left. I tucked the pack into my leather jacket to save them for later, since I didn't know when I'd be able to buy more.

Cameras were no doubt having a field day watching me approach the slot three times before I finally worked up the nerve to shove my meatworks hand in. Why couldn't it scan my prosthetic instead— make that stupid hunk of metal do something useful for a change? Jim said they couldn't scan prosthetics, but you know what? I'd given it some thought, and I decided Jim's full of shit. Because what about people with two robo-arms? What do they do? Stand there outside until they can follow someone else through, and then get accused of trying to mug them?

One more try. A broad circle, like I'm sneaking up on myself, just passing by, shoulder tenses, and before it's too late, before I can puss out, in with it. He shoots, he scores. My hand was only in the scanner for a second, and the British voice said, "Welcome, Mr. Poole," like I'm a member of the fucking royal family. The door slid open.

I wasn't hit by a blast from a furnace that never shuts off like the old place on T-street. No, I just had that damn voice talking to me while arrows on the wall lit up and herded me down a sterile hallway. As I followed, the officebot said, "If you'd like to send a package larger than fourteen ounces, say yes, now. If you're here to pick up a package, say yes, now. If you'd like to open a P.O. box, say yes...."

"I want to talk to someone."

"I'm sorry. I didn't understand that. If you'd like to send a package...."

"You don't sound sorry."

The hall opened into a waiting room with a dozen seats arranged in three rows of four. The first row faced a bank of monitors, and the second two faced monitors installed on the seats in front of them. It was kind of like getting on an airplane, only without the plane. Five other people sat, some tapping their requests into the system, some leaning back with their eyes closed, waiting to talk to someone. I parked myself in the seat that was blinking at me, and set about keying my request into the monitor in my face. Once I finally drilled down to the option of *mail missing*, it did a quick calculation and flashed the message, and the speakers said, "Estimated wait time for Desmond Poole, one hour, thirty-eight minutes."

I groaned, slouched in my seat, spread my legs out as far as they would go beneath the seat in front of me, and tried to decide whether or not I was grateful that I was too damn uncomfortable to nod off.

"Did you know, you can reduce your wait time by up to seventy-five percent?"

"Shut up."

"Start your query from the comfort of home. Type USPS into your housebot for a full menu of options."

"Fuck you."

"When you get here, you'll be sorted to the front of the line."

"Fuck. You."

An older, thick-necked guy with a buzz cut turned around and gave me the stink-eye—evidently he'd never heard the word "fuck" before—and I decided to drop it. I slouched back into my seat, gazed up at the ceiling, and fantasized about a helpful person finding my check somewhere on the floor where a mailbot had let it slip out of the stack. Because simple mistakes like that had to happen sometimes. Right?

That's what I told the post office chick who finally saw me two hours later, a black woman with blonde hair extensions. Her windowless office was small and stuffy and crammed with papers, and her desk was inset with three flat horizontal monitors scrolling data. One was covered in coffee rings. She scowled down at the middle monitor and read off my address. She seemed a lot quicker on the uptake than the guy at the old place who couldn't read my handwriting, so I was grateful for that.

"Okay, Mr. Poole," she said. "Did you bring an old Social Services envelope with you?"

"I didn't know I was supposed to."

"There's a code on the bottom. It would save a lot of time if we could scan it." She slid out an old-fashioned keyboard and started to type. She was fast. The keys made a clickety noise. After she dug for a good long while, she said, "Which batch is your check in? The one that come on the first?"

"The fifteenth."

The keys went silent. I looked up. She was staring at me. I stared back. She said, "It's the seventeenth."

"I know." I kept the "duh" out of my voice as much as I could, since it seemed like if anyone could help me, it was her.

"It's not missing if it's two days late. That's just...late."

My heart started pounding. "Yeah, but, it's never late. Not more than one day, and that's only happened maybe twice since...." I glanced down at my robo-arm and tried to swallow, but it felt like my throat was closing.

When I looked back up, she was staring down at the prosthetic, too. I couldn't really get a read on what she was thinking—she was one of those black chicks whose every expression was some shade of serious. But eventually she pressed her lips together and said, "I'll look."

The seizing in my throat let up some.

The keys made their clickety noise. I watched, riveted, as her hands moved over them while her eyes stayed glued to that middle monitor. Finally, finally, she saw something that made her eyes widen (slightly), then she sat back and said, "It's easier to trace gov'ment mail. Their mailroom bot codes it all, scans it all in. They keep records, if you know where to find 'em. Here's what they got on you. Something the fourteenth of last month, probably your September check. Something on the eighteenth. Something on October second. Then something on the eighth. Three things on the tenth. That's it. Nothing on October fourteenth when checks went out."

"That's all they tell you—'something'? Not what it is?"

"They're letters, not parcels. That's all it says."

A letter. As in a letter from Jim stamped *Check Enclosed* with no fucking check inside. That stunt pissed me off just thinking about it. When had that been? Right after my second Gimp Night at the Steiners' house. When was that? Two weeks ago? Already?

And the last cluster of correspondence…that would've been the cascade that began with cheering me on for attending Gimp Group, then shooting me back down for hooking up with Corey.

"Did you get any mail from Social Services after that?"

"I dunno. I could have. It's hard to keep track."

"You need to talk to them. Could be some reason why your check didn't come. Why it never got sent."

Could be. Once I got the double-barreled breakup from Jim—first, the letter with the key in it, and then the one that told me I'd get a new social worker too—I figured there wasn't much more the mail could tell me.

Surprise, surprise.

✻ ✻ ✻

The day was pretty ripe by the time I bused it downtown, thanks to the two-hour wait at the post office. Buffalo Social Services Northwest was in a low, mean office building that must've been designed by a nihilistic defector from Soviet Russia. It was as stolid and joyless as everyone who worked there, including the Fishery Resources on the first and second floors and the Deeds and Records on the third.

The lobby smelled like B.O., and half the officebots were dark. Without even playing the old sneak-up-on-myself game, I marched up to one of the functioning bots and stuck my left hand inside. The monitor flashed my old drivers license photo and my name, with a touchscreen button below that read *Confirm*.

I confirmed that I was me...though I looked about a million years younger in the picture that had been on the license that I didn't even own anymore. I'd been thirty-two. I was thirty-three now.

I'd had two hands then, when I was thirty-two.

I confirmed that the guy in the picture, the one with the wise-ass smile and the bleached forelock, the one who could still drive, was me. Even though he really wasn't anymore...the Social Services lobby was not exactly the time and place for a philosophic debate. The monitor flashed, *Do you have an appointment, yes/no?*

I hit *yes*. Of course, I didn't. But the only way I'd get to talk to anybody would be if I made it look like there was a screwup in the system.

Accessing....

The elevator dinged open behind me, and a cluster of low-paid office drones got out, talking about who'd bought a square on a football pool and who hadn't. I looked at the tiny time readout in the corner of the officebot monitor. Four thirty-one? No way. They *closed* at four-thirty.

Accessing....

Fat fucking chance. I turned on my heel and slipped around the football brigade, and flashed my prosthetic through the gap in the closing elevator doors. The sensor caught it. The doors opened up again, and I stepped inside. Since everyone else would be waiting for a down elevator, my upward trip didn't stop at Fishery Resources or Deeds and Records. It opened on the fourth floor of the world's dourest office building this side of the Kremlin, and I shuffled out and reminded myself that I was not there to see Jim. Because it sure as hell felt like I was picking him up (back when I could still drive) on my way home from work. And we were gonna have a few beers, maybe, and then go back to my place and get busy.

Social workers milled around at the safety glass door that connected the office to the fourth floor lobby. I looked at them, rumpled, tired, in ugly ties and worn shoes, as eager to get out of that place as I was. And I realized I didn't even know who my social worker was anymore.

Only that it wasn't Jim.

He'd always had an uncanny way about him—and his mojo was still intact. I thought his name, and there he was, behind the greenish glass with its honeycomb wires. James Murphy. So broad-shouldered that his off-the-rack dress shirt strained across the upper arms, and crept up his wrists to let his tattoos peek out.

James fuckin' Murphy.

He was talking to some co-worker chick in a suit. Laughing.

His smile died when he saw me standing there in the open elevator door.

The co-worker he'd been talking with kept chatting until he said something quiet to her, and she looked over at me to see what was what. Hard to say what the face she made was all about. Pity, maybe. Disgust.

Jim strolled over slow—no hurrying him—and his cronies didn't hold the elevator for him. As the door closed on them and left the two of us alone, he shoved his hands in his pockets, looked me up and down, and said, "Desmond."

"I don't suppose there's any chance my new guy hasn't logged out of his terminal yet so he could answer me a quick question."

"Your new guy...."

"You know. My social worker."

"Maritza Collins?"

Fine. My new *chick*. Whatever. "Yeah. She around?"

Jim's face did something like his co-worker's had when she'd given me the once-over. "Maritza's on vacation this week."

"For a whole week? Geez, must be nice to work for Uncle Sam. What am I supposed to do while she's gone?"

"You didn't call, did you?"

"Like I'm gonna waste time dicking around with the phone. I barely made it here before you closed as it is."

"Your social worker's not here. You didn't pre-arrange your visit through your housebot since you refuse to have one. You couldn't be bothered to call." He glanced up at a digital readout on the wall. "And on top of that, it's four thirty-five. Desmond...you asking me what you're supposed to do? I could answer that question, but we'd be here all night."

Suddenly, I couldn't even look at Jim anymore. If I looked at him, I'd remember what he smelled like. His skin. His hair. And I'd realize how much I missed smelling it. I looked down at the linoleum as if it was fascinating.

He'd drawn a big enough breath to keep listing another half-dozen of my faults, but when I stood down, he did too. "You really needed to see Maritza?"

"I'm here to straighten something out, not to stalk you. I'd never flatter myself by thinking you'd be willing to give me the time of day."

A few beats, and then he said, "It's four thirty-seven, now."

Like I needed to be reminded that not only did I screw everything up with the hottest guy I'd ever fucked...I missed that damn wit of his, too. "So when does she come back?" I said.

"Monday."

"Fuck me," I muttered. Rent wasn't due for another couple weeks, but I had five bucks and change to my name. To my knowledge, the liquor store didn't offer a line of credit. And I only had three cigarettes left. "Can I see someone else? It can't wait 'til Monday."

He thought about it for a minute—and believe you me, he wasn't trying to sort out what the answer was. Jim already knows everything. No, he was weighing the pros and cons of helping me out. I kept on staring at the floor and looking as humble as I possibly could.

"Is it your check?" he said finally.

I nodded.

"Okay. We should try to clear it up before the weekend."

He walked back toward the safety glass doors and scanned into the officebot. I was right behind him, fighting the urge to run my hand down his hip—and not just because we were at his work. It wasn't my place to touch him like that anymore, in public or in private. The officebot balked, and he needed to key in—twice—to confirm that he knew he would not be paid for any overtime he worked. Then he turned to me and said, "You'll need to scan, too, since it's after hours. Policy."

I swallowed my anxiety and let the thing read me. The door slid open, and the bot piped in some canned music that sounded familiar, but not, to cover the rattle of a misaligned blower in the HVAC system. Then I recognized a hook. Dead Kennedys.

Shit—that meant Jim and I were probably alone. Either that, or one of his co-workers recently went hardcore, and since they were all a bunch of Beyonce fanboys, that wasn't very likely. And being alone with Jim was making me crazy in a way that I totally hadn't seen coming.

His office looked the same: a mess. Which didn't seem right. Because how could it be the same, when so much had changed?

The officebot had logged him into his terminal by the time we got there. He sat in his chair. I sat in mine. He was pretty calm. I tried to look like I wasn't warring with the urge to strip that necktie the rest of the way off and start gnawing on his throat like he liked. "Let's see...." My file was right there, too. As if the officebot wanted to get me out of there as fast as it could so I didn't get a chance to ogle Jim. "Maritza called you ten times before she left. Your answering machine didn't pick up."

He glanced up at me, and the sort-of-pitying look on his face made my randiness wither. He didn't bother asking if the machine was broken (as far as I knew, it wasn't) and if I'd been home while the phone rang, and rang, and rang.

I had.

"She was only required to try four times," he said.

"They have a policy for that?"

Jim ran his hand through his hair. He had enough hair to do that, since he'd grown it out. Since the last time I'd touched it. "They have a policy for everything."

He grabbed one of the dangling metal balls of a perpetual motion machine on the desktop, pulled back, and let go. The ball swung down and hit the others, and then the ball at the far end swung up. *Clack. Clack. Clack.* Out of synch with the Musak version of Holiday in Cambodia. When I couldn't stand not knowing anymore, I said, "Does the terminal say whatever it was she wanted to tell me?"

Clack. Clack. Clack.

Sigh.

Finally, Jim met my eyes and said, "You were supposed to see a career counselor. When you didn't do that, the system assigned you to a re-training program. Which began on the thirteenth." *Clack. Clack. Clack.* "Which put a stop on your check when you didn't show up."

I slapped my hand over the metal balls to shut them up, and said, "So, what? I'm screwed?"

That response was just begging for a Jim Murphy-style dig, but he didn't take the bait. "I can set it up so your check gets cut when you sign back into the officebot in the lobby and let it know you're going to the job site tomorrow. I'll expedite the payment so you get it by Friday. But, Des, if I do this and you don't show up when you're supposed to...then *I'm* screwed."

"I don't get what this whole re-training thing is about, anyway," I told him. "All kinds of people—two-handed people—live off Disability for the rest of their lives. And now I've gotta go through all this bullshit—"

"Desmond?"

"Yeah?"

"Shut the fuck up."

CHAPTER 7

Digi-tech might have started out as a bunch of do-gooders like Pam Steiner, who let a bunch of gimps graze their way through all her husband's junk food one night a week while Cripples Anonymous took place in her family room. But I think by the time I darkened Digi-tech's doorstep, they were your typical assholes who'd won some kind of government bid. The warehouse was full of robotics components, all the tinkery moving parts that make bots do their thing. It was also full of people making those parts. And still more people watching the other people who were making those parts. It wouldn't have surprised me if there was yet another tier of people watching the people-watchers, but if there was, those guys were probably off in some air-conditioned room where the lowlifes like me couldn't see 'em.

"Mister Poole," the woman at the check-in desk said. She glanced at her clock. Eight fifty-nine—I was early. Because how could I sleep in when the look I'd seen on Jim's face was haunting me? You know. The one when he told me I could royally screw him...with the implication that he thought it was a very real possibility. "Fill this out—it's two-sided—and when you're done, report to Luis, over there by the welders."

I glanced where she was pointing with her clipboard. That'd be the spot where all the sparks were flying around.

My basic information was already on the piece of paper. Name. Address. Handicap...that spot said RBE, short for a "right arm-below-elbow" amputee. Real catchy. What wasn't filled out was all the hard stuff. The essay questions. Name my greatest skills. (*My winning personality*). Any challenges I anticipate. (*I will take them as they come*). And the reason I wanted to work there...I didn't suppose I'd score any points with, *they're forcing me,* so I wrote, *self-esteem*. That's one of those catch-all terms that means nothing at all, but the mere mention of it leaves all the socially conscious liberal types nodding sagely and scratching their chins.

My new supervisor, Luis, was a double-amputee with a five-fingered prosthetic for his right hand and a rotating clamp thing for the left. Thankfully, he didn't try to shake hands, because then I most definitely would have walked out of there. Whether my job desertion screwed Jim or not.

He took my clipboard with his clampy hand, smoothed a wispy mustache with his fakey hand, scanned my info and said, "You were an HVAC technician? Good. Then you know how it all fits together."

Yeah. The useless bone's connected to the lame bone. "Uh-huh."

"You know how to weld?"

"Haven't done it since shop class." And I wasn't particularly good, even then. "Most HVAC systems are galvanized. Held together with bolts instead of welds."

"Fabricator-installer is the job to have, *bato*." He was so enthusiastic about it, you'd swear it was his religious calling. "Good money. Real good money."

Okay. I could do with some real good money. Before work, I'd gone through my garbage and dug out eight different cigarette butts in hopes of getting one good drag off each of them to get me to the bus stop. So dangling money in front of me at that particular moment was like flashing a T-bone steak to a starving Rottweiler.

Luis leaned in and confided in me, though he'd only known me all of two seconds, "The trick is to let someone else do the standard installations. The custom jobs—that's where the money's at. How much you think you can charge someone for a custom gardenbot?"

"I dunno."

"Take a guess."

"Uh. A thousand dollars?"

"Psh. A mid-level model right out of the box starts at eight-fifty, without installation."

"Look, I haven't been shopping for a...I live in an apartment."

"Try eight thousand bucks."

I turned the sum around in my head and said, "Okay."

Even more conspiratorially, he said, "Think about it. You pay six hundred, wholesale. You build a special housing so it fits in their brick wall or their rock garden or whatever. Then all the rest? That's markup, my friend. Over seven grand. All yours. For what—a little cutting, a little welding, hook up a few wires, and there you go."

"Wow."

He glanced at my chart meaningfully. "And I'll bet you already know how the wiring goes."

Even back when I'd had two hands, I'd never exactly been all that eager to show up for work. Then again, I'd never hauled in seven grand for a little cutting and a little welding.

It was a good thing Luis had managed to get me all starry-eyed about the prospect of having a marketable skill—otherwise I would've flipped when he jammed a welding gun over my prosthetic. "Just wear it around, get used to the weight. For today, you'll shadow Ben over there. He does a good pull-joint. He'll get you up to speed on how to do your settings. Then, after lunch, we'll set you up with some practice pieces. MIG welding's easy, you'll get the hang of it in a week."

I nodded, like I still had visions of sugarplums and seven thousand dollars dancing in my head. It was tiring work, though, watching this Ben guy weld. Lunch couldn't come soon enough, even though lunch for me was an air sandwich and a trip to the drinking fountain. Imagine my surprise when I turned around and found one of the other welders standing behind me with his welding mask flipped up—and there was old Georgie Argusto from the Crowley Avenue Boys, minus all his eyebrow piercings, and dressed in navy coveralls. A hefty kid, tall. A few years younger than me, with big Italian features and a five o'clock shadow that grew back in ten minutes after he shaved. "Georgie," I said, like he'd snuck up on me in some kind of dream. I checked. He still had two hands, just like I remembered. "What're you doing here?"

He glanced at me and quickly looked away. Tried to pretend he hadn't seen me although it was obvious he had. Georgie might be big, but he was no mental giant. If he hadn't done that, made eye contact and then done a piss-poor act of not knowing me, I would've figured maybe I was remembering wrong. Maybe he was just another member of the Argusto clan, one I hadn't actually met. But the way he absolutely refused to look at me, I was sure.

"Come on, Georgie. Don't be a dick."

Georgie curled his lip and gave a little shrug. "Don't tell nobody I'm here."

"Yeah, okay." Here I'd thought the problem was me—hell, it usually is. What a relief he was embarrassed not to see me, but to be seen.

"I was on Disability for bipolar...but some fuckhead over at Social Services decided I needed a job. And here I am." He looked down at his coveralls. "It ain't too bad. I guess."

Georgio Argusto. Of all the guys, I knew him the least, but even so, bipolar would explain a hell of a lot. He'd never been one to kick back and relax. He was too busy climbing viaducts and tagging train cars to hang out and shoot the shit.

He took a drink from the water fountain, then nodded for me to follow him outside. We scanned out at the service door, then parked ourselves on an old corrugated metal loading dock that was still warm from the morning sun. He shook out a smoke, saw me looking at it, then offered me one. Winstons. But I wasn't complaining, since my plan had been to poke through the ash trays and see if I could find any with a few drags left on 'em.

"What's going on these days?" I said. And what I meant was, *I know I wasn't really a full-fledged part of the crew, me being gay and all. Even so, does anyone give a damn what happened to me—anyone at all? 'Cause I haven't seen a single one of you since that night.*

Or maybe what I really meant was, *what did Biggie say about me? Does he even know I'm alive?*

I met Tony Bigliani in the fourth grade. He gave me my first cigarette. Sounds romantic, I know...but back then my body wasn't as inured to nicotine as it is now. When that cigarette made me hurl my meatloaf and tapioca pudding, Biggie also gave me a new nickname: Puke. It lasted through September, when the Vietnamese transfer student took the heat off me by getting pegged with Gook. Apparently it's too confusing for nicknames to rhyme. I'd outgrown it anyway. By then I could smoke circles around any other ten-year-old in Riverside.

I didn't ask about Biggie specifically. Instead I asked general questions about the old gang to get a feel for what had happened since that fateful night last spring. Georgie smoked, and told me who was in jail, and who was out of jail, and who was on the outs with the rest of the guys for knocking up someone else's chick. Because if you're gonna be doing that shit, at least pull out before you shoot.

Nothing about Biggie. I couldn't tell if he was hiding something or he was just too oblivious to think I'd care. I'd smoked my cigarette down to the filter. Instead of asking about Biggie, I looked at Georgie's pack and said, "You got another one of those for me?" and he tapped one out. I lit it and took a good drag, and decided that maybe Winstons weren't too bad after all.

"Don't your new arm work?" he blurted out, so suddenly I flinched.

"It works."

"You lit it left-handed." He pulled out his own lighter and fumbled with it in his non-dominant hand. "I can't do shit with my left hand." Finally, he got the lighter going, awkwardly. "It's like you can hardly use that thing at all. That ain't how everyone said it would be. I thought them robo-arms were supposed to work as good as a real hand."

I shrugged, and the stupid hunk of junk whirred and positioned itself like I was trying to hitchhike. I gave him a sarcastic thumbs-up and said, "Yeah. They're fucking fantastic."

* * *

I usually grab a burger on my way home from the bus stop, but I was too broke even for that. I went a quarter-mile out of my way to a corner store and grabbed a couple packets of ramen noodles instead. Fifty cents each—since when? I could've sworn they were ten for a dollar. Maybe in a real supermarket. A short trip for someone with a car, but for me and my gimpy bus pass? An hour-long mission, easy. I bought three. Could've afforded five, but I told myself I felt more secure with a buck and a few quarters in my pocket.

The change in my routine—grabbing dinner somewhere new—threw me off just as much as reporting to an actual job had. I approached my place from the wrong side of the street, without a burger in my hand, with no wrapper to throw over the fence. Which sucked, because I was keen on seeing how long it took the neighbor's gardenbot to come out and clean up after me. Maybe get a look at its housing, and see if it was just a pre-fab unit, or if any customization had needed to take place to fit it into its setting. The bag of ramen hung from my prosthetic. I squeezed the bag's contents with my meatworks hand and considered unwrapping one of the noodle blocks for the sake of having something to throw, but I figured I'd just end up with noodles everywhere and a lost flavor packet if I went that route. Besides, there was plenty of trash in the gutter.

I bent over the curb and looked for something big enough to attract the gardenbot's attention, and saw a dozen slimy cigarette butts someone must've dumped from their car ash tray. You know your nicotine fit's bad when that starts looking good.

I kicked myself for smoking that cigarette Georgie gave me for the road once I got off the bus. I'd thought I was jonesing bad then. That was nothing compared to now. As I hovered there, bent over, looking for something to throw, wondering whether or not I'd let any butts with a drag still on 'em slip my notice that morning (maybe, in the bedroom ash tray), a car door slammed and a voice I'd know anywhere called out, "Des-mond Poole. Showing off your best side, I see."

I straightened up and turned. Corey approached, decked out in his Harrington and his stovepipe jeans, and a jaunty little gray tweed cabbie hat to top it all off. He was a sight for sore eyes. And there I was, garage chic, with black grunk under the nails of my left hand without even performing any actual work with it, just from being in the shop all day. "Hey. You got a cigarette for me?"

He marched up, hands in pockets, and glanced down at the gutter clogged with leaf slime. "You drop your pack?"

"All out. And broke 'til Friday."

He shot the gutter one more look, but didn't pry to find out what I'd been looking for. His robo-arm gave off its quiet whirs as his arm muscles signaled his activators and his activators moved his prosthetic fingers, and he pulled out a pack of smokes and grabbed me a Camel Light as easily as Georgie had coughed up that Winston. He even cupped those robotic fingers around the cigarette when he moved to light it for me, just like a real hand. He didn't flick his lighter with it, then again, it'd been his non-dominant hand that got eaten by a conveyor belt. Though if it had, I would imagine he'd have that lighter fired up in no time flat, even with his robo-arm. Corey's clever that way.

Me? I'd just learned to smoke with my left hand. Since I had a bag of ramen hanging from the right, it made sense. Maybe I should start carrying ramen everywhere. I'd get less questions from people like Georgie, wondering why I hadn't figured out how to work the damn thing yet.

"I tried to call, but your answerphone wasn't on."

I forgot about the gardenbot next door and headed for the vestibule, with Corey right behind me. "Yeah. Remind me to fix that."

"And by fix, you mean...hit the little on-button?"

"You enjoy being a smartass too much."

"That's what you love about me."

My key slid from the lock and skittered across the metal, but I chalked it up to the smoke stinging my eyes. It was just an expression, this *love* thing. Like you love sleeping in an hour when daylight savings time is over, or you love it when you find a free sample in your mailbox. Love him? I'd known him all of two weeks.

"So where've you been? I've been sitting out there for an hour seeing if you'd turn up."

Really? If that'd been me, I would've gone home once he didn't answer his doorbell or his phone. "I was at a job."

"No way." He trooped upstairs behind me and groped my ass while I got my apartment door unlocked. "What kind of job?"

"Welding," I said around the cigarette.

"No wonder you smell like machine shop. I think I like it. Kinda rugged. So, what's the deal, you're earning a few bucks under the table, or what?"

I finally got the door open and took the cigarette out of my mouth. Funny, how I could hardly stand parking them there with the smoke wafting into my eyes, even when I was dying to take a drag. "Nothing like that." I'd never be so ambitious. "Social Services is making me go."

"Serious? And you didn't get out of it?"

"I just said I spent the day at work, didn't I? What do you think?"

He followed me into the kitchen, where I de-bagged the ramen with a lot of rustling plastic, then turned the packet over to see how much water to boil. A whir, a grab, and Corey snatched it out from under my nose. "If you need to read the directions, you're sorely out of practice."

"I'm too hungry to argue with that."

"Relax. Have a drink. I'll cook it for you."

"There's nothing to drink. I told you, I'm broke. I didn't get my check."

"Aw, fuck. Who's your caseworker—Jim Murphy? That guy's a fucking Nazi."

While occasionally I did itch to tell Corey to shut the fuck up—I'd never needed to seriously bite back the impulse as much as I did at that very moment. Jim was a big boy, and he didn't need me to defend him...plus, the mere sound of his name made me go all funny inside. I knew if I said anything back, no way would it come out as playful. So I smoked his cigarette. And I watched him boil water.

"They'll do that," he said. "After four months—it's been longer than four months since you got the arm, right? Yeah, that's what they do, ship you off to vocational rehab like you're some kind of slave labor." He put the pot on the stove with his robo-arm and turned on the gas with his meatworks hand. The blue flame appeared in a whoosh. "I wish I'd known. I could've helped you get out of it."

"Yeah? How?"

"You don't see me working some bullshit job, do you?"

"I thought you got some kind of settlement."

"Not nearly as much as you'd think, not a hand's worth, if you know what I mean."

I did.

"You need to get some more diagnoses," he said. "Depression's a good one. Hint that you want to kill yourself when you see the shrink, that'll usually do it. There's other stuff you can do too—phantom pain, trouble sleeping, anxiety...you get the idea."

"I haven't seen the shrink in two months. At least."

"You've got to get in there. If your caseworker thinks you're at risk, he'll push you through the system and get you in to see the shrink. Who'd you say your guy was?"

Jim had never been adamant about me visiting the shrink—then again, Jim knew how much I hated that pasty little butterball. He'd watched me drink myself into a puking stupor after the first couple of mandatory visits. It just then occurred to me that the constant rescheduling of my psychiatric appointments might not be entirely coincidental. My caseworker knew me *too* well.

Though he wasn't my caseworker anymore, so all bets were off. "Marissa...somebody. I don't remember. She's new. There's probably a letter around here somewhere."

"Depression's totally your best bet. I've got a book you can use to read up on it, figure out what you're going to say. Then, if she does a home wellness check and sees you haven't cleaned up lately, you're golden. So don't clean the apartment for a few days."

I hadn't been planning on it.

"And if she asks, just say it didn't seem worth doing."

It didn't. "Let's not talk about it. It's too depressing."

Corey ignored my lack of enthusiasm for the subject in his totally Corey-ish way, and as we slurped our noodles and broth at the coffee table, he went on and on about different things I could say or do to stack some more diagnoses on top of my existing RBE. I didn't have much to say in return. I probably looked like I was too busy smoking five more of his cigarettes to weigh in on the discussion. He tipped back his bowl and drained his soup, and watched me smoke for a minute or two, then finally dropped his right hand to his crotch and said, "How sweet do you think my jiz will taste, now that you've swallowed all that salt?"

While it's seldom to never that I pass up dick, I felt exhausted, in the bone-deep way of a guy who hasn't worked for the past seven months and then been conscripted into hard labor. Or at least watching other people perform hard labor.

Corey unbuttoned his fly. "I bet it's just like a vanilla float."

"I'll take a rain check. I'm spent."

"C'mon, Des-mond. Don't be that way." He pulled it out and showed it to me, already fattening up in anticipation of the feel of my tonsils. "After I waited at your doorstep all this time...and even cooked you dinner."

His meatworks fingers slid up and down the stiffening shaft, while his robo-arm rested on the back of my couch, stationary and silent. I tried not to look at his dick. But impulse control wasn't exactly my forte. Corey's got a hot dick. I couldn't deny that.

He watched me watching him, and smiled. And stroked. And said, "Just a little taste. You know you wanna."

I savored the last few drags of his Camel, took another sidelong look at the ruddy head pushing out from his loose fist, and decided I didn't have anything to gain by denying myself. I slid down to the floor, knelt between his feet, and wrapped my mouth around him. He did taste sweet, but not because my mouth was salty. He'd spiffed himself up before he came over. His skin tasted like soap. His clothes smelled like clean laundry. And a hint of aftershave lurked around him, just a trace, that I needed to be right on top of him to pick up on. Sweet? The kid was a fucking lollipop.

He petted my head with his meatworks hand while I sucked him off—he knew better than to start in with the other one again. "You're not horny at all? Aren't you getting all hard feeling that cock in your mouth?"

I'd be a liar if I said stirrings hadn't begun. And him, saying it like that, well...it was more than just stirrings, listening to him talk about it, what with all the breathing and sighing he was doing, the hot little sounds that told me he dug the way my mouth felt.

"C'mon, man. Touch yourself while you deep-throat me. I want to watch you stroke it."

He was stiff enough to stay in my mouth while I struggled my pants down around my knees and started beating off for him. I handled my boner left-handed now. Just like my lighter.

"Yeah, like that." Corey cupped the back of my head and forced his dick a little deeper.

Schwing.

I got off on the thought of him forcing me—whaddaya know. I beat off harder. It was quiet for a while, just him breathing, me breathing, and the wet sound of his cock battering my throat, and the softer sound of my hand flying on my meat. He started squirming and arching his back, and I crept closer to the brink too, just from the feel of him getting ready to shoot.

He gave a little moan then, and I started jacking off hard. And then he said, "Fingerbang me. Please."

Shit. It was the "please" that did it. Nothing gets my rocks off like making a guy beg. My dick throbbed when I let go of it, but the thought of Corey writhing around on the end of my finger was enough to keep the juices flowing.

Even when he said, "With your other hand."

If I'd had maybe ten fewer strokes, I would've totally backed off. Corey, though, he's a pro at springing shit on me once I'm past the point of no return.

"Please," he said again, so soft I almost couldn't hear it.

It pissed me off, the way he was so good at using me to get what he wanted, but that anger just added more fuel to the fire. I twitched the residual meatworks of my right arm in an attempt to get three of my fingers to fold down, but no such luck. Most people with roboarms did it all the time. Ringing doorbells. Pointing. But not me. I just trained my left hand to do all that shit.

I grumbled, and he grabbed my hair and fucked my throat more urgently. "Please, Desmond, do me. I'll come so hard...."

Gah, he knew just what to say. I tried folding some of the fingers down with my left hand, even though I knew that'd never work. You can't start the motion from that end. The sensors only go one way, from my stump to the bot. The fingers sprang back up. Finally, in desperation, because I'd be damned if I let him finish without me, I managed to replicate the shrug that'd caused the stupid thumbs-up gesture I'd given Georgie at lunchtime. I pulled my mouth off his dick just long enough to spit on it, then I pressed that silicone-covered metal stub home. He howled, and he thrashed, and no, he hadn't been exaggerating. He came so hard it practically shot out my nose. And that's what I focused on. Him. Peaking so hard he was a helpless wreck.

That's what tipped me, finally. Focusing on him.

CHAPTER 8

It surprised me that I got any sleep at all with Corey in my bed, since I was used to having the whole thing to myself. That, and I was used to being at least half-drunk when I turned in. But between working all day and shooting my wad, I slept like a rock. A bird tweeting outside my window finally woke me, and then the realization that it was pretty bright in my bedroom. And then the realization that I had somewhere to be.

I did one of those classic sit-up-and-gasp moves. Corey'd been clinging to me like an octopus. He disentangled, and rolled to face the wall. "Too early."

"Fuck." Eight o'-fucking-clock and I needed to be there by nine. "Fuck." Shower? No time. I started pulling on clothes from the floor. "Fuck."

Corey rolled to face me and said, "What're you all worked up about?"

"I'm gonna be late."

"For your jobby-job? Where's it at?"

"In Kenmore. At nine."

"Calm down, Des-mond. I'll drive you. There's plenty of time... unless that clock is wrong."

I glanced at the clock. Eight oh-two. I'd always assumed it was right. What if it wasn't? What if it was slow? I hopped up out of bed with nothing on but a dirty sock. "Fuck."

"Go take a shower," Corey said. "You got coffee? I'll put coffee on."

I turned in the doorway and watched him grudgingly work his way out of the covers. Sleep hadn't been kind to his hair, which he usually kept in a mid-60's Pete Townsend forward-combed shag. Now it was mashed flat on the pillow side and sticking straight up in back, nearly emo. He pushed himself into a sitting position on his robo-arm, natural as you please. The actuators whirred quietly into the sheets as he straightened the fingers. Then he cocked his head and looked at me, hazy with sleep. "Thinking about playing hooky?"

I'd be lying if I said I wasn't tempted. But as distracting as Corey looked, all sleepy and naked (and I'd never imagined him waking up beside me, but there he was), I still had the image of Jim fresh in my mind—the one where he told me he'd be screwed for expediting my check if I managed to fuck this up. I said, "Coffee sounds good," and headed for the bathroom.

Once I had my prosthetic in its usual spot—lying across the closed toilet seat lid—I pushed open the shower curtain with my stump and turned on the water. I held the soap in my left hand, obviously, but in my haste to get in and out in two minutes, did a lot of the soaping up with my residual arm. It was probably the most I'd used my right arm all week. Once I'd dried it well enough to powder it and squeeze the prosthetic back on, I staggered out half-wet to the smell of coffee, and decided clean clothes were probably my best bet, since I wouldn't need to wait on the Hertel bus.

"I'm betting you take it black," Corey said, when I made a pit stop into the kitchen.

"Yeah? How come?"

He handed me a full mug, then trailed his meatworks fingers up my bare forearm. Goose bumps rose behind the trail of his touch. "Either I'm a really perceptive judge of character...or you don't have any sugar or cream."

"Smartass."

"You know it." His hand skimmed my side as he turned away to finish getting dressed himself, and I let out a breath. I'd set myself up big-time for one of those "that's what you *love* about me" comments.

I'd just dodged a bullet.

Corey's car was new, a Chevy Servo with everything bot-run, from the windows to the radio. You can always tell who's driving a bot-mobile. They're the ones stuck going the speed limit. He scanned his meatworks hand into the dash, and the carbot said, "Destination?"

"Digi-Control in Kenmore."

A route lit up on the dash, and Madness blasted from the car stereo. He spun down the volume and said, "Scan in if you want to hear something different."

"It's fine."

"You realize I've never seen you scan in anywhere."

"Last night I scanned in to your ass just fine."

He laughed as if he thought I'd been joking. We breezed by the bus stop in no time flat, then pulled into a fast food drive-through. My mouth started watering. He said, "I heard that's an actual medical thing, too."

"What is?"

"Aversion to robotics."

I grunted, and he ordered four egg-and-sausage biscuits without asking me if I wanted anything. Which was good, since I couldn't pay for them, not until my check came. It would be there when I got home from work—I consoled myself with that thought. When Jim said he was going to do something, he made it happen. Corey pulled through and paid, then took out one sandwich with his robo-hand and gave the bag to me. "There. Breakfast and lunch."

Saliva was pumping so hard it practically ran down my chin. "Thanks."

"You did spring for dinner. Though I did all the cooking."

I wolfed down two of the biscuits, then wrapped up the third in the paper bag and tucked it into my inner pocket for later. I wouldn't get home soon enough to cash that check, but I had enough for a couple more packets of ramen, and I could be at the bank bright and early Saturday morning and get some actual money.

We made it to the shop with time to spare—me showered, with food in my belly, not even hung over. It was nothing short of a miracle. "So you wanna hit the bars later?" Corey asked as I opened the car door with my left hand. "There's an open mic with a couple of cool bands that're supposed to play."

"Eh. Probably not. After I'm through here, I'll just want to stay home and unwind."

"That's cool. I'll bring the booze."

I'd been about to clarify that I wanted to unwind *alone*, but when I thought about it, vodka sounded mighty tasty.

"I'll see what I can dig up on getting out of work," he said. "This job-training thing is such bullshit."

He gave me a little wink as he pulled away, and left me standing there at the factory door with ten minutes to spare, the remainder of his cigarettes, and a head full of confusion. Because he sounded like me—or, more precisely, what I imagine I sounded like when Jim was forced to listen to me. And for some unfathomable reason, I wanted to disagree with him.

Luis noticed that I clocked in a few minutes early, and he seemed pleased. And I was pleased with myself for pleasing him. And I wondered if those would be my first few steps on the road to self-sufficiency that Jim had managed to engineer for me, despite the double-barreled breakup. Which led me to wondering why I hadn't felt nearly as optimistic before, back when I'd been your typical, two-handed HVAC installer. After all, hadn't I possessed the skills to do these high-paying custom installations before? No doubt they would've been easier with two hands. But the motivation had never been there before. And that changed everything.

I shadowed this guy Marco for about an hour, and then he decided I could try a few practice welds myself, just to get the feel of the machine. Even if I'd been holding the welding gun in an actual hand, the speed of the wire feed was controlled by foot pedal. All I needed to do with my gimp arm was aim it—no fancy flexes of my shoulder or control of my actual prosthetic required. Just a matter of keeping it steady. Once we went through all the machine settings, I did some push-joints and some pull-joints, and though it'd been years since I held that sparking welder in my hand, it came back to me easily enough that I lost myself in the process of making a perfect weld, not too skimpy, and not spattered and slaggy, either. Just right.

I was so wrapped up in my weld that I nearly jumped out of my skin when I heard the crash and scream.

All around me, guys dropped their tools and ran to go see what had happened. I was stuck to the welding gun, and it took me an extra couple of minutes to unhook it from my prosthetic. I spotted Georgie pacing back and forth behind the crowd that had formed around the accident, and I asked him what happened.

"I dunno. I think he had the safety off."

I rubbernecked into the crowd. Whatever had gone bad, it'd happened with one of the robo-welders, the machines that do the bigger welds, and do 'em quick and consistent. I crept into the crowd even though part of me was silently screaming to myself, *What the fuck? Turn around! I guarantee you don't want to see.* That was probably my common sense part—and I wasn't accustomed to paying it much heed.

The guys at the front of the crowd were too tall to see past, and maybe that would've saved me, not seeing it, whatever had just happened. Except for two things.

The smell. Like pork chops.

And the sound. Someone up front yelled, "Get an ice pack—maybe they can save the fingers."

Hall. Door. Cold air.

Down the street.

Another street.

Save the fingers.

Another street. And another one. Houses. Suburban houses. All the same.

The smell of cooked meat.

A crosswalk. A park. More houses.

Cop car. Flashing light.

Save the fingers.

"Desmond Poole?"

I stopped walking and looked up. It was just a couple of Kenmore cops, white and middle-aged and relatively harmless. One of them said, "Are you Desmond Poole?"

"He's supposed to have a robo-arm. Can you see his hands?"

"They're in his pockets. But yeah, that looks like him."

The cop got out of the car. I tried to remember what I'd been caught vandalizing this time. Don't say anything. They can't arrest you if they don't read you your rights.

"Mr. Poole? Can you hear me?"

"He could have a weapon. Watch out—I don't like his eyes."

"Me neither. Mr. Poole, nice and easy now, take your hands out of your pockets so I can see them."

"I'm calling for backup."

"Nice and easy."

A scuffle. Me, face-down, with two hundred pounds of Kenmore Cop on my back. Handcuffs. The back of a cruiser. Radio sounds. The white, vertical slab front of their municipal building. The inside of a cell.

"Desmond? What happened?"

Jim?

Vaguely, I remembered that he was still my emergency contact. And then I experienced a moment of disorientation where I wondered if I was still in a hospital bed with tubes in my veins and a compression bandage on my fresh stump.

I looked down at my hands. Two. But one was meatworks, one robotic. The plasticuff dug into my meat hand. My other hand could've snapped the vinyl—if I knew the right series of shrugs and twitches to make that happen. I flicked my arm muscles, and the robo-hand gave the finger. Where the fuck had that gesture been when I needed it the most?

"Desmond?"

"An accident," I said. My voice sounded funny—pinched, like I needed to swallow.

"That's what Luis said. There was an accident at the shop, and you walked right out. And he chased after you, but you didn't say a word. Just kept on walking."

"I guess."

"You guess. What does that mean—that you don't want to talk about it? Or that you don't actually remember?"

"I dunno."

"Because if you're faking some shit to get out of working, swear to God, I will never forgive you."

I swallowed a few times. What—hadn't my swallow-reflex been working while I was on my little stroll? And how far had I gone, exactly, before the pigs picked me up? Fucking hell, all those things Corey had said about pretending to be crazy must've gotten to me, 'cause I was starting to think I might really be certifiable. "My recollection's a little vague," I mumbled.

* * *

Jim lowered his voice and said, "Dr. Hewitt's coming. And the way this all turns out is up to you. Keep laying it on thick, and you just might get out of working. You might also find yourself committed."

A part of me thought Jim was the one laying it on thick. But that part felt small, and very far away. When I didn't answer, he cradled his forehead in his palm and let out a shaky breath. "That's not what you want, right?"

"No." I valued my freedom too much. I remembered that, at least.

"Then don't talk suicidal," he whispered. "Whatever you do."

Details of the station began surfacing, like the floor that had just been washed with something rankly antiseptic, and was still a bit tacky, and the sound of phones ringing down the hall. I still felt vague. But the vagueness was taking on some semblance of reality. I'd been making a pull-joint—I remembered watching the sparking wire through the helmet, and even though my gimp arm was sore from holding it steady, it wasn't a bad kind of sore. I didn't mind it.

And then there'd been screaming.

I shook my head and focused on some initials carved into thick paint. Not gang symbols or graffiti tags, just a couple of clumsy letters by someone who wanted the world to know that he'd spent time in suburban lockup.

"Mr. Murphy." The shrink's voice, as he greeted Jim, carried down the hall, as powerful as an opera singer's. It was totally at odds with his physical appearance—short and round, with a well-receded hairline, and fleshy looking features that always seemed somehow moist. Just to look at him, you wouldn't think he was a person with any authority. But the minute he opened his mouth, everyone around him scrambled to do his bidding. He paused beside Jim, and said, "My paperwork says Mr. Poole isn't in your caseload anymore."

"He isn't. Maritza's on vacation."

"Ah." He scrutinized a printout he was holding, and Jim loomed over him.

Jim's pissed off. Funny, how I could tell by the way he was standing, and me only watching him with my peripheral vision. Especially with half my brain somewhere in la-la land. But I knew he was mad at the shrink, just like I knew my ass was starting to get numb from sitting in the same position too long.

"According to the report," Hewitt said, "he was exhibiting dissociative behavior."

He looked to Jim, as if he expected some sort of confirmation. Jim just stood there, stony—which wasn't much like him. I was curious about it, but not enough to perk up and pay attention. I don't know that anything short of a miracle would've really got my attention.

When it was obvious Jim wasn't going to throw him a bone, Hewitt shuffled some papers, then looked up at me and said, "Mr. Poole, do you know where you are?"

"Kenmore," I said. It came out flat.

"And do you know who I am?"

"Looks like you're Dr. Hewitt."

His eyebrows did a wry twist as he kept shuffling through my paperwork. So much paperwork. "Can you tell me what day it is?"

"Friday." And my check would be in my mailbox when I got home. It damn well better be.

"You haven't been in to see me in over three months. We'll need to rectify that."

I shrugged the shoulder of my meatworks arm. It wasn't safe to shrug them both. You never knew what shrugging the right shoulder would make the robo-arm do.

"Can you tell me anything about what happened at work today?"

"There was an accident." *Try and save his fingers.* "I dunno. It's…I dunno."

"How do you feel?"

"I dunno."

"Remember the primary emotions. Happy, sad, angry and afraid."

Not only did I not know how I felt at that very moment, I couldn't even recall feeling any of those things. Ever. I remembered the visual aid we would work with in his office, the sheet of paper that had two dozen different words for fear on it—like they didn't all mean the same damn thing when you came right down to it. I could remember that piece of paper that was supposed to make me pinpoint how I felt. But I didn't actually feel anything. "I dunno," I said again.

"Are you having thoughts of hurting yourself?"

I shook my head slowly. To be honest, I wasn't having many thoughts, period.

"Are you angry?"

I kept shaking my head, slowly, side to side. "I'm not anything."

He flipped papers, and read a bit here and there, and then said, "This incident's similarity to your own accident triggered an acute stress reaction. The numbness will clear itself up in a matter of days, if not hours. Your memories might resurface..." he paged through my data, "or they might stay a bit shaky, given your history. But you're hardly a danger to yourself or anyone else—so there's no reason for them to hold you here."

"That's it?" Jim said. He was just as loud as Hewitt, but only because he was pissed off. "What's he supposed to do, just go back to work like nothing happened? Aren't you going to give him any meds for it?"

"All he needs is some rest...and an assignment somewhere a little less hazardous, next time occupational therapy places him."

"I'll let Maritza know." Jim's voice was like ice.

"And get him scheduled to see me. These support-group hours he's been racking up might satisfy your office's mental health requirements, but talk therapy is not indicated for PTSD. He needs to see a real doctor."

"So you can cut him loose after he's had an acute stress reaction and tell him to go get some rest?"

"What more should I do—follow him home? Tuck him in?"

Jim chewed on his response and said, "We're not seeing each other. That was before his accident."

"Any insinuation you drew from my statement is of your own

interpretation," Hewitt said. "We both know it would be just as much against departmental policy for me to reference your personal life as it would for you to be involved with a client."

I'm not sure why the good stuff insisted on happening while I was too blown away to care about it. Jim is a rock. It takes a lot to get to him, a hell of a lot. And I'd never seen anyone get under his skin like Dr. Hewitt. Normally, I would have asked him about it—especially given how long it took for him to sign me out of the police department. But instead I just sat there as Jim dealt with the red tape, and as we drove past Digi-Control, past the post office, past the place where I normally grab my burger, and around the turnoff to the side street where I live.

Where Corey's metallic blue Chevy Servo was parked in front of my house.

"Can we go to your place?" I blurted out.

I think it surprised me as much as it surprised Jim. After all, I could have told him to just drop me off. That I was tired. That I needed to get some rest. But I knew that no matter what I said, he probably would have at least seen me in. That's how he is. And while Corey wouldn't have been surprised to see Jim there—especially once he heard how my day had turned to shit—I just wasn't up for explaining Corey to Jim.

He slowed to a roll as he eyed me, and then said, "Okay," and eased on the gas.

I slumped a little so my jacket didn't show above the passenger window and turned my head away as if I was checking out the house across the street. Another turn, and disaster was avoided.

At least for the moment.

CHAPTER 9

Jim's got a place in Black Rock that used to be a drug house. It's a small, ugly box of a building that ran him maybe twenty grand at the auction block, and another ten to make it livable. The little old Polish lady next door who'd been there all her life was leery of him at first. Until she saw him getting in his car and driving off to a job every weekday morning—then she warmed up pretty quick. He had renters on the other side with a dog that barked morning, noon and night, but maybe those guys were gone by now. Every once in a while he got a knock on the door from some tweaked-out idiot who couldn't see it wasn't a drug house anymore. And then the next day he'd end up scrubbing spray paint off his new siding.

Most of the houses in that part of Black Rock were built too close together for driveways, but the parking spot in front of Jim's house was open. When he was at home in a wife-beater and jeans, he looked like he could kick your ass from here to next week, so the thugs with their half-dozen half-working cars found other places to park them all since, unlike the wandering druggies who could have come from anywhere, they'd be pretty easy for Jim to find.

Jim parked in the empty spot. He probably would have opened my door for me if I let him, but even though my head felt cottony, I managed to let myself out of the car. There was something different about his house, but maybe it was just the change of season. There'd been snow piled up to the windows last time I'd seen it, whereas now it was drifting leaves and newspapers.

I think he normally would have picked up a few stray fast food wrappers and plastic shopping bags that had blown onto his lawn as we crossed it—no gardenbot here—but he was too busy worrying about me to give two shits about the grass. His front door opened right into the living room and the stairway to the second floor. The housebot was mounted front and center beside the stairs. He scanned in, then turned and looked at me awkwardly and said, "Maybe you shouldn't."

Someone telling me *not* to scan in? Shit, maybe I really had snapped.

A grunky kind of industrial song came on, and Jim pushed a few buttons for quiet, then pulled off his necktie and dropped it on the floor. His old black cat Simba slunk around the corner, stretching a front leg, then a back leg with spread toes, as if she didn't want to seem too hurried about greeting us. She wove through his ankles a few times, then mine (as if the months that had gone by since the last time she'd seen me were hardly worth noticing), and then calmly strolled back to wherever it was she hid out and observed the goings-on at Casa Jim even more unobtrusively than the housebot.

"Are you hungry?" Jim said. "Do you want a beer?"

I probably was hungry. "A beer."

He went to the kitchen and came back with a couple of beers in one hand and a half-full bag of tortilla chips in the other. "Don't just stand there," he told me. "Sit down."

I was still standing beside the front door. I wandered in and sat on the couch.

"Here." Jim grabbed my leather jacket and helped me shrug out of it. "Park your thumb." He slipped the jacket off and tossed it on his recliner, then sat down next to me and opened both the beers. I took a sip, and then another. I'm not a big beer drinker—too much carbonation and not enough alcohol—but when someone puts a drink in my hand, it doesn't occur to me to not drink it. He plowed through a few chips. I drank. He drank. And finally he said, "You're not feeling suicidal, are you?"

I shook my head.

He ate a few more chips, then held the bag up for me to encourage me to do the same. I did my right-left thing, and it took me extra time to process that neither sticking my prosthetic in the bag, nor attempting to pick up a chip with my meatworks hand without letting go of the beer was a viable option. I put my beer on the coffee table, took a tortilla chip and ate it, then realized I was starving and started devouring them.

I polished off what was left in the bag, finished my beer, and turned the empty bottle around in my hand a few times.

"It's weird," Jim said, "seeing you this quiet."

I nodded.

"Is it true your support group doesn't help you at all?"

I tried to determine if I was better or worse off for my time at Pam Steiner's house, but it seemed like too much information to process at the moment. "It's a royal pain to get there," I said.

"I figured it might help to meet other people who were going through the same thing as you."

I thought about the way Corey's prosthetic clattered against mine while he was buried in my ass. "I dunno. I guess."

Jim sighed long and hard, and took a pull of his beer. "I guess it was stupid of me to get you out of seeing Hewitt."

I actually laughed at the thought of that—nothing elaborate, just a quick "ha," but the sound of it startled me, as if there'd been someone else in the room with us who chose that moment to pipe up.

"How is that funny?"

"I always figured you knew how to work the system." I couldn't make sense of what he actually chose to make the system do for him, no. But it was no big surprise that he could bend it to his will if he put his mind to it.

"Hewitt's a jag. If there was anyone else for you to see, it would be different. But it's just him. On the whole northwest side, just him."

The thought of there being only one shrink in the city struck me as improbable, but of course, that's not what he meant. Hewitt was the only free shrink I could see through Social Services.

"What's the matter," I said, "is he too quick to whip out his prescription pad for your liking?"

"So that's what this is about? You're worried you're missing out on the good drugs? Believe me, the strongest thing he'd give you is an antidepressant. Nothing that would leave you feeling good in the short-term. Nothing you'd be able to sell."

Figured. I supposed you didn't get to be Social Services' top shrink by handing out pills like they're candy. I grunted.

Jim stood up and went to his bookcase, which was crammed from top to bottom, some shelves even two-deep. A jumble of stuff, from an old encyclopedia to some skin mags to a sack of detective novels he'd scored for a buck. His old college textbooks were in there too, somewhere toward the bottom. Heavy things that anchored the shelves in place.

He flipped through a couple of books, and I remembered I still had a few of Corey's smokes in my jacket. I worked my way through them while he read, crouched on the floor. He'd always been huge, but now, with me getting accustomed to Corey's wiry build, Jim seemed even bigger. His dress shirt had a pleat in the middle of the upper back, and it spread open so wide when he moved his beefy arms, the fabric had snapped taut.

"Acute stress reaction," Jim read out loud. "Pretty much just like he said. Even that it'll go away by itself in a few days." He closed the book and scowled at it. "I hate it when that arrogant fuck is right."

Left-handed, I sorted through the empty cigarette pack, and the empty beer bottles, and the empty bag of chips, though I wasn't sure what I expected to find. Jim put the book away, stood, brushed off his pant legs, and sighed hard. "I'm just gonna let Maritza deal with this. You should have your check...she can get the rest of it all squared away by next month."

"Okay."

He shot me some kind of pained look, but I didn't know where to begin sorting it out. Was I supposed to beg him to take me back—professionally, that is? When he admitted that he knew how to pull the office strings, maybe that's what he'd been hinting at.

Or was it just a general kind of anguish he was trying to project?

Because how was I supposed to deal with his suffering if I couldn't get a handle on my own?

"I should probably go," I said, scooting toward the edge of the couch cushion in an attempt to gather the gumption to stand. Corey would be gone, right? Or would he? Maybe Jim would just drop me off...or maybe he'd want to get a look at my shitty housekeeping to prove to himself what a wreck I've been. I'd walk home then. It was walkable. Not convenient. But walkable. "I could use some air."

"Why are you so pissed off at me?" Jim asked.

"I'm not."

"You have no right to be. I would do anything for you." He planted his hands on his hips and looked up hard at a crack in the ceiling, and his voice shook a little when he said, "And the harder I try, the more you hate me. So I'm done."

"Would you stop it? I don't hate you."

He took a few breaths and regained his usual voice, then said, "I couldn't just leave you at the police station."

"No, I...I'm glad you came. I don't know what the fuck happened. That was some fucked-up shit."

He came over by the couch and tilted the shade of a lamp beside me so the bulb lit up my face. He went down on one knee and stared up into my eyes. "You weren't faking?"

"Faking what? I don't even know what that was."

He made a grab for my hands—one meatworks hand, one prosthetic. I still felt stunned and sluggish, and he managed to catch both of them, and clasp them together. "When Luis said there'd been an accident—I thought it was you. Why else would he call me? I thought it was you."

The lamplight was shining over Jim's features too, and his eyeball gleamed wet. It takes something big to move him to tears, something like a funeral.

My funeral. That's what he'd been steeling himself for. Beneath the shock, I felt weary at the thought of Jim walking on eggshells, waiting for a reason to dust off his church suit. Deeply and profoundly weary. "I'm okay," I told him, and when I pulled my left hand out of his grasp, he let me. And when I ran my fingertips down his cheek, he let me do that, too.

Even though, like the rest of me, my fingertips were kind of numb...Jim's face felt the same as it always had.

He looked away when I touched him, like the visual contact was too heavy to sustain, but he leaned his face into my hand. I cupped his jaw and ran my thumb over his stubble. It was harsher than Corey's, close-packed like sandpaper. He turned and pressed his lips to my skin. His hot breath filled my palm. The feel of it lingered, as if I might be able to hold it like a physical thing. "Don't go," he said into my meat hand, then he paused and waited for me to react. When I didn't flinch away, he stood and pulled me to my feet, chest to chest with him. "Stay."

He took me up to his bedroom. It looked the same, mostly. But it felt different. "Do you want a shower?" he asked, but I shook my head. He stripped off the clothes I'd worn to work that morning, the nonskid, steel-toed oxfords, the navy double-knee Dickies, and the short-sleeved work shirt. The type of thing a guy who'd show up to fix your furnace might wear. Which was the type of guy I used to be. Before I was a cripple.

Then his hand closed around the wrist of my robo-arm, and he said, "This too?"

I actually considered keeping it on—but, hey, this was Jim. Not only had he seen my residual right arm more times than even my doctors, he'd seen it looking a hell of a lot worse, when it was all stitches and scabs. I performed the one shrug I always got right, and freed my meatworks from the robot. Maybe it is all space-age lightweight plastics and alloys...but it's still a hell of a relief to set down the burden.

He sat me down on the edge of his bed in my briefs and socks, and then he stripped down to his boxers. While I wondered what the deal with the underwear was all about, I couldn't figure out how to ask without sounding like I was challenging him. He climbed over me and held up the covers so I could get underneath, and when I lay back, the guy-smell of Jim on his bedding cradled me just as surely as his pillow did. He settled against my side, with a leg hooked over my thigh and a brawny arm thrown across my chest. He couldn't have been particularly sleepy—what was it, maybe seven? But no doubt he was exhausted.

I know I was. I fell asleep like I'd just been sedated.

The room was a bit darker when I woke, but my body clock told me I'd been out for a while. It was early, then. Not late. My head hurt from sleeping in a strange bed—and then my heart hurt a little too, from thinking of Jim's bed as a "strange" bed. He'd shifted away from me during the night, and now he was wadded up against the wall with most of the covers balled up in his grasp as if he was worried some tweaker would break in and steal them. He still had his underwear on. So did I.

Despite the crick in my neck and the fact that I wasn't hungover, I felt suspiciously like myself—more than I had since the whole commotion at Digi-Tech. Dr. Hewitt was probably right. Whatever shock tactics my body was employing on me, it would get bored with them soon enough and return to the status quo.

I sat up, scratched my balls, and cast back on the events of the previous day. As far as I could tell, it had gone something like this: woke up tangled up in Corey, let him drive me to work, something bad (this was vague), a long walk, a ride in the back of a Kenmore Baconmobile, some time in lockup, and a quick chat with Social Services' only free shrink. And I knew what the bad part in the middle was, but I also knew better than to recall it. You know when you've got a CD with a scratch in it, and there's a song that's skipping? You can try to force it to play, and you might get lucky and end up with just a few mangled bars. Or you might end up looping on something so damaged you've gotta unplug your damn stereo and take the fucking thing apart with a screwdriver to get the disc out.

I looked over at Jim. A pair of tattooed hammers, crossed in a goose step, covered him from shoulder blade to shoulder blade. Corey'd shit a brick if he saw it; he didn't know the half of it when he'd called Jim a Nazi. Now Jim's back was a lot hairier than when he was seventeen, and the sig runes on either side of the poorly executed white power symbol had pale stretch marks running through the tat where he'd outgrown it. The only thing he'd ever told me about that piece of ink was that he was glad it was on his back so he didn't have to look at it every day and remember what a stupid little shit he'd been.

It was comforting to think that I wasn't the only one who needed to forget things.

I let myself out without waking Jim, and started the half-hour slog back home. Black Rock looked like a war zone at sunrise, with nothing stirring but the plastic bags on the wind and the seagulls fighting over spilled garbage. It was nippy out, almost frost, but I warmed up fast enough from walking. I felt a few quarters in my left pocket. Enough for a ramen breakfast, but the corner store didn't open 'til nine. That was fine. I was more worried about making sure my mailbox had a check in it than putting noodles in my belly.

So worried, in fact, that I almost missed a message on my front walk.

Not that a front walk is anyplace to leave someone a message, mind you. But it was such a dramatic gesture, it would've been a shame if I'd just walked right over it in my hurry to grab my mail.

The word WANKER was scrawled across the sidewalk in letters three feet high—metallic blue letters whose origin was a spray can in an auto body touch-up kit. It didn't look as if Corey'd had much practice with tagging. He'd spaced the lettering all wrong, so the final R landed partway on the neighbor's lawn—where the lawnbot was rolling back and forth over the cured paint in an attempt to vacuum it up.

I had to smile. Most guys would've called me a jerk or an asshole or a dick. Leave it to Corey to get mad like a rudeboy.

CHAPTER 10

The first order of business when I got home from the bank was to put away my TV dinners before they thawed. I slipped my vodka into the freezer beside them. Pretty soon I'd need to defrost the damn thing—it seemed smaller every time I filled it. But not today. After the night I'd had, I was just too damn wrung out.

Since it seemed like the root of all my most recent problems was my answering machine, once I'd squared away the groceries, I manned up and turned the damn thing on. It picked up when Corey called around noon. He sounded hungover. "Way to fucking leave me hanging, Des-mond. Where were you last night? I got plenty of places to go too, y'know. For your information, I just got home." He breathed into the phone for a couple of seconds, then said, "Call me back, you retard."

He hung up, and the machine beeped, and the number one flashed on its readout.

I hadn't really considered answering the phone and telling him I'd been in lockup. That would've seemed like I was making excuses, and I didn't want to start acting like I thought I needed to explain myself to him. He decided to go get his dick polished somewhere else—fine. Maybe he actually had, or maybe he was just saying he did to yank my chain. But either way, it wasn't like we were fused at the hip.

I nuked a salisbury steak, swallowed it down so hot it burned the roof of my mouth, then warmed up another one and ate that, too. More slowly though, with some chewing. Just as I was picking the last bits of stuck-on cherry cobbler from the dessert compartment, the phone rang again. Jim, I thought, as my heart started pounding hard. And it was nothing to get all worked up over, I told myself. He'd come and freed me from the clink. Of course he'd do a little follow-up. Because Jim Murphy is nothing if not thorough. And professional.

But when the machine played the message through, it wasn't Jim at all. "Mr. Poole, this is Dr. Hewitt. I'm going through your records and I see we're long overdue to touch base. I'd like to get you in today, if at all possible—"

I picked up the handset before I could talk myself out of doing it. I hated the Social Services system, and I hated the phone, but more than that, I hated this wreck of a human being I'd become. And I probably did need to talk to a shrink about it.

We set up a time, and I had a quick shower and shave before my appointment so he didn't misdiagnose me as some kind of paranoid schizo who thinks germs are his only friend. Since it felt like I might be strong enough to pick at my emotional scabs today, I didn't want us to start digging in the wrong spot.

The neighbor's gardenbot had given up on erasing Corey's spray paint effigy by the time I headed back to the bus stop. It probably needed to charge. I glanced over the hedge to get a peek at its housing while Luis' seven thousand dollar markup played through my mind...but then I remembered the industrial accident that had me visiting a shrink today to begin with, and I realized I was about as likely to become an independent gardenbot installer as I was to see a Ramones reunion tour.

By the time I dashed up the steps to Hewitt's second-floor office ten minutes late, I found him standing in an empty waiting room, scowling at me over his reading glasses. "I was just about to...." His voice started out booming, but he trailed off when I planted my hands on my knees and sucked air. "Did you run here?" he said in a normal volume for him, which was still slightly loud.

"Fucking Elmwood bus."

"I see. Come in. Sit down. Catch your breath."

The other offices in the chopped-up Victorian were all dark. Hewitt was tight with the pills, *and* he was willing to show up on Saturday? No wonder he was the city's favorite charity shrink.

He filled a coffee mug with water from a small water cooler in the corner and set it on the table in front of me. I pulled the neck of my T-shirt up over my face to blot my forehead. My freshly-shaved upper lip prickled hard enough to bring tears to my eyes. And while I pulled myself together, he flipped through my file. Once I stopped gasping for air, he said, "Do you own a car?"

"It's in storage."

He began writing on a legal pad, something long. A lot longer than my three-word reply should've merited. "Is it in a drivable condition? Passed inspection?"

I nodded.

"The reason it's in storage?"

"I need to re-take my road test."

He looked at my robo-arm. "Why would you say you're avoiding that?"

Because I avoid everything. I wanted to shrug, but worried I'd only end up giving him the finger. "I might not pass."

"Is it a stick shift?"

"Yeah. A four-speed."

"So the things you'd need to do mainly with your prosthetic hand would be to start the engine and work the shift. Is that accurate?"

"I suppose."

"Are you not capable of working the shift with your prosthetic?"

I shrugged—but only the shoulder of my meatworks arm.

"Did you take the test and fail, or have you not even tried?"

If I hadn't seen for myself how much he and Jim loathed each other, I would've sworn my ex had fed him the question, because that sounded exactly like something Jim would ask. "I don't have the scratch for insurance right now anyway," I said. "The ten-dollar Gimp Pass works just fine."

He looked down at his pad and wrote something really long. I finished my water. When he looked up, he said, "You didn't scan in to the officebot."

Fresh sweat prickled my upper lip. "Oh. I just figured you'd want to get started right away."

"And how much time would you approximate it takes to scan in?"

"I dunno."

"Take a guess."

A few minutes? Hell, I didn't know. I lowballed it, since it seemed like he expected me to guess high. "Thirty seconds."

"Three. It typically takes three seconds to scan into an entrybot, if it's just a regular scan with no additional queries. Why do you suppose you overestimated the duration by ten times the average?"

"Just because something doesn't take a long time doesn't mean it's not a pain in the ass. That's why there's a fly on the front of your underwear, when it wouldn't take more than a second to just pull 'em down."

He looked me in the eye for a moment. Then he wrote some more.

I sagged back into the couch and stared up at the ceiling, and I wondered if maybe Jim'd had the right idea when he shuffled me out of my psychiatric duties.

"I'd like to have you scan in now," Hewitt said, but with his booming voice, it was more of an order than a request.

"Why? You get overtime for coming in on a Saturday?"

He folded his hands and watched me attentively, without replying. I sighed, made a big show of pushing myself out of the low couch, shuffled over to the stupid officebot and stuck my meatworks hand in. Three seconds? Yeah, probably. More or less. Jerk. I clomped back to the couch and sat down hard, and looked at him like, *what now?*

"Your file says you don't have a housebot."

"Riverside. You know how it is. Cheap rent, shitty apartments."

"But you have plumbing? Electricity? Heat?"

"What's your point?"

"That unless you're living in a historic landmark, building code states very clearly that a functional housebot should be on the property, if not an individual unit in every apartment, then a basic scanner in one of the building's communal places."

"I had a housebot. It broke. You don't need to make a federal case of it."

"On a level of one to ten, one being perfectly at ease, and ten being unbearably anxious, how would you rate your anxiety when I had you scan in just now?"

"I wasn't anxious. I just didn't feel like standing up after I finally got comfortable."

"I see. So you're at a *one*?"

"Yeah. A *one*."

"All right. Scan in again and tell me if that *one* changes."

"This is your idea of therapy? Making me poke my hand into an officebot for an hour?"

"Your anxiety doesn't sound like a one to me. Is it a one?"

"I'm not anxious. I'm pissed off."

"On a level of one to ten—"

"Five. Six. I'm a pissed-off *six*."

"You haven't always been anxious around robotics, have you? I see you were an HVAC technician."

"I'm not anxious."

"And was your housebot functional at this point, when you were installing heating systems?"

"I guess."

"I see." He wrote for a painfully long time, then said, "My recommendation is that you stop attending the support group and set up an evaluation with an anxiety disorder specialist, Dr. Ivery." He moved some papers and began typing into a terminal that was set into his desk, like the lady at the post office. I hadn't even realized it was there. I thought shrinks had secretaries to do that kind of stuff for them. "I see she's available next Wednesday. Ten o'clock in the morning. Downtown. You can make it?"

"What is this about? That freakout I had at Digi-Control? That was fucked-up, but you were right. I came out of it. I feel like myself again."

"That incident concerns me, yes. But there's something more subtle going on here. Something that affects the quality of your day-to-day life, and it needs to be addressed before it gets any more severe. Dr. Ivery will perform a screening to determine if you're robophobic."

Robophobic? No way. Here I'd figured I'd just been depressed all along. Or that I was an asshole. Someone would corroborate either one of those theories, I was sure. It just depended who you asked.

"You can let Mr. Murphy know you have my permission to skip tomorrow night's support group, since I presume he won't log into his officebot until Monday morning."

"But Jim's not my caseworker anymore. Maritza is."

"I assumed he might be concerned when you didn't—"

"We aren't seeing each other anymore, you know." He seemed so glib about it, like he also *assumed* Jim and me were fucking. Why? 'Cause we're fags? And that's what we do? Fuck anyone who'll take our spooge? "We aren't dating anymore. We haven't been together since before...this." I held up my prosthetic and felt the middle finger start to rise, but I flicked the gesture into a fist...which probably looked just as threatening.

Hewitt didn't look particularly threatened. "Are you sure? There must be some reason he's bending over backwards to enable you."

"I'm with someone else now," I snapped—and then I realized that by trying to protect Jim from Hewitt's scrutiny, I'd painted myself into a corner of needing to let Jim know about Corey myself, before Hewitt beat me to it.

Hewitt's glittery little eyes regarded me from the fleshy expanse of his face, and it looked like he could tell he'd just got something out of me I hadn't even admitted to myself. That I was seeing someone—someone other than Jim.

Up until then, I suppose I hadn't really owned it. Fucking shrinks. They know all those goddamn sneaky tricks.

CHAPTER 11

Thankfully, as the city's favorite free shrink, Hewitt had a full schedule. Even on Saturday. So, he couldn't prolong my agony. I made my way out of his office and onto the street. Normally I would've been happy to be wandering around on the Elmwood Strip with nothing to do and a fresh wad of cash in my pocket. There were hip restaurants, just a little too dirty for the yuppies to overtake 'em, and salons that'd dye your hair green, and resale shops with outrageously tight pants in the window. You could even score vinyl, if you were willing to listen to some clerk drone on about how the Stones hadn't been cool since Exile on Main Street.

I paused by a pay phone and lit a smoke, and tried to wrap my head around the conversation I'd just had with Hewitt. He told me he thought I was robophobic. I told him I wasn't seeing Jim anymore.

Fuck.

I hefted the phone book that was dangling from a short chain and saw that the S section was relatively unmolested—the Steiner page in particular. There were good ol' Hugh and Pamela up in richie-rich Parkside. And there, in the entry above them, was Corey.

Unless he'd moved since the phone book was printed, he lived right down the strip in Allentown. I could even walk, if I was feeling ambitious. I heard the whine of air brakes and saw a bus headed in my direction, and a bus shelter just a few yards away from the phone.

I could flash my Gimp Pass and be at Corey's place in five minutes easy. It seemed like a good enough plan, for having just been pulled out of my ass. Before I could talk myself out of it, I found myself on the corner of Elmwood and Allen. The liquor store there was no piss-smelling dive like you'd find in Riverside or Black Rock—it was an upscale joint nearly a block long, with imported-this and special-edition-that. I blew twenty-eight bucks on a bottle of Icelandic Reyka.

Hopefully that would be enough, since without an explanation of how I'd landed behind bars, my previous night's Reyka offense was probably more like a sixty-dollar Stoli Elit apology.

I found the building—the mailbox in the lobby read *Steiner*, which was encouraging—and I grit my teeth and scanned into the housebot so I could buzz Corey's unit. After a pause that was long enough to make me think I should go find his car to determine if he was actually there and just avoiding me, the intercom clicked on, and he said, *Desmond?*

Not in that playful way he usually did, either.

"Yeah, hey. I was in the neighborhood."

Doing what? Never mind. What do you want?

"Just wanted to see you."

A long beat of silence when I wondered if maybe he'd closed the connection, and then, finally, *Okay, c'mon up.*

The lock buzzed, and I let myself in.

Corey's building was just as old as mine, and not much better-kept. It was just in a hipper part of town. The patterned hall carpets were worn thin down the center, and the sounds of TV filtered through the walls. The first floor smelled like incense, and the second floor smelled like cat. The stairs creaked. The banister felt tacky. And Corey's second-floor front door was decorated with stolen black and yellow police tape stapled neatly around the doorframe.

I knocked. He yelled, "Just a minute," and I waited. I heard water running, and then footsteps. He opened the door as far as the chain. I looked at the chain stupidly, and attempted to picture myself forcing my way in.

"Hey," I said.

"We already went over that."

"Oh."

"So? What is it?"

I looked through the gap in the door. His hair was wet in front, like he'd just rinsed his face, and his eyes were red-rimmed. He must've been pretty damn hung over. I held up the Reyka. "Hair of the dog. What do you say?"

He looked at the bottle and frowned. "What the fuck—you can't call first?"

Shit. I glanced over his shoulder to see if he was alone. He seemed like he was alone—what I could see through the four-inch gap. He was dressed in his usual T-shirt and pegged jeans, but he was barefoot, like maybe he'd just thrown his clothes on when I hit the doorbell. "You got someone over? I'll share."

"No, I...fuck you."

"Okay." I did my best attempt at a charming smile. When I gave the bottle a hopeful slosh, he relented and unchained his door.

Since I had a good sense of how close I was to being tossed back out, the second I was over the threshold, I backed Corey into the wall and gave him a kiss—a slow one, only hinting with my tongue. He tasted like mouthwash. He must've been way more hungover than I thought.

His body felt tense. Instead of putting his arms around me, he pressed his palms against the wall. The actuators of his robo-arm gave a little whine when he spread the fingers. It felt right that he should make me earn his forgiveness. I cupped his face with my meat hand and kissed him real nice, working his groin with the top of my thigh until, finally, he sighed. "Don't go thinking I'm not still mad at you," he said against my cheek—but he ran his fingers down the back of my leather jacket as he said it, pausing at my ass to feel it through my jeans.

"I know." I kissed him again, and lingered on his lower lip. "I fucked up."

He shifted so he was straddling my thigh better. It felt like he was willing to let himself think with his dick, which was a big relief. I tilted my head and went in for his neck. Strange, to feel stubble on him while I was freshly-shaved. I teased his throat with my teeth, then sucked the hotspot to the verge of a hickey. His breathing went jerky. He was still mad, though. Turned on, but mad. "Ten minutes," he said. "That's the longest I wait for you, from now on."

I said, "Okay," against his neck.

"Ten minutes, then I'm gone."

I ran my fingers down his cheek, down his chest. Tweaked his nipple through his T-shirt. He breathed harder, and I gave his crotch a nice grind. "I'll make it up to you."

"It'll be a bitch, come winter. Standing there in the snow waiting for the bus. Remember that."

"Do whatever you want—whatever it takes to even things out again. Smack me with your belt. Piss on my face. I don't care. I probably deserve it."

"You'd just get off on it." He ground himself into my leg. He was stiff inside his jeans, now. "Sick fuck."

I raked my teeth over his neck. "Totally sick."

He pushed at me with his shoulder, and I backed up a couple of steps and wiped the spit off my mouth with the back of my hand. He looked down at our crotches, where we each had a bulge casting a shadow against the denim. "Strip. Then get on the bed."

I suppose I'd expected him to strip down, too. But he didn't. He just watched me. It made me nervous, undressing in front of him like that while he was staring at me, but I remembered to park my thumb. And I stripped myself down without too much fumbling.

His apartment was an efficiency, and the bed was a futon that took up most of the space in the room, butting up against the wall on one end and a big-screen TV on the other. Maybe when the futon was folded up into a couch, there'd be enough space between it and the screen to actually watch it. But just barely.

I stepped over some shoes and empty soda cans and sat on the edge of the hard futon.

"Not like that. Face-down. Ass in the air."

A shudder coursed through me as I wondered exactly how pissed off Corey actually was. I hadn't known him all that long. Maybe he was gonna take me up on that belt offer. And maybe he really was gonna whip me. Hard.

As I got my knees under me and pressed my face into his sheets, the twinkish smell of him enveloped me, shampoo and youth. He didn't feel so harmless lurking there behind my bare ass, though. I told myself he was unlikely to do anything that would cause any permanent damage. Even so, with the tension of not knowing, I found myself starting to shake.

He said, "Show me that hole." His voice was husky.

The thought of being anal-probed by a vibrating robotic finger made my breath catch—and not in a good way. Sweat stung my upper lip. I wiped it against the sheet.

"Do it," he said.

And I was shaking like a prosthetic on a cleaning cycle, but I reached back with my left hand and spread my cheek. He took the other side with his meatworks hand, and then I felt it. Not metal.

Breath.

He held himself there, just breathing me, and it was the tiniest whisper of moistness over my hole—and I swore I'd never felt anything that gentle so keenly. I groaned loud enough that it would've been funny if the whole thing wasn't so fucking intense.

"I don't get you," he said. The words played over my spread hole like a caress from a damp finger, and I bit the sheets to keep from groaning even louder. "Leave me hanging on a Friday night, then show up here the next day with a leaking foot-long boner, looking to get laid."

"That's not why I came here. I just wanted to see you."

"Maybe. Or maybe you don't know what the hell you actually want."

Corey Steiner, hot little rudeboy, jealous? Why he'd care what I did with my sorry ass was beyond me. Plus, it wasn't as if guys were lining up to poke the gimp. He knew I hadn't been with anyone since I got my damn metal. I'd told him so.

And Jim and me, we'd spend the night with our underwear on.

"Isn't it obvious what I want?" I said. "That boner's got your name all over it."

He gave a scoffy little laugh that shot a thrill through my asshole and straight up my backbone, then straightened up and unhitched his pegged jeans with his robo-hand. "I don't have any poppers."

"That's okay. Just take it slow. Or don't. Pound me, if it makes you feel any better."

"Nah, you don't get off the hook that easy." He reached for a pump bottle on the nightstand and grabbed a few squirts of Wet. He teased my hole with it, and my metal hand whirred itself into God-knows-what stupid position from the way I was flexing my shoulders. His fingers pushed in with a slick, wet sound that punctuated my gasping, but he stayed quiet. I might've thought he wasn't enjoying himself since he wasn't even breathing hard, but then he lined himself up and I felt how stiff he was, like he was aching to pork me, and I walked my knees out wider to offer up my ass.

It felt different from the last time he'd done me. We'd been face to face then. Now it felt deeper. Not quite as painful, but it still smarted some. His hand was still slick when he gave me the reach-around, and it went from painful to perfect. I was slippery and hard and stretched open wide. I was face-down with nothing to do but enjoy the ride—and he rode me until the sheets were damp. I almost didn't warn him, since he might be angry enough to ease off at the tipping point, but at the last minute I huffed, "Oh, fuck, I'm gonna—" into the sheets.

He didn't back off. Just kept right on fucking me, and jacking me, and then I was coming hard, big, beautiful spurts, three good ones and a few more happy contractions after that. He milked my spent dick while he fucked me faster, harder, and finally he shot his load, deep inside my ass.

When I rolled over, I saw he was still dressed—he had his jeans around his thighs, and that was it. I patted the bed and said, "C'mere. Lay with me so I can feel you."

He undressed without saying anything, threw his T-shirt over the wet spot, and climbed into bed with me. He fished the master remote out of the clutter on his nightstand and powered on the massive TV, which played the type of cheesy black-and-white horror flick I could watch a hundred times and never get bored.

The housebot had picked it out for us, Corey and me, based on our preferences. It was perfect.

I watched him out of the corner of my eye. Was I supposed to say something? Did he want to *cuddle*?

Why did everything need to be so fucking complicated?

It seemed as if he was waiting for me to take a stab at talking, so I cast around for something to say, and finally came up with, "Well?"

"Well, what?"

"Are you still pissed off?"

He rolled his eyes, muted the TV, and reached for his Camels. He lit one and took a drag, then passed it to me. The filter was damp from his lips—and of all the wet and sloppy things we'd just done, somehow that intimacy hit me the hardest. Jim would have simply given me my own damn cigarette.

"I think you like me," Corey said. And I started to laugh, because it sounded like such a conceited thing to say, until he added, "But I think you can't deal with my arm."

"I like you," I said. With feeling. "Nothing we can do about our arms. Either of us."

He took back his cigarette and perched his ash tray on his stomach. "Well, we can't grow the fucking things back, no. But we can choose to make the most of what we're stuck with." He glanced at his robo-arm, which was cradling the ash tray just like a real hand. Then he looked at mine, which had fallen to the futon beside me, positioned as if someone had turned it off while it was attempting sign language. "Or not."

"You're never gonna believe this—Dr. Hewitt, the Social Services shrink? He says I'm robophobic. It's that bullshit made-up thing you told me about yesterday, right?"

"You were at Dr. Hewitt's?"

"Just up the street."

"I know where it is." He scowled at my arm. "On a Saturday?"

I took the smoke from him and steeled myself with a nice, long drag. Smoke streamed out of my nose when I said, as casually as I could, "I kinda fucked up at work yesterday. Walked out. Blew my chances of ever going back."

"What do you need a job for? You're disabled."

"Then why are they so keen on making me punch a clock?"

Corey crushed out the cigarette, set the ash tray on the nightstand, and slipped his arms around me. One meat, one metal. I held him and rested my head against his smooth chest, and I listened to the whooshing throb of his heartbeat. He un-muted the TV. A couple of actors in suits were having a standoff with guns, though it was lots of talking and no shooting at all, and since everyone was dressed up so spiffy, I couldn't tell who the bad guys were supposed to be. Not that I guess it mattered. It was just a cheesy fifties horror flick.

I didn't think there was much else to talk about, but then Corey said, "I like you too. And I think we're good together." I gave him a squeeze, and he said, "I want to be more than fuck buddies. I want to be your boyfriend."

His sincerity left me all warm and gooey inside. And firmer and firmer on the outside. "I guess I beat you to the punch when I told Hewitt I was seeing someone."

"You told Hewitt about me?"

"Just that I was seeing someone. I didn't name names. Whatever secrets you got are safe with me."

He reached over the side of the futon and picked up the Reyka where I'd left it on the floor, and held the bottle between his bare knees to crack the seal with his meatworks hand. It was a pity to drink such spendy vodka at room temperature. He must've been dead set against emerging from our cocoon of new-boyfriendom just yet. Not even to get some ice, with his kitchenette maybe eight feet away.

We passed the bottle back and forth a few times, then he closed it and slid down farther into bed to hold me, and cover my mouth in vodka-tinged kisses. Even though I'd just blown a fat wad, I felt stirrings again. Who knew I'd be able to keep up with a young kid like Corey? Even if it turned out I couldn't, it seemed like I'd have a hell of a good time trying. He pressed a bare knee between my legs and we made out like that, sloppy and naked, while the music swelled on the TV and guys in pinstripe suits finally did shoot their guns, at a guy in a robot suit.

Hilariously sad, what they thought robots would look like, a half-dozen decades ago. Big metal boxes with ductwork for arms and legs, and square heads. No silicone grippy parts. No whining actuators.

Corey walked his fingers through my leg hair while I pondered the lumbering silver machine on his big screen, and then he kissed my chin, and said, "It's not bullshit."

"What isn't?" I asked, but the Reyka was warm in my belly, and he'd rolled me onto my back to trail kisses down my chest on his way downtown, and pretty soon, all that mattered was the feel of his mouth making all my troubles drift away.

CHAPTER 12

The idea of being with Corey twenty-four hours a day was something my brain initially balked at. Then again, *intelligent* isn't the first word out of most people's mouths when you ask them to describe me. Plus, I'm a loner. A rebel. And, yeah, a gigantic fucking cliche.

While I didn't set out to strike up a relationship with the guy, truth be told, hanging out with him was phenomenally easy. I stretched out in his fold-a-bed futon and luxuriated in the smell of coffee teasing my nostrils from over in the kitchenette. "You must like it thick," he said into his pillow. "Smells strong."

And with every day I lingered in Corey's hip Allentown efficiency without scanning out, it got a little stronger. His housebot was busy integrating my predilections with his. It seemed as if both of us were cool with the results.

I picked up the remote control (left-handed) and hit the music button. The Clash. The housebot had decided it was "our" band, punk-roots enough for me and Ska-enough for him. Train in Vain... apparently this was "our" song, with its "stand by your man" lyrics.

I expected my brain to balk about that, too. Nope. Being half of a couple came pretty easily to it, actually, as long as the other half allowed me to do what I want, when I wanted, and didn't nag me about petty little bullshit stuff. Why had that been so hard with Jim fucking Murphy? Maybe we'd both been too old. Too set in our ways.

Too stubborn. Obviously I'd been working too hard trying to fit an RCA cable into a quarter-inch jack when I tried to mix it up with Jim in a way that didn't just irritate us both.

Corey rolled to face me and fit himself against my side, all smooth skin and grogginess. His morning wood prodded my thigh. His hair smelled like vanilla, or maybe almonds. He was snoring again before I had a chance to figure out if he wanted to bone me or if he just needed to take a leak.

And that was easy about Corey, too. The sex. Because if I wanted to fuck, then great. We'd fuck. There was no "exhausted, just let me rest my eyes" or "seriously messed-up day" or "can't get my mind off this goddamn case" like there was with Jim.

If I didn't want to fuck? Hell, I have a dick, right? Of course I always wanted to fuck.

Our robo-arms were pinned between us, so I needed to turn toward Corey to cup his dick. His snores faltered. He flexed his hips and pushed himself into my hand. I kept my face in his hair. Not only did it smell good, it excused me from pasty early-morning kisses. The music crept up louder—sweet, the neighbors must have been at work. We could be as loud and nasty as we wanted...not that the presence of neighbors ever kept us from yelling out whatever we wanted, anyway.

His fingers walked to my spine and started stroking around my vertebrae, one at a time, lower and lower. All the while, he humped my hand, slow and unconcerned. The urgency wasn't what it might have been a few days ago. We both knew how it was all gonna end. And I liked that, the leisureliness. It seemed to fit with us—like the Clash, and the B-movie reruns the TV chose for us, and the strong black coffee.

"I'm still knackered," he murmured. "Are you awake enough to fuck me?"

My emerging boner throbbed at the thought. "Get on your back." He did, and I straddled him, and climbed up his chest to get myself some head before I settled into the main event. Just as I fixed my elbows on the back of the couch, the housebot interrupted Mick Jones to say, "Monday, October 21, 9 a.m."

"Imagine," Corey said, "right now all the suckers in this world are sitting down behind their desks at their jobby-jobs." I was about to entertain the thought that I'd had a job just the week before, for all of a day and a half. But then he said, "C'mon, Des-mond, feed me your hot dick. Choke me with it."

His stubble rasped against the head while I aimed, missed, aimed again, both of us too lazy to use our hand. Both of us too sure of the outcome to worry about how long it took to get there. His robo-hand's actuators whirred, and I told myself not to dwell on the fact that he touched himself with it. Most amputees did. They even made special silicone jackoff sleeves just for robo-hands, since it was half a step up from yanking yourself off to do it with your prosthetic. I hadn't known that, before I got with Corey.

It wasn't the type of thing Social Services printed in their helpful brochures.

He turned his head and snagged my cock with his tongue, and I prodded it into his mouth. Such a pretty face, all big, dark eyes and quirky smiles. He ran his tongue around the crown and I pushed in farther. Hot mouth.

"Incoming call for Desmond Poole," the housebot said, just before the phone rang.

I rolled off Corey's face. A year ago, I wouldn't have thought anything of having a phone call follow me around. But ever since my hand waved bye-bye, I'd grown unaccustomed to sticking my remaining hand into any machinery-filled slots in the wall, so calls just end up lost somewhere at my apartment.

"Come back," Corey whined playfully. "Let the answerphone get it."

Gotta love how he says "knackered" and "answerphone" as if he thinks he's a limey. He doesn't do the accent, but he's adopted the vocabulary as his own. His over-the-top cuteness calmed me down, and I settled myself against him and listened to the speakers rather than finding the phone and picking it up.

"Mr. Poole, this is Dr. Tricia Ivery. You've been referred to me by Dr. Hewitt to evaluate the severity of your robophobia and determine a course of treatment. I'm calling to confirm our appointment this Wednesday at 10:30, and also to give you some preliminary instructions. Normally, I'd have you call me back...." Papers shuffled. She'd probably just come to the part in my permanent record that said I wouldn't pick up the phone unless I'd been drinking steadily for about four hours. At least.

"It's my recommendation that you refrain from wearing your prosthetic limb until we go over some relaxation techniques. In fact, if it's at all possible, put it in its box and don't even look at it. Keep a compression sleeve on your residual arm until then, and bring your prosthetic with you to the appointment so we can do some exercises with you looking at the device without touching it."

"Is this for real?" Corey cried out. "The treatment for robophobia is *looking* at the arm? And they pay someone to make you do that?"

I shushed him, because the super-shrink was saying something about some paperwork. "...messengered to your house before I realized you weren't there. You'll need to get that filled out before I can see you. If you have any questions...." She left her number and hung up.

"I don't have a compression sleeve," Corey said. Because I'd been conveniently able to use all his other stump-care products, like the lotion and the antiperspirant and the chafe cream, but he'd lost his hand three years ago—and he didn't tend to hide his arm on himself in a drunken stupor. Of course he didn't own a compression sleeve.

I grudgingly swung my legs out of bed and headed for the coffee pot. "It's fine. I should head home today anyway. My Sea-Monkeys are probably evaporating."

"But look how hard I am for you," he pouted. He modeled his dick for me, holding it in his meatworks hand. The tip was pinkish-red and shiny, and the sight of it cradled in his fingers made me want to swirl my tongue over its smoothness. To feel his pulse throbbing in the distended veins as I shoved into his ass. To hear the way his breath faltered when he was getting ready to bust.

"Well...I could come back later."

He perked right up when I said that, hopped out of bed, and ducked into the bathroom. I listened while he pissed out the liter of Stoli we'd consumed the night before. As he washed his hand, he called out, "I'll drive you. We'll be there and back in less than an hour."

I poured my black coffee while the housebot found a selection from London Calling to entertain me with, and then I poured some for Corey. And I turned over the notion that if I were to make my escape, the time for me to say, "No, that's okay, I'll take the bus," would be now. But instead I added two sugars to Corey's cup and went back to wait for him on the futon.

* * *

Fast-forward, Wednesday morning. Paperwork? Check. Clean underwear? Check. Disability card? Check.

Box of arm?

Check.

It looked like I was on a collision course with promptness for my meeting with Dr. Ivery—especially since Corey hadn't even seemed to notice the tent I was pitching in the sheets. He turned to the Sea-Monkeys that sat on his bookshelf between his comic book collection and his porn. "Did you feed our pet plankton?"

"No." I hadn't needed to. Not since I'd decided it was easier to bring the little plastic tank with me to Cory's pad than to feel guilty about neglecting them. He loved those things. Found them the perfect spot away from the radiator. Gazed at them as they did their manta-ray moves on the non-existent currents. And the way he fed them, I thought we'd come home from the bar some night to a six-foot shrimp smoking our cigarettes and trying on our clothes.

He pulled off the salt-crusted top and tapped in a tiny scoop of Sea-Monkey food. "Eat up, kids. And clean your plates. There's shrimp starving in China who'd kill to have this tasty grit."

I supposed it was all for the best that he didn't ambush me and have his way with me before my appointment. God only knows what those wily psychiatrists are capable of making me confess to. Coffee, a stale bagel, and we were out the door and halfway to the doctor's office before I even knew what hit me. Corey's car stereo blasted Fishbone at us. Its mix had never been alerted to the fact that I could only deal with so many trumpets in one day. I'd never scanned in to the carbot.

And why start now?

The music made it easier to not talk...and for me to try to piece together the reason he was so eager to get me to the shrink. Given the fact that Corey only does the bare minimum he can get away with to stay on Disability, his enthusiasm made me leery. By the time he pulled into the lot and put the car in park, I couldn't help but ask him, "What is it you think's gonna happen today at this session of mine?"

He looked at me, startled. "Uh, I dunno. Y'know."

"If they 'cure' me, I won't get to stay home and play house all day. They'll make me go get a job."

He made a scoffy little laugh that sounded unplanned. "You're in no danger of finding a cure in one sitting."

"What's that supposed to mean?"

"C'mon, Desmond. You're so freaked out by your own prosthetic that you can't even look at it without professional help? Not exactly employee-of-the-month material."

I rocked back in my seat like he'd just slugged me. Since when did Corey think I needed actual help? He was usually the one coaching me on how to play up my "depression" to milk my benefits. He ignored my reaction and got out of the car. When he noticed I hadn't moved, he walked around to open the passenger door for me. "What? You're not gonna see the shrink now? You want me to take you home?"

"Is this about me, or you?" I swung out of the passenger seat and stood so he wasn't talking down to me. "What do you care how I feel about my hunk of junk. What difference does that make to you?"

"Huh?"

"You know what I think?" Even as I said it, the past couple of days clicked into place. The way I hadn't seen any action since I boxed the arm. The way he engineered for a pillow to cover my residual arm before he kissed me goodnight. "I think you just want me to screw my arm back on 'cause you can't deal with the sight of a fucking stump."

"Oh, piss off." He crossed his arms and looked like he was doing his damnedest to cook up another limey insult. "No way."

I almost planted my hands on my hips...funny how certain gestures come back even if you can't perform them anymore. "You were all over me until the headshrinker told me to take off my arm."

His eyebrows bunched down and he backed up a couple of steps.

"I was...worried about you."

"Oh, please."

He looked away. The hands-on-hips thing...he managed to do it. He scuffed a bit of broken glass along the asphalt with the toe of his natty brogue, shifted his weight, then said, "If that's what was happening...fuck. I didn't do it on purpose."

The excess promptness for this appointment was ticking down, fast. "We'll talk about it later."

I turned toward the sliding doors, but he snagged me by the sleeve of my leather jacket before I could exit the conversation. "Holy fuck, Desmond. That's exactly what I was worried you were doing to me. That when you looked at me, you wouldn't be able to see *me*. All you'd see is some guy with a robotic arm."

Jesus Christ. "I see you."

He nudged me back against the hood of his car. Over his shoulder, I watched the people across the street in the mailbox-copy shop peering at us through the plate glass window with *Overnight, Ask Us How!* scrawled across it. But Corey was looking up into my eyes so earnestly, I couldn't exactly pretend that the mundane stuff I saw over his shoulder was so fascinating. I met his eyes.

"You know I'm crazy about you," he said. "Right?"

I sighed. "We're fine."

"I don't want to be *fine*." He jammed his thigh between my legs and wrapped his meat-and-metal arms around me. "You and me, we should be fucking awesome."

I'd be lying if I said his intensity didn't stir up some dusty old feelings inside me that I'd figured for dead a long time ago. The passion. The hope. I drew a breath to tell him we were better than just fine, that fine was a stupid word anyway, one that should be reserved for sandpaper and nit-combs. But before I could get the words out his mouth was on mine, and his tongue was parting my lips, and his arms, meat and metal, were holding me tight like he never wanted to let go.

I didn't get a boner from it or anything. But it was still a hell of a kiss.

We walked toward the building—toward my appointment with

the phobia specialist—hand in hand. The sliding doors bounced our reflection back at us, as well as those of a couple of blue-collar guys in the mailbox shop pointing and laughing at the big fags and their parking lot melodrama. If I'd had a second hand, I would've flipped them the bird.

Or, heck, even a decently functioning prosthetic would've sufficed.

CHAPTER 13

Dr. Tricia Ivery's office smelled like old-lady perfume. Which was weird, since she was only forty or so. I think. Hard to tell with skinny chicks, since they've got a caved-in mummy look that adds a good decade to their age, whether they smoke or not. If they dye their hair, which I'm guessing Ivery did (unless she was naturally greenish blonde), then those bony girls could be anywhere from thirty to sixty for all I can guess.

Maybe the smell wasn't her. Maybe it was one of the gazillion candles that lined every flat surface in the room—dusty candles with white wicks that had never once known the touch of a lighter. I considered picking one up and smelling it. But since my left hand was busy holding a box that contained my fake right hand, sniffing the candles wasn't really an option.

"A phobia," she explained, "can be defined as an intense fear reaction to a stimulus that isn't necessarily dangerous. Sometimes the fears are hardwired—like the fear of the dark. But then some, like yours, are brought about by a trauma."

I nodded, half-listening.

"Your trauma involved scanning robotics, and so the fear is understandable. But you've expanded that fear to include all robotics, even those powered by a current that's weaker than a phone line, or those with non-moving parts. You're a technician..." Correction. I *was* a technician. "...you know these facts intellectually. But you've conditioned yourself to have a reaction that's out of proportion to the stimulus."

"Okay," I said. "They got drugs for that?"

"Considering the incident at the job site last week, I think our safest course of action is systematic desensitization. It's gradual. Results won't happen in a single breakthrough session. You'll need to practice twenty minutes a day. But that's not such a high price to pay to be able to work your housebot again, is it?"

Because it seemed like she expected me to, I said, "Sure."

The first step in the process was making a hierarchy of my fear, which seemed pretty stupid, since the low end of the spectrum involved mundane things like walking through an automatic door and programming a coffeebot. But somewhere around imagining sticking my remaining hand into a housebot scanner I got a little antsy, and thinking about poking around inside a bot assembly with a volt meter made my throat flutter.

Once the good doctor had her list, she said she needed to teach me to relax—pretty lame, considering I'd spent the last three days in bed watching monster movies. Dr. Ivery was just as earnest as Corey was, though, so I went along with her spiel. *Clench and release your eyelids. Clench and release your jaw. Clench and release your neck muscles. Clench and release your...arm.*

The pause was slight, but I'll bet she'd almost said *arms*, plural.

Make a fist.

Yeah, whatever.

Once she'd determined I was relaxed, she had me picture myself making coffee. I pictured Corey's coffeepot. And not just because mine was manual. His was fresher in my memory. Weird. I tried to picture mine, and it seemed like it should have been more vivid. But my apartment, in my mind's eye, seemed like an empty husk. Well, maybe not completely empty. There'd be plenty of spent fifths on the floor and an avalanche of yellow envelopes by the door. But nothing living present, except the ants on the countertop.

"Your state of anxiety," she prompted, "On a scale of one to ten?"

"Zero," I said. And then I corrected it to, "I mean, one. Not anxious."

Me. Corey. In his apartment, together, like a real couple. It didn't make me anxious at all.

I could deal with a boyfriend who had a robotic hand. For real.

How about that?

"Imagine walking through an automatic door. Can you picture it? Good. Now squeeze your eyelids shut tight...and relax."

I could imagine it all right, me walking through the front door that reflected the rubbernecker reaction I'd received when I swapped spit with *my new boyfriend* out there in the parking lot. And that big-eyed boy and me, a rocker and a mod (which maybe was like Romeo and Juliet forty years ago, but today we were each just a different flavor of retro alternative) walking side-by-side. Hand in hand. And we looked good together, damn good. Him and me.

Dr. Ivery had me do the visualization followed by squeezing and tensing on other low-anxiety things. The checkbot at the store, which has a laser reader rather than a scan-slot. A flat rubber street-cleaner crawling along like a wandering speed bump while the traffic drove over it. And before we got to anything that involved moving parts or limbs thrusting inside, Dr. Ivery said, "Okay, that's time. Here's your homework. I'll patch a relaxation sequence into your...wait a minute. You don't have a housebot. What do you listen to music on?"

"A boombox." From the late eighties.

"I think I have a...." She dug in her desk drawer. "Here it is." She handed me a cassette tape. "Hopefully it still works. If not, take this printout and follow the written instructions as best you can. Stay in the lowest tier of the hierarchy, and do twenty minutes, twice a day, starting tonight. There's a checkbox for you to mark once you've done it. And we'll meet again Monday to check your progress. I want you to have nine practice sessions in by then."

I took the sheet in my left hand, then realized my robo-arm was sitting in a box on her couch. "So can I put my prosthetic back on?"

"Oh no, not until after our next appointment, at least. You need to start slow. Will you need a non-robotic limb in the meantime? I can probably have the prosthetist fit you with a temp on Friday."

A fake limb might make Corey feel less like he was facing off with a mirror image of himself—minus the hand—but getting fit for a sleeve is a royal pain in the ass. I didn't want to bother with it if I could get back to my regular routine in a week or so. Corey would deal with it. Especially after that chitchat we'd had in the parking lot. And the public display of affection afterward.

I folded the instructions one-handed and stowed them in my pocket, and headed back out to the waiting room to rejoin my man. There must be some way to break the news to him that he'd be dealing with the sight of my stump for another week. Maybe over lunch. Or drinks. Or....

Corey had a weird look on his face when I emerged from Dr. Ivery's office. He stood. And so did another guy who was seated on the opposite side of the room.

Another guy who, I now realized, was Jim.

Jim fucking Murphy.

And the look on his face wasn't exactly promising, either.

"Jim," I said. Even I had no idea what I meant by that single word.

He looked at me. He looked at Dr. Ivery. He looked at Corey. And then he looked at me again. And maybe he wasn't currently wearing his signature skin-tight tattered Fear T-shirt, or his spiked leather jacket. But even in an office drone shirt and striped tie, menace rolled off him like heatwaves off July asphalt. He looked at Dr. Ivery again, no doubt weighing the effect that whatever he was dying to say to me would have on his professional reputation.

And then, apparently, he told himself, *Fuck it*.

"Now you've got Corey Steiner chauffeuring you around?" he said.

"What's it to you?" Corey said to the side of his face. "You dropped both of our cases."

For all that Jim paid attention, Corey might as well have been invisible. Jim's pissed-off gaze was all for me.

"You own a car," Jim said, "but instead of taking some responsibility, some initiative in getting your license back—"

"I don't want to get into it here," I said. I almost told Jim it was none of his business. Not only had he broken up with me back when I had two hands, but he'd had my case transferred out of his caseload for "fraternizing" with a member of my Gimp Group...and he'd even mailed me back the key to the lock around my neck.

Which...I was still wearing.

Fuck.

If zipping up my jacket would have covered the lock, I might have been tempted to do it. That would only call attention to it, though. Besides, my left hand was currently holding a bag with an arm in it. "Look," I said, and I tried to be as gentle about it as I could. I owed him that much for getting me out of suburban lockup. "I'm with Corey now. So if he drives me somewhere...maybe it's because he wants to."

"*With* Corey," he repeated, inflectionless.

"Right. *With*."

Jim's eyes went narrow and hard. "Right. With. You two are just fucking perfect for each other."

"What's the matter, Mr. Social Worker?" Corey taunted. "Sounds like you're jealous."

Jim smiled—not at Corey, at me. About the least pleasant smile I'd ever seen. "He doesn't know, does he?"

"Know what?" Corey said.

While intellectually, I knew that Jim hadn't been planning on making things between Corey and me even more precarious than they already were...intellectually, I also knew a standard housebot was incapable of grinding off my remaining hand.

"I'll need you gentlemen to clear my waiting room," Dr. Ivery said. "This is not an appropriate place to have this discussion."

"Believe me," Jim said. "Desmond doesn't think anyplace is appropriate for telling people things they need to know."

"Your tone is hostile," the shrink said, "and it's making me uncomfortable. I won't ask you again. Leave. Now."

While Jim was the one she'd been talking to, it was Corey who suddenly spun around and flew out the door. After he made a little chokey-sound, during which I presume he realized my prior relationship with Jim went a lot farther than a social worker and his cripple. Which I took as my cue to leave. "Corey, wait...."

I ran after Corey. Jim was right behind me. I could feel the treads shake as he pounded down the fire exit stairs hot on my heels. I called back over my shoulder, "Just 'cause he's too dark for you doesn't make him off limits to me."

We spilled out into the parking lot, Corey, then me, then Jim. "I don't give a flying fuck that he's Jewish," Jim spat. Huh—I'd presumed Corey was part-black, but Jewish worked too. "He's an overprivileged freeloader half your age."

"What do you care who I'm with?" I snarled. "Earth to Jim. You-left-me."

"Is he teaching you a thing or two about how to keep the benefit hose spraying out monthly checks? Is that the reason you suddenly developed a debilitating phobia?"

Corey strode over to his car and got in. I paused, and yelled back over my shoulder, "Only you would be cynical enough to think I'd fake something like this. You think I faked getting my fucking hand lopped off, too?" With that grandiose parting remark, I turned to open Corey's passenger-side door. The handle snapped ineffectively. Still locked. I waited a beat for him to pop it, then tried it again.

Snick.

The idea crept into my consciousness, as I beheld the reflection my own panicked-looking face in the tinted window, that maybe the door wasn't locked due to negligence.

The window powered down, and my reflection sank out of sight, replaced by Corey's glaring eyes. "How long?" was all he said.

"It's been like a year since I was with Jim. I swear. Like I told you the first night. I haven't been with anyone else. Not since the accident. And not since I met you."

"No, not how long since you broke up." His gaze shifted very, very slightly, dropping to the padlock at my throat. "How long were you together?"

What the fuck did it matter? "A couple of years."

"A couple of yea-rs," he repeated, drawing out the final word in that way of his where he could insert extra syllables into anything. "Right." His robo-hand dropped to the control panel on his door, and the window whirred back up. My reflection looked confused...and then slightly alarmed, as he put his car into drive and rolled out of the parking lot.

Jim's beater station wagon was right behind it.

I wondered for a minute if Jim was gonna do something rash,

like ram Corey's new car from behind. But instead he just turned onto a side street before even the first red light...which then flipped to green for Corey, and let him cruise away without even slowing.

And then I was alone.

So Jim was pissed off. And Corey was pissed off. And probably Dr. Ivery, too. At least I understood what her beef was. She didn't want to see big bad Jim Murphy go nuclear in her office. As for Corey, though, and as for Jim—I tried to wrap my head around their problem. But I couldn't see where I was to blame for whatever was pissing either of them off.

When I reached for my pocket to make sure I had my Gimp Pass with me, my prosthetic, dangling by my side in a plastic bag, whacked me in the knee. I sighed, and looked up to scope out the nearest bus stop—and instead caught a glimpse of the mailbox shop across the street.

The guys behind the plate glass window pointed in my direction and laughed.

CHAPTER 14

In my absence, something had died in my apartment. Either that or my refrigerator chose the half a week I'd spent at Corey's place as the perfect time to break down. My initial thought was, "Not my problem. The landlady will replace it."

But then I realized that refrigerators that functioned independently of housebots were hard to come by these days, and that she might very well decide to bite the bullet and rewire my whole place. Not only would she then raise the rent...but I'd be stuck with a fucking housebot. And me, not even properly desensitized.

I stepped into a half-inch deep puddle of water courtesy of the freezer. Well...that was one way to defrost it. The smell was worse when I opened the door, thanks to the quart of now-chunky milk in there. I don't drink milk. But Corey had a thing for "tea" in the afternoon, which had seemed like an easy enough way to make him happy. Now look how it stunk up the place.

That was probably a metaphor for something. But you'll drive yourself crazy giving all the metaphors in your life the attention they demand.

Not only was I not in the mood to hear some fucking housebot commentating my life again, I wasn't up for a bunch of guys in work shirts and steel-toed shoes tromping through my apartment replacing things that worked perfectly well for the most part—things that didn't dictate what you could or couldn't have based on some fucking algorithm. The thing to do, obviously, would be to fix the refrigerator myself. True, my expertise was more with air conditioning than refrigeration. But still...I knew how to do that shit.

I was a trained professional. Or I had been. Once.

Though it occurred to me, as I hooked a garbage bag onto my stump to begin clearing out the rotten cold cuts and moldy leftover pizza, I had no idea how to hold my tools left-handed—and worse, if I wasn't even supposed to wear my damn prosthetic, I'd need to do it with only that hand.

I turned on the cooktop vent, opened my windows and hauled the fridge-rot outside, all the while weighing the pros and cons of attempting a repair with my left hand and my stump versus going against Dr. Ivery's advice and strapping on my robo-arm for a few hours, just long enough to open up the casing and see what the problem was.

Then again, how much did I need a refrigerator, really? I could always grab a soda at the gas station, one of the big ones, and fill the cup with ice. That'd be enough for cocktails.

I was heading back inside, pondering the fact that Social Services would have a field day if they knew I was seriously considering "going without" as my best option for the refrigerator situation, when I realized the pounding I heard in my apartment building wasn't one of my neighbors attempting some kind of DIY project, but someone knocking on a door. The door to my unit. No big surprise since I'd left the outer door propped open so that any old derelict could wander on in...or any old angry boyfriend. I approached and said, "Hey." Because saying anything more specific to Corey Steiner seemed like a land mine just waiting to blow up in my face.

He turned to me, startled to find me coming at him from the hallway side of the door, and said, "What's that smell?"

While I was tempted to tell him it was the decaying corpse of my dead dreams, I decided it wasn't the time or the place to be cute. "The fridge shit the bed."

"Nice."

I went in and he followed me inside. "You want tea? I had to toss the milk...how about coffee? The coffee's still good."

Corey shook his head and didn't move to sit down. "No, nothing." He shifted something small and plastic in the crook of his arm. The Sea-Monkeys.

"What is that?" I said. Although, of course, I knew damn well.

"They're yours. Figured you'd want custody."

"Corey...don't do this. You want to be mad? Fine. But you and me just got started. Don't break up with me."

He looked up sharply. Maybe he'd been ready for me to smartass my way out of the situation. Or to minimize it. Or sweep it under the carpet. Clearly, he hadn't expected me to beg. "You push my buttons, Desmond. And not just the good ones."

"I only want to push the good buttons," I said. "I just need more practice. That's all."

Corey looked at a spot of nothing on the wall. "If this is the way you fat-finger my keypad, I'm scared to think what you could do to me with practice."

"I'm sorry. Really." He put his weight on one leg, like maybe he was coming around to my way of seeing things, although he wasn't quite convinced. "You gotta cut me a break," I explained. "It's not like I can find a time machine and I can go back and un-date Jim for you."

"That's what you think? I'm mad you had a relationship with him?"

What, was I supposed to agree with Corey? Disagree? Fuck me, he argued like a chick. "Something like that."

"It didn't occur to you," he said carefully, "at any point, when I was saying, 'That asshole Jim Murphy,' or, 'the most self-righteous social worker in the world,' or, 'that fucking dickhead Nazi,' that maybe... just maybe...you could have mentioned the two of you were lovers for two...fucking...years?"

"Right. 'Cause you would've taken it so well."

He sucked in a great big breath, and he sighed a shaky sigh. And his eyelashes gleamed damp. "Just tell me one thing."

Great. I'm sure whatever it was would be a doozy. "Yeah?"

"The padlock around your neck. Is it Jim's?"

He'd been fixated on the fucking padlock since day one. I had the key—damn it, it had been in my hand—but I'd dropped it somewhere over by the couch, and then I'd forgotten about it except in passing when I wasn't in a spot to dig for it, and now look where it got me. Should I tell him that? I had the key. We could unlock it then and there. And that would be that.

Except that wasn't what came out of my mouth. Instead, I said, "No. It's not."

He looked at me so hard I'd swear he could see right through my thick skull, deep into the folds and wrinkles of my brain. And then his face twisted, and he screamed, "Liar!"

He moved—fast—and something smacked me in the forehead before I even realized he'd thrown it. Wet. Salty. I blinked away brine as he whirled around and banged through my front door. "Wait," I called out, starting after him, but my vision blurred, and what I had in my eyes really sank in. Those blurry shapes clinging to my eyelashes were more than just drops of water. I moved to grab the door frame as I yelled, "Corey!" but I didn't have a hand on, just a fucking compression bandage. I toppled over, and carpet-burned my left hand trying to catch myself.

"Wait," I begged into the carpet. It stunk like cigarettes.

But down the stairs, the outside door slammed, and Corey Steiner was gone.

* * *

I was drunk when I took the refrigerator apart. Not drunk enough to care that my Stoli wasn't cold, but drunk enough to attempt a major appliance repair in the middle of the night with nothing but a butter knife. My plan for a continual flow of fresh ice from the gas station soda fountain had proved to be majorly flawed, since it involved me leaving my house on a regular basis.

Working the fridge away from the wall one-handed was a bitch, even though the thing was empty. Years of greasy strings of dust and dead spider husks coated the coils, and the wall behind it. The rank smell was almost enough to sober me up. I pried the housing off the capacitor and briefly considered shocking some sense into myself by discharging it with my bare hands...but I only had one fucking hand, didn't I? Besides, it would be more likely to scramble my nervous system than to kill me. I had a resistor lying around somewhere. And some insulated screwdrivers.

The *Closet from Hell* is deep and narrow, and it's situated under the stairs leading to the third floor so that the ceiling is nothing but right angles to clock your head on. I sustained three or four solid head-raps in my search for a toolbox. I hadn't used it in so many months, it was buried deep. And the layers that covered it were practically worthy of an archaeologist's study. On top, the short-sleeved shirts I had no intention of wearing anymore. Under those, a pair of Jim's jeans. Lower still, fresh gimp supplies, still in their packages: bandages. Gauze. A cotton sheath. A gel sheath.

I knocked them aside with my stump and dug deeper.

Winter hat. A glove. The one I didn't need—the right one—of course. I threw it over my shoulder. An old porn stash: Colt Men, Buckshot Boys, the best pages stuck together. I vaguely remembered them, but the recollection was hazy enough that they'd be good now for a few more pulls. I threw those toward the bathroom. Finally, there at one of the lowest layers, was gear. My home toolbox, which I grabbed and hauled out of the pile with the full intention of getting back to my repair job...until something else caught my eye. A softball glove. I'd never been good—I smoke too much to run worth shit. But it had been something to do with the guys from the bar to get our drinking started a little earlier from that refreshing and seemingly endless cooler that gushed vodka lemonade from the spigot.

Something to do with Jim where I might actually see him smile.

Theoretically, I could still play softball, in the spring, once I was cleared to wear my robo-hand again. Catch with the left hand, nothing new. Throw with the right. Perfectly doable—Corey had demonstrated how easy it was to throw something accurately with a robotic limb, as the dried Sea-Monkeys I picked out of my eyelashes could tell you.

But without Jim...what was the point?

I woke up sprawled on the pile of closet junk with a crick in my neck and my face stuck to Jim's jeans where, apparently, I'd still been drunk enough to cry myself to sleep. I fucking hate it when I'm a maudlin drunk, though at least no one had been there to witness me carrying on. As I unglued my tongue with a cup of black coffee, the idea crept up on me that maybe my pathetic blubbering had rehydrated the brine shrimp. I took a long hot shower, face-first into the sprayer, and I considered whether it would have been easier all around if I'd just let that capacitor zap me after all.

To my bleary, stinging eyes, my apartment looked even worse than usual. Not only was the residue of my normal day-to-day existence littering the floor in the form of empty bottles and junk mail and takeout bags and crushed cigarette packs, but now there were refrigerator parts. And all the shit I'd dug out of the closet. I hardly knew where to start, but despite my headache, I sensed that crawling into bed and hoping it would all go away was not an option. After all, my new social worker (Maritza Somebody?) might take it upon herself to do a wellness check when she got back from her vacation. And the last thing I needed was to get myself committed.

Empty bottles were easy enough to sort out. Those went first. Between the bottles and all the food I'd thrown away the day before, my designated garbage bin was now full. When was garbage day? I had no idea. I went back in and filled another two bags, and snuck them into my neighbors' bins.

By mid-afternoon I had a clear space in the living room. While I could have shoved everything that had spewed out of the closet back into its niche under the stairs, I figured I might as well have a look at it all in case there was something I could get rid of while I was on a roll. I left Jim's damp jeans wadded in the corner, though. I figured that in terms of deciding what to do with those, I had nothing but time.

Clothes. Short-sleeved shirts…garbage. Wound-care supplies… garbage. Shoes. A pair of outrageously tall fourteen-hole Docs that made me look like a badass, though they were a bitch to get out of at the end of the night. As if I had anyone to impress anymore—as if I could deal with fourteen fucking eyelets and only one hand to lace them. Garbage.

But there beneath the clothes that nowadays would just leave me feeling like a poser, I found other things. Quiet things. My high school yearbook. A Jackson Pollock ripoff I'd painted before I realized I wasn't the first talentless dumbass to try to pass himself off as an abstract expressionist. A Polaroid Instamatic that had belonged to my uncle.

So. Once upon a time, there'd been hobbies in my life.

The camera was heavy—substantial and distinctly non-robotic. I thought I remembered hearing Kodak had discontinued the film... but also hearing that they'd changed their minds and brought it back a year later. I parked my cigarette in my mouth, turned the camera around in my lap and braced it with my stump while I flicked off the lens cap. Figuring the batteries were dead so there'd be no actual chance of the thing working, I held it up in the general vicinity of my face and snapped the shutter.

There was a flash, and a square photo whirred out. I set the camera down and pulled the photo, and even though it supposedly didn't make any difference, I shook it. Habit's a funny thing that way. At first, I assumed the old film was to blame for the image that took shape—because I'd ended up with a shot of my old man, the long-dead rummy nobody missed, whose image had somehow managed to stick inside the camera all this time.

Of course, that haggard, red-eyed bastard in the Polaroid was actually me. I put the camera back in the closet and shut the door.

Normally I'd see if I was up for another drink, or maybe crawl back into bed. But today my momentum wasn't hampered by my disgust. Instead, I was gripped by a steely determination to see this thing through—whatever *this thing* might actually be. With a choice between warm tap water and hot coffee, I chose the coffee as my afternoon fuel. My tools were just like I remembered them, though they felt foreign in my left hand. The hand-skills are only a small part of the job, though. It's the mental skills—knowing what powers what, weak spots, cause and effect—that are the main thing you tap into when you're doing a repair.

With all the extra rigmarole of strapping an insulated screwdriver to my stump by a bandanna I tightened with my teeth, it took me half an hour to discharge the capacitor, rather than the two minutes I would've spent on it with the use of both hands. Whatever. It wasn't like I was lacking for time.

It sucked through and through—both having only a stump

to brace the parts with, and trying to work all my tools with my non-dominant hand. But even though it was frustrating, I managed to lose myself in the task: solving this thing where no one was going to end up hurt. Too bad real life wasn't like that, but there was no relationship capacitor to discharge. Only shocks.

It was late by the time I determined the compressor relay was shot. I was dizzy when I stood, not from alcohol poisoning (or not entirely) but from lack of food. A cup of instant noodles filled my gut, and buffered it from the vodka that was warm enough to make me shudder. There wasn't enough booze left to black me out, only enough to get me maudlin again when I considered that I had no way of getting to the far-flung parts store without Jim or Corey driving me. And the fact that both of them probably would've been secretly relieved if I'd just electrocuted myself with the capacitor.

In the morning, I found dried noodles stuck to the toilet rim, looking like I hadn't even chewed them. But I felt surprisingly good. Puking will do that for you sometimes. For all the hauling I'd done the day before, my apartment didn't look any cleaner. Just different. The yellow handles of my screwdrivers and pliers were more cheerful than the empty bottles that usually covered the floor.

I still needed a relay. Which meant I needed a ride. A cab would cost more than the part itself. And I wasn't even gonna start on Jim or Corey. I turned on the TV so I could think and I parked myself on the couch, and I pondered calling some of the old Crowley Ave Boys. They'd still know who I was, right? Georgie Argusto had remembered me. He'd even given me about half a pack of smokes when I was flat broke. Maybe he'd give me a ride.

Then again, it was Friday morning. And Georgie Argusto had a job.

Fuck.

Corey was the only person I could think of who would be home—although, if I let it slip that his availability was the main reason I'd called him, no doubt he'd be twice as pissed off at me as he already was...with me still waiting for dormant Sea-Monkey eggs to spring back to life beneath my eyelids the next time I felt sorry enough for myself to give in to the temptation of waterworks.

Which had been happening a fuck of a lot lately.

Okay, if not Corey, maybe someone else from Gimp Group. His brother, his sister-in-law? They probably both had jobs. Plus if I was on the outs with him, chances were his family would be none too thrilled with me. The soldier guy? I didn't know his name. Plus he was back in the Middle East or something. The car crash lady? Again, a name would have been helpful. That left...who?

Ken Roman. The smirking professor with the tattered prosthetic.

Not only did I remember his name...but he'd given me his business card, back there in Pam Steiner's slick-floored vestibule. Which meant he actually wanted me to call him.

It was just a matter of finding the damn card.

I suspected it had fallen into the black hole between the couch and the coffee table. That area hadn't been subject to my latest clean sweep, so I cracked open the last garbage bag and got to work in that quadrant. More vodka bottles. Yellow Social Services envelopes everywhere—and I would need to be extra-careful with anything paper, so I didn't accidentally toss Ken's card. As I looked at each envelope (*Love, Jim*) I started sorting them by date, figuring it might be a good idea to piece together things I needed to know about the last couple of months, but pretty soon there were too many of them to make heads or tails of, and I ended up just stacking them all inside my half-full laundry basket.

The lowest level of detritus was all the smaller stuff. Amazing how many cigarette butts escaped the ash trays, and the cracked saucer, and the salsa jar lids. Popcorn—I couldn't remember the last time I'd eaten popcorn. My stomach rumbled. There, just under the edge of the couch, a bottle cap. Jim's? He was the beer drinker. Not me. I got down low to see what else was hiding under there...and came face to face with a key.

The key.

The padlock needed to come off. Thing was, if I showed up at Corey's bare-necked and green and wanting a ride, he'd take it all wrong and figure I was using him for his car. I couldn't risk it, not with his hair-trigger temper. What I needed to do was get my shit together and do something nice for him. Cook him a dinner, a real dinner, a couple of nice steaks and a bottle of wine. But first things first. I snagged a greasy business card out from under the couch so I could see about fixing my fridge.

CHAPTER 15

Professor Ken Roman pulled up to my building in his silver Toyota coupe, which seemed a bit too small from him, but undoubtedly got amazing gas mileage. Imagine my surprise earlier when I called his office to leave a message and he told me he wasn't currently in class, and that he'd be delighted to give me a ride to the parts store.

Delighted.

Normally, I'd figure that meant he expected a BJ for his trouble, or at least a handie. But there was something edgy about the way he'd said it—I could just picture him smirking—that led me to believe whatever he really did want in return was nowhere near as straightforward.

I climbed in, kicked aside some greasy single-serve pizza boxes to make room for my feet, and said, "Thanks for the lift." The car smelled like oregano.

"The Steiner Clan's matriarch didn't mention why you weren't at last night's meeting." He looked at the empty right sleeve of my leather jacket and raised an eyebrow. "And now you're going au naturale."

"It's been an eventful week."

He turned onto the Thruway and waited for me to elaborate. I didn't, initially. But Ken didn't beg for details. He just whistled...not even really a melody, just a quiet string of scales going up and down, until finally, just to hear him stop, I said, "They're not forcing me to go to Gimp Group anymore."

"Gimp Group. I'd love to see Pam's face when you call it that."

"You've got a job." I figured "professor" might have even paid pretty good. "What's Social Services holding over your head to make sure you show up?"

"Oh, my attendance isn't mandatory."

I sat with that awhile, until the whistling started again. Then I said, "You go because you *want* to?"

He smiled a wry smile to himself.

I turned that idea around a few times, then said, "You got the hots for Pam?"

He laughed out loud. "I can barely stand to be in the same room with her. And the feeling is mutual."

Maybe he liked the car crash lady. Or maybe it was Hugh he was after. Corey's brother was a good-looking guy. But before I could ask, Ken said, "I'm not trying to pick up anyone at the Steiner house. It's not about sex. It's about...connection."

"You don't connect."

"Indeed, I do."

"But in group, you sit there and you don't say a word."

"I hear myself talk all day long. I go to listen. They're my tribe, the other amputees. Just being among them feeds my soul."

How anyone could forget the big smirking guy in the corner was eavesdropping on their conversation and actually open up was beyond me—but apparently Ken's M.O. panned out for him. I asked, "You hear anything about...Corey?"

"Let's see. *Tell him he'd better not be late to Nana's birthday...Yeah, I already did...Tell him again.* That's all."

I got a little chill from that, because it sounded so much like Pam and Hugh Steiner it was almost like he'd taped the conversation and played it back in his own voice. Maybe he had something like photographic memory, only with speech. And then I wondered what I'd said to him over the course of our acquaintance. Not much. Probably. Although my recollection of our conversations was vague at best. I was lucky I'd even remembered he'd given me his card and which part of the living room garbage heap it was likely to be in.

And, of course, the thought that Corey had a "Nana" and I didn't even know about her was bothering me, too. Because that's the type of thing your boyfriend would know. Not some guy who comes to your house once a week, takes off his shoes, and parks himself by the fireplace, smirking.

"So why aren't you wearing your robo-hand?" Ken asked. "Is that what you need this special part for? A little customization?"

"This? No, this is for my fridge. I can barely work the damn prosthetic as it is. Can't see tinkering with it." Not like Corey had done with his, turning it into a big vibrating probe with a flick of his shoulder.

"Then you're having a problem with the amputation site...?"

"Turn here," I told him. "There, the place with the green awning."

Ken pulled over and cut the engine. He ignored the fact that I was obviously avoiding the subject of my prosthetic, pulled a folded newspaper out from between the seats, shifted his bulk, and said, "Take your time. I don't have any classes after lunch on Fridays."

When he didn't follow me into the shop, I felt myself relax. I hadn't realized I'd been tensing.

Louie behind the counter did a triple-take before he registered who I was, and then he greeted me with some surprise and remarked that he hadn't seen me in ages—and then he got a little too smiley as he remembered why, and tried to figure out how to not-look at the empty space below my right sleeve. I faced my right side away from him to spare him the anguish, and kept my shooting the shit to a minimum. I dug the old relay out of my pocket, noting that the cassette tape from the shrink, Dr. Ivery, still hung heavy there. While Louie located the replacement part, I wandered the aisles. But I didn't need anything else. I only wanted to get my fridge running. It wasn't as if I planned to make a habit out of fixing things.

Once I got back in the car with Ken, he pointed out a café on the corner, and said, "They look like they have good pastries."

"I really need to fix my—"

"Come on. I skipped lunch to drive you here." He squeezed out from behind the steering wheel and heaved himself from the car. It rocked as he transferred his weight from the seat to his own two legs.

I hadn't eaten any lunch either...or breakfast, for that matter. And my stomach was doing that acidy thing that could really stand to be soaked up with a bagel or a muffin. Grudgingly, I followed.

A tray with a steaming cup of coffee and a couple of gigantic pastries on it sat beside the register, while Ken scratched his stubbly gray beard and said, "...and one of those brownies—the big one, there, in back."

I wondered if he'd lost his hand to diabetes. Although I thought diabetics had problems with their eyesight and their feet, but I wasn't exactly an expert so I couldn't say for sure.

"And for you, Mr. Poole? I'm buying. And this fine young lady has assured me the bear claws are excellent."

"Um...coffee," I said, because the whole place reeked of coffee, and I couldn't see going without. "And a bagel."

The chick behind the counter was maybe twenty, with a pierced eyebrow and chipped blue nail polish. Hard to tell if she had a cute haircut or good wardrobe sense, given that her hair was in a ponytail and she had on a brown plaid waitress uniform shirt. She was busy reading the buttons on my jacket, though, so I figured her for a wannabe, if not a full-fledged, safety-pin-pierced punk rock chick. Then she saw me noticing her noticing me, and her cheeks went a bit pink. "Plain?" she said. "Whole wheat? Blueberry? Poppyseed?"

"Plain's fine."

"Toasted? Cream cheese?"

"Yeah. Sure."

"So did you see Green Day the last time they were in town?" She bent to dig a bagel out of the case. "I heard the opening bands were... good."

Her face had gone eye level with my empty sleeve, and now her eyes were big enough to fall out of her head. She dropped a bagel on the floor, and it rolled, rolled, rolled—all the way over to the espresso machine before it finally thumped to a stop—without her even noticing it was gone.

"No," I said. "Not a big fan."

"Yeah," she said quickly. "I was working." She grabbed a new bagel and turned away to toast it with a lot more focus and attention than she actually needed.

I took my coffee to the table in the far corner, where Ken sat watching the exchange. Either he was smirking faintly, or he actually wasn't, but his face had frozen that way when he was a kid. Because if anyone should find that exchange to be pathetic, it would be a fellow gimp.

"You were just about to tell me what happened to your arm," Ken said.

My robotic arm? Or my real one? Either way, it was none of his business. Free bagel or not. "No, I wasn't."

Then he smiled wide, for real. "I never wear my robotics at home. I found an antique prosthetic at a flea market—a hook. Very useful. But not the sort of thing one wears in public...if you know what I mean."

Did I? I didn't think so. But maybe I didn't want to.

Punkie girl brought over my toasted bagel, took one look at Ken's tattered robo-arm reaching for the sugar dispenser, and literally ran back to the counter—and then kept right on going, past the espresso machine and into the staff-only room.

Ken chuckled and poured as much sugar into his coffee as the cup would hold. "I see a lot of that, fall semester. Especially among the freshmen. They're still teenagers—practically children. Haven't learned how to be diplomatic quite yet. But once the add/drop period is over, and all the students who find the hand too distracting have transferred to Earth Science or Intro to Philosophy, the ones who are left in my class get over it soon enough."

I took a bite of my bagel, realized how long it had been since I'd had solid food, and then began wolfing it down as fast as I could chew it, thankful for the lubrication of the cream cheese and burnt coffee. Had I dodged the bullet of the "where's my arm" conversation? It seemed I might have. Ken was packing away his food just as quickly as I was, though his motions were leisurely, as if he was utterly convinced the bear claws and brownie had nowhere to go but his expansive belly. And though his motions were unhurried, the bites he took were huge.

"How is it," he said between bites, and I thought he meant my bagel, but then he added, "getting around with only one hand? You were right-handed originally, weren't you?"

"How do you think it is?" I swallowed a few times. "It sucks."

"The body is a strange and wondrous thing. Plenty of people adjust to losing a limb. Plenty of people are born without them to begin with, and they make do."

I'd never known anyone to be born without an arm or a leg, but I figured that arguing with him would only make him dwell on it, and I focused on my coffee instead.

"I go to the flea market at least once a week," he said, "sometimes two or three times. If you're interested, you can tag along. You might find an intriguing hook. Or a vintage hand. Plastic. Or wooden, if it's old enough...in fact, I know a collector who had something like that from the 1920s—might still have it, if he hasn't sold it yet. Whalebone fingers. I tried it on. Too small for me. I could have had it adjusted, I suppose, but tinkering with an antique like that would only ruin it. Seemed like a shame, nearly a century old. But you..." he looked me up and down, "it might fit you."

I stared at him hard, trying to figure out what he was getting out of all of this. And I came up with nothing. "I'm getting my robo-arm back," I told him. Just as soon as it didn't make me crazy.

"Ah," he said, as if he understood...everything.

* * *

It turned out that the relay was the only thing keeping my ancient refrigerator from running. It also turned out that I didn't have the patience to put the damn thing back together one-handed. I unwrapped my stump and slipped on my robo-arm. It felt strange after being off for two days, but not bad. My meat hadn't shifted. I was just aware of the sleeve touching me, in the way you might be aware of a new pair of shoes.

And maybe my control of it wasn't as bad as I usually make it out to be. I was able to do my thumbs-up and steady the compressor with the grippy silicone while I maneuvered the relay into place with my left hand. I also pressed my robotic forefinger against the screw slots and wondered what it would be like to have one of those fancy tool attachments. Sure, I'd need to wear a bigger battery pack. But coming at the screw right-handed, even with a robo-arm, felt more natural to me than fumbling a manual screwdriver in my left.

Of course, if I wanted something like that, I'd never be able to afford one myself. I'd need to work somewhere that would subsidize it. Like the Digi-Control shop I'd worked at...all of a day and a half.

Once the big harvest gold beast was up and running in the middle of the kitchen, I noticed it was pretty damn loud, and took it apart again to see what the deal with the fan was. Warped. If Corey didn't hate me, I'd have him drive me down to the parts store. Or Ken Roman, if he wasn't so damn creepy. But I pinched with my robo-hand and took up flat-nosed pliers in the other and straightened out the blades as best I could, then laboriously put the refrigerator back together.

It was still pretty loud. Just a different pitch. I itched to replace the damn fan, not because the noise bothered me—I could always drown it out with the TV—but because it was against my nature to leave a piece of equipment limping along with a shoddy part inside.

Jim was another one I would normally grab a ride from—before the double-barreled breakup. Before the key in the mail and the Gimp Group announcement that he'd tossed my case file in someone else's in-basket. And although I could have told myself that he'd just shown up in Dr. Ivery's waiting room because he was a control freak, fact was, I knew the real reason he'd come was to make sure I was okay.

Given the scene in that damn waiting room, I suspected if I asked Jim for a ride now that I'd burned through all his goodwill, I would only end up with a lecture about how I had a perfectly good car being stored in Mrs. Zelko's garage down the block, and why don't I get my license back and drive myself.

And this is the sneaky thing about Jim. Even with this lecture being delivered only inside my own head with no help at all from him...I found I had zero rebuttal.

Why don't I?

Mrs. Zelko was off playing pinochle, or whatever she did on Saturdays, but the $25 per month I tithed to her bought me a key to her dusty garage. I turned that key left-handed. And there she was, the primer-gray Gremlin I'd had since I was seventeen years old—the car that, by all accounts, should no longer run. I ran my hand over her peeling hood. If I re-connected the fuel line, I bet she'd chug right back to life. Just like the fridge.

CHAPTER 16

On Monday morning, I woke with the realization that I would need to get my ass in gear if I wanted to be at Dr. Ivery's office in time for my appointment. And also that I'd fallen asleep with my prosthetic on. And also that I was out of coffee.

And also that I hadn't done a single thing on her homework list.

I took a quick shower and very nearly screwed on my robo-hand once I dried and lotioned and powdered my residual arm. But I didn't have the balls to tell Dr. Ivery I thought she was wrong, and that I wasn't actually *afraid* of the prosthetic. After all, she was the one with fancy degree-type letters after her name, not me. So I wrapped my stump in a compression bandage instead and threw the limb in a plastic bag to take with me. Maybe I could get "permission" to put it back on after today's session, though I planned on wearing it home whether she gave me the go-ahead or not.

I got there five minutes late—fucking Niagara bus—and realized I probably should have at least peeled the plastic wrap off the cassette tape in case Dr. Ivery told me to turn out my pockets. But it wasn't as if I was in juvie, right? Or an AA meeting, or any of those other things I might have brought upon myself. I was there for help. Not punishment. And so of course she wasn't gonna search me and make me feel like an idiot.

Hopefully.

"Let's get started," she said briskly, and then shot a pointed look at the clock.

"About that," I said. "I think it's time for me to drive again."

"Do you own a car?"

"Yes."

"Is it robotic ignition?"

"No—it's not robotic anything. It's a '78 Gremlin—"

"Then I don't see that it will interfere with our progress. Let's take a look at your worksheet."

It was still folded in my pocket, untouched. "I forgot it at home. It's on my fridge. Which, actually, I fixed this weekend, and I think it was kind of a turning point for—"

"Bring this with you next time," Ivery said. She pulled out a duplicate of the sheet I had ignored, and said, "How many times did you do the relaxation?"

I almost said, "All of them," but even I could see that would be an obvious lie. She'd told me to do nine, so I said, "Eight. I missed one on Friday. When I took a trip to the parts store."

"And on a scale of one to ten, was there any shift in your level of discomfort when you imagined the top of your lowest tier of robotics interactions once you'd had some practice with the relaxation?"

"Not really. I mean...going through an automatic door, the kind that just opens without a scan-in, isn't much of a problem for me. The anxiety was already at a one."

"So you're saying you experienced no anxiety doing the exercise."

Was that a trick question? If I said no, none, would she know I hadn't bothered to do it? "That's not what I said. It's just that, I think robots in general aren't—"

"There was no shift?"

"I guess...it got easier. During the last couple of tries."

"If it was low to begin with, I'll put down that you shifted from a two to a one." She filled out the new form for me. "All right, now we can move on to your second tier of anxieties. These involve touching the exterior of a robotic appliance or device—kitchen items, games, and keypad-activated machines. Let's get a baseline level of your anxiety when you think about using a microwave."

"My microwave isn't robotic."

"A stove, then."

"Nope. It's an antique."

"Television?"

"Uh...no."

"It's worse than I thought," she said. And she wrote in my chart for a very long time.

"But, see, that's not really a phobia," I tried to explain. "I'm not *afraid* of a smart coffeemaker. It's my stubbornness, is all. Old stuff is cool, it's classic, and I just don't see why I should be forced to have robotics in my house if I don't want to."

She continued to write. I don't know if she was ignoring me, or if I'd just added more fuel to her fire.

"I think my biggest problem is scanning in to a housebot—and that makes sense, right? Because that's how...."

Scribble, scribble, scribble.

Eventually, she looked up, and said, "I'm going to have you visualize that you're setting your Hooverbot to vacuum the carpet while you're at work. Picture the keypad...."

Even when I'd owned a Hooverbot at my last apartment, I never would have trusted it to go about its business if I wasn't home to watch it. I've always dropped too many important things on the floor. I said, "Uh-huh," without making any effort to picture it trundling across the rug, and I lied and told her my zero-level anxiety was at a two, since it seemed like we'd never move on to the things that mattered until I showed some sort of "progress" on my "lower tiers." Things like my inability to work my goddamn robotic arm, and the fact that it actually did freak me out to stick my hand into a scanbot.

We repeated the process on a TV remote (I used to own one, but it wasn't technically robotic, plus I destroyed it with my robo-arm) and a Bathroom Buddy (mine was so crusted with lime I found it easier to use cleanser and sponge. Even one-handed.) And then we did the relaxation, tense and release, and went through it all again. The vacuum. The TV. The Bathroom Buddy.

"Now," she asked me, "where is your anxiety level?"

"Zero. Uh...I mean, one. I think I'm ready to move on to my prosthetic."

"Oh, no. That's much too fast. Your progress can backslide if you go too fast. You won't be ready for your arm again until next week, at the soonest." She pulled out a small box and set it on the edge of her desk. "First, we'll need to work on interacting with a simpler robotic. One that doesn't involve you inserting your hand or arm into it."

The box was all pastel pink and blue, with a cartoon of a smiling... thing...on the front. "What's that?"

"This little bot is used in high schools to dissuade teen pregnancy by making the kids aware of how much work it is to care for a newborn. It's called the Parent-Egg."

"You know I'm gay, right? There isn't any danger of me accidentally—"

"Ignore the packaging. What's important—I'll set it to sleep through the night—is that it will give you the practice you need interacting with robotics on a regular basis, without the threat of the specific action that's at the heart of your phobia: insertion."

This was not happening.

"When it needs something, it will cry. If it's flashing red, you press the formula button. If it's flashing blue, you rock it. And if it's flashing green, you talk to it."

"Look, really...."

"This isn't up for debate. Practice your breathing, care for the Parent-Egg, and fill out this form to track your progress, or else I'm letting Maritza Collins know you're not cooperating with therapy."

"But—"

"Don't break it. There's a four-hundred dollar price tag attached that will come out of your monthly benefit check if you throw it, kick it, or try to disable it in any way." She opened the box and rolled the white plastic oval onto her palm. "And if you decide to stash it somewhere and ignore it until next session like you did the chart...I'll know. All actions are recorded."

"That's awfully punitive."

"The program doesn't have the resources to waste on participants who won't prioritize their own self-care."

"In other words, my benefits now depend on the approval of a robotic egg."

"The whole blasé attitude might come off as charming to men with tattoos and leather jackets, but you should seriously consider the ramifications of failing this assignment." Ivery handed me some kind of homeless shelter brochure with models on the cover made up to look even more down-and-out than me. "A little food for thought."

I managed to keep from rolling my eyes.

Before she re-boxed the egg, she pulled a key from her desk drawer, stuck it in a tiny slot in the oval chassis, and turned. The bot let out a high-pitched squawk. She returned the key to her drawer.

"Wait a minute," I said. "How do I shut the thing off?"

She gave me a hollow smile. "You don't, Mr. Poole. That's the whole point."

* * *

Although I didn't have "permission" to wear my robotic limb, I was sick and tired of having my only hand occupied with carrying it around in a plastic bag. Once I got myself settled at the back of the bus, I snagged the edge of the compression bandage with my teeth, pulled off the dressing, shoved the robo-arm up the empty sleeve of my leather jacket, and gave my stump the practiced twist that would fit it into the sleeve of the device.

When I looked up, a blue-haired old lady sitting by the back exit was watching me shrug into my arm, wide-eyed behind her thick bifocals. She didn't look away when she realized I saw her. She just nodded. Maybe people who've lived that long have seen enough that they're impossible to shock. People like Jim, too, who dealt with crazy fuckups day in and day out. Maybe that's why he'd stuck by me so long...and why it took him three tries to break up with me. But who's counting?

The egg started whining as I let myself back into my place. I opened the box top and saw it was flashing red. I pressed the button with the baby-bottle icon on it. The whining stopped.

I put it on the couch and headed back to Mrs. Zelko's garage. It was tempting to siphon a little juice into my Gremlin's carburetor, just to see if she turned over, though I knew I should probably replace the shocks first. At least there was an automotive store within walking distance. Pricier than one of the big one-stop places. But I wouldn't need to beg anyone for a ride.

And then there was the matter of actually doing the repairs. It would take me a lot longer with my left hand and my prosthetic—because I'd be damned if I waited until the end of my week-long sentence with the egg to get going on the project. I needed to work on the car. I'd go nuts if I didn't.

I popped the hood and considered the spark plugs. If I could get my pinch-gesture perfected, enough to use my robo-arm like an ad hoc adjustable wrench, putting the Gremlin back on the road might actually be fairly doable, after all.

I was flying high, euphoric over the prospect of a night on the town with my primer-gray lady, and self-satisfied enough as I traipsed back up to my apartment, I hardly even minded that one of my lame neighbors had set their smoke alarm off.

Until I opened my front door and realized the shrill was coming from my apartment.

I looked up at the pale round circle on the wall where my smoke detector used to be—but, no, it was still gone. The safety fairy hadn't made a visit while I wasn't looking. I tried to follow the sound, figuring maybe there was a carbon monoxide detector somewhere that I'd managed to never notice. I narrowed it down to the living room, finally. And then underneath the couch, specifically.

Where a blue light was blinking, on and off.

"Are you kidding me?" I jammed my left arm under the couch, but the egg was backed against the wall, flashing and bleating. "Come here," I told it. Dr. Ivery had failed to mention it was able to move. "Get the fuck over here."

Talking to the egg was one of the three things I was supposed to do with it, right? But I didn't see how the hell it could hear me over its own damn siren.

"Here, eggy. C'mere, little eggy-weggy. Come to Desmond...*fucking fucker fuck-egg!*"

It kept right on shrilling and flashing.

"Come on out and I'll give you a nice, solid...rocking."

No dice. It must've had a sensor that could tell I wanted to punt it across the room—four hundred dollar levy or not.

"Fine. Be that way. But don't think I'll forget the fact that you made me move the couch on your account."

CHAPTER 17

If I looked too hard at the whole process of getting my license back, I would probably decide it was more than I could handle and settle down on the couch with a drink, a jerkoff magazine and an old sock. But I did need to look at the big picture, at least vaguely, squinting the whole while, if I wanted to determine step one.

Because maybe I could do that right now. Step one.

I needed a license. And for that I needed to re-take my road test. And for that I needed to learn to drive again with my robo-arm at the helm—Ken would probably be *delighted* to ride along while I re-mastered that skill. But even the act of practicing for a road test seemed completely out of reach, given the fact that I could barely work my own damn arm.

I looked down at the silicone-covered motor where my wrist used to be, and I sighed.

Step one would be to figure out how to use the arm.

It wasn't as if no one had ever attempted to teach me, too—that was the scary part. I'd spent weeks, months, being ferried back and forth to physical therapy by Jim. And I could barely park my thumb well enough to get dressed.

The perfect person to teach me the arm's fine gestures was the same guy who'd informed me that I pushed all his buttons—all the wrong ones. But if I gave Corey a few days to cool down, and then I sweet-talked him good? Maybe it would work. But it would take time.

Ideally, I'd teach myself. All I needed were some instructions. But it seemed to me I'd thrown out all the pamphlets and the photocopied exercise sheets the day I got them, though I needed to check to be absolutely sure. Another three-hour expedition into the closet under the stairs revealed that my memory was, for once, accurate.

I found the Instamatic camera, the softball glove, and Jim's old jeans, which were still damp.

The notion of swinging by Jim's, browsing his gimp library and returning the jeans crossed my mind, but I nixed it. I had the feeling that Jim, with that way of his, would know what they were wet with the second I put them into his hand. Still, he might have something on prosthetics, or at least in that dismal office building he worked at, he'd be able to find a pamphlet or a brochure. Maybe that shaky hope didn't merit a bus ride, but it was a good enough excuse to call.

He answered in four rings.

"Uh...hey." It occurred to me I probably should have rehearsed what I wanted to say. Now I sounded awkward. "I was just wondering if you had any of those books...y'know. About how to use the robo-arm."

He was silent for so long I almost thought he'd hung up on me. But finally, he said, "Why?"

"It would just be easier. That's all."

"What would be easier?"

Driving? Functioning day to day? Feeling like maybe I had something to wake up for in the morning? Hell, I didn't know. "Just...things."

I heard stuff moving around over on his end of the line, and then he said, "Yeah. I've got something. I'll bring it by."

It's a five minute drive between Jim's place and mine. Five minutes, apparently, was the perfect amount of time to realize what a sorry state I was in without giving me enough time to do dick about it. I stunk. My hair was rank. I had oil under my fingernails and I hadn't shaved in a week. A normal guy—that is to say, a two-handed guy—might hop in the shower. Not me. Removing the arm and getting the stump dry enough to safely re-engage would take at least ten minutes, and even slinging a garbage bag over the damn limb would take too long to secure. A quick swab with a washcloth was all I had time for. That, and a fleeting encounter with a toothbrush that was so dried out it made my gums bleed. Jim wouldn't notice that, would he? Maybe. It was Jim, after all. He notices everything.

I stood by the intercom, waiting for the buzz, then told myself I didn't want to seem too eager. I scooted the Parent-Egg to one side of the couch and sat. And then I decided, screw it. When the buzzer buzzed, I'd count to five, and then I'd answer. Nobody could possibly know I'd felt compelled to time myself. Not even Jim.

So I stood by the intercom, wondering what I'd say when he did ring. For fuck's sake, who the hell plans what they're gonna say to the intercom? Whatever was up my ass that night, apparently it made *me* that guy. The one who felt the need to weigh the pros and cons of words like "hey" and "what's up" and "yeah."

As I mouthed the words "c'mon up" in an attempt to see if they sounded natural, I realized Jim was uncharacteristically late. Funny, the things that went through my head. Maybe he'd known I needed extra time to clean up, and I should have opted for a shower after all since he'd so graciously given me those few moments to recoup some dignity. Unfortunately, I could no longer be sure if Jim gave a rat's ass about my dignity or not, and the notion crept in that maybe his motivation for keeping me waiting was at the other end of the spectrum entirely. Maybe what he wanted was to make sure I stewed.

I was good and pissed off by the time I began to wonder if maybe neither of those scenarios was true, and maybe some fried tweaker had crossed paths with Jim somewhere between Black Rock and Riverside, and that old station wagon of Jim's was nowhere near as sturdy as it had been before the undercarriage rusted out...sirens, ambulances, a crowd of mouth-breathing gawkers, I saw it all. And in the midst, bleeding out deep red on graying asphalt like a fallen Titan, was Jim.

I grabbed for the door, right-left, then slowed long enough to park my goddamn thumb and yank on my leather. With a massive tug, I left-handed my front door open. Although I saw the book, there was so much momentum propelling me that I tripped over the damn thing anyway as it fell into my apartment with a soft whump.

Robotic Limbs: Hand and Arm

I stood in the hall and stared down at the stupid book, fighting the urge to kick it. My asshole neighbors were never very careful about shutting the outside door, and honestly, neither was I. Of course Jim could slip in and out without me being any the wiser. That was no big shock. But what did surprise me was my profound, nearly debilitating sense of disappointment that he hadn't bothered to hang around long enough to see me.

What the hell was my problem? There it was, the missing manual, the magical tome that would help me get my life back, inasmuch as it was possible. No reason to be so glum since I had what I wanted.

Didn't I?

An egg-bleat disrupted my train of thought—not that I was too keen on exploring it further, anyhow—and as I glanced back at the useless bot, I saw the whole place afresh, as Jim might see it. Before the fridge died, my mess had been so deep that it had created a sort of visual static. But now that I'd de-junked, the things that were out of place stuck out like an unparked thumb. The newly decluttered coffee table now held an empty vodka bottle and three half-full ash trays. A pair of dirty boxers was draped over the arm of the couch. And on that couch, there sat the egg, the useless hunk of circuitry the system had saddled me with to make some grotesque point about responsibility. Or maybe just to piss me off. Or maybe, I realized, because I was actually expected to fail at my assignment, thus saving upstanding taxpayers the expense of keeping my sorry hide alive.

The egg bleated again, more loudly now.

Maybe it was for the best that Jim hadn't stopped in.

* * *

At four hundred dollars, the Fucking Egg was, in my opinion, overpriced. After only a few days, I'd determined the "needs" were on three cycles. Food, every four hours. Rocking, every five. Talking, every two.

Parking it in front of the TV took care of the talking requirement. That was pretty lifelike, I supposed. Food only required the press of a button. And I could rock it with my foot while I was trying to perfect my pinch.

My robotic fingers were set to apply a maximum of a hundred pounds of pressure, although the arm was capable of a lot more—strong enough to shatter a brittle remote, but too weak to unscrew a corroded bolt. Probably to curtail the amount of accidental castrations they'd end up with in urgent care from the gimps who'd figured out how to jack with their prosthetic. I'd be able to do basic mechanics with the weak grasp, but I wouldn't be able to use it as a real wrench unless I had the limiter tweaked. For now I'd settle for being able to pick something up with the damn thing.

Problem was, I was making my fist all wrong. I needed to curl the thumb in first, then bend the remaining fingers around to stabilize whatever I wanted to grab. But I just couldn't get the two in synch. The diagrams in my book were as good as I could expect, but I've always been more of a hands-on guy. Reading a schematic would do in a pinch—having someone show me how something was put together then taking it apart myself was the only way I actually learned anything.

With just me and the book and the robo-arm, it took me all day to master a wimpy pinch—and if that sounds disappointing, believe me, it wasn't. It wasn't a grasp, exactly. Finally, though, I could pick something up if I needed to, and I could hold on to something if I was careful.

Turning an ignition key would take more work—after all, that motion was pinch and twist—but at least I was on my way.

Unfortunately, the only one there to celebrate my accomplishment with me was the Fucking Egg. And it appeared to be asleep.

Since Jim had done his book drop with all the grace of a drive-by shooting, I didn't consider calling him for more than a minute or two. But Corey...if he'd had enough time to cool down, he would be happy for me. Right?

I dialed his number, and instead of a ringtone, I heard a chime. A robotic voice came on the line and said, "You are currently scanned in at the location you're attempting to call, DESMOND POOLE."

I was? I hadn't been there for at least a week, but I supposed it was entirely possible I'd never scanned out. And I hadn't scanned in to Corey's car. Or the shrink's office. Or anyplace with a scanny-door, like the shiny new robotic post office.

"If you would like to re-set your current location to your home number, press one, now. If you would like to ring through, press two, now. If this is an emergency, press zero, now. If you would like to hear these options again, press four, now. Or, simply hang up."

Too many options. What I'd been prepared to say was that I was sorry. And that I wanted Corey to give me another chance. And that I'd love it if he could demonstrate a few simple prosthetic gestures for me. But now I was faced with the knowledge that my phone line had been feeding to Corey's place all week.

What if he'd been talking to my shrink on my behalf. Or to Jim? Gah. Corey would never forgive me. And that scared me.

"Please make a selection. If you would like to re-set your current location to your home number, press one, now...."

Pull it together. It doesn't mean anything. After all, what could anybody tell Corey about me that he couldn't figure out for himself after spending a few days together?

Just proceed as planned.

"If you would like to ring through, press two, now."

I pressed two. Corey answered. "Hello?"

"Hey." I didn't think Corey and I were at the "it's me" stage. Not like me and Jim. "It's Desmond."

While I didn't *expect* to hear his lilting "Des-mond Poole," maybe, in the back of my mind, I'd been *hoping* he might greet me with it. So, of course, instead he said, "What?"

"What's going on?" I said, as casually as I could. Because I hadn't planned on responding to anything quite that terse.

"Counting down the minutes 'til happy hour...and don't take that as an invitation. Just an indication of how sorely I was hoping to find a drink. And a friendly person to drink it with."

"I'm friendly," I said. "Why don't you save yourself some trouble and have that drink here, with me?"

"Where are you calling from, Opposite Land? 'Cause as far as I remember, you're nothing *but* trouble."

He had me there. "Okay. Save yourself a few bucks at least."

When he didn't have a snappy comeback for that, my first thought was panic. He'd been toying with the whole boyfriend-scenario not long ago, and now he was so pissed off with me he wouldn't even share a drink? But then my eyes went to the gap in the wall where the Sea-Monkeys used to live, and I realized that maybe I should be grateful for the pause. At least it wasn't an out-and-out refusal.

When he finally spoke, his voice sounded small, like he couldn't even bring himself to talk right into the phone. "Why did you call?"

I could tell he'd smell a lie a mile away. Corey was a sensitive kid, and he had no patience for bullshit. Still, he'd be ticked off if he knew I was angling for prosthetic lessons—even though that was the first thing I'd noticed about him, the fact that he could work his fake hand like an extension of his own body. That couldn't be all, could it? Because if anything, his competence should have repelled me. True, the robo-hand was part of him—but it didn't define him. Initially he was a startlingly attractive fellow gimp, but now when I thought of him, the metal was no longer the first thing that came to mind. It was his stupid Britishisms, his afternoon tea and the way he rocked his natty brogues. It was the way he lingered over me with a soft look in his eyes when he brought me coffee in bed. It was the way his eyelids fluttered shut when he was buried deep in my ass, searching for that perfect rhythm to stab me into dying my little death. Yeah, Corey could show me how to work the prosthetic—but so could half the trainees at Digi-tech. The real reason I'd dialed his number was that I missed him.

I was attempting to figure out how to say so without sounding too pathetic when the Parent-Egg let out a squeal. "Oh, sonofa—"

"What the hell was that?" Corey asked.

"My fucking homework."

"Blimey. It sounded like an abstinence egg."

"Give that man a cigar." I attempted to hit the feeding button with my toe and knocked the Fucking Egg over instead. The bleating intensified. "Hold on, the phone cord doesn't—" I lunged and grabbed, not realizing I'd actually led with my robotics until the very last second, when I pulled back for fear of crushing the egg's plastic housing. I released the handset and it smacked the wall, swinging wildly on its curly cord. I dove on the egg, thumbed the button left-handed, then tossed the annoying robot on the couch and grabbed up the phone again. "Don't hang up. If they find out what a piss-poor parent I am, I'm completely screwed."

"What can they do," he scoffed, "give you detention?"

"They don't want to waste 'program' money on me unless I get with the program."

"What program—the psychotherapy, or the Disability benefits? That isn't legal, is it? They're bluffing. It can't be legal."

One person who'd be able to answer to the legalities was Jim, but I knew better than to bring him up in casual conversation. "It's just a week, desensitizing me to robotics or some such shit, and then I can give this thing back and—" The egg toppled off the side of the couch, lit up red and shrieked.

"Not sounding good," Corey said.

"How the fuck do these fucking things move? Shit, it's rolling under the couch again...."

By the time I got the egg situated well enough to stop blinking and screaming, Corey was gone. I left one message apologizing for letting the phone drop, but that was all I could do. Back before the robots controlled the telecom lines, I would've encouraged him to pick up by repeatedly calling so it rang a few times, then hanging up before the machine could grab it. But according to his housebot, he'd scanned out. So pestering him was useless. In my heart of hearts, I was hoping the reason he'd scanned out was that he was willing to take me up on my invitation after all. But I didn't really believe that. I must not have. Because the relief that surged through my veins when he buzzed my non-robotic intercom twenty minutes later nearly knocked me on my ass.

I was surprised to find him darkening my doorstep again—surprised and grateful—but there he was. He hadn't prettied himself up especially for me this time, but even his most casual duds stood out from the crowd, stovepipe jeans, high-tops and a mod target shirt. Relief gave way to wanting as memories of our lazy week in his one-room efficiency flooded me, and I moved in for the kiss.

I caught a whiff of vanilla, and that was all, as he dodged neatly and slid into my entryway. "Keep a lid on it, Bucko. I'm here to check on the Parent-Egg, not get my fillings probed." He shoved a plastic bag at me. "Plus I've been meaning to give you this."

"What is it?"

"Open the bag and see."

I reached for it and almost did a right-left...but since I'd been practicing, I'd gotten better at making sure my thumb was approximately where I wanted it to be. Instead of switching course, I carried through with the motion and snagged the bag's handles with my four robotic fingers extended, then clamped down clumsily on the handles with my thumb to keep from dropping the bag. Corey noticed... but he didn't say anything. Just observed.

With the handles clamped securely, I pried open the side of the bag and took a peek. Inside was a brightly colored box, red and blue and yellow, covered with cartoons and photos and lettering. *Amazing Sea-Monkeys*, it read. *Deluxe Habitat.*

I said, "You didn't have to—"

"Yeah, I did. I felt like Medea." I imagine the reference was pretty obvious to someone more cultured than me, but I wasn't much for opera, or ballet, or whatever it supposed to be about. "I'm sorry."

"Well...so am I. Truce?" I held out my left hand to shake—even though that meant shaking with Corey's prosthetic—but before we could seal the deal, a plaintive whine rose from the vicinity of the TV. Fucking Egg wasn't flashing, yet. But it had a slight greenish glow to it, as if it was just about to start. "What the hell?" I said. "Green is for talking. And it's right in front of the goddamn set."

"The shopping channel?" Corey said. "Really?" We both approached the bot and squatted down in front of it. "Hey, li'l sprog," Corey crooned to it, and the whining stopped.

I was relieved for half a second, but that feeling only lasted until my dread caught up to me. "It understands?"

"Not exactly. Not words. But tone of voice, duration, crap like that." When I sighed, he said, "I take it you've been swearing at Junior this whole time."

I quelled the urge to say *fuck*. "So you've dealt with one of these before."

"I was my homeroom's best egg-mommy. Earned three hundred

bucks manning the nest for all the kids who wanted to score an easy A for the semester."

The age difference between Corey and me didn't usually seem like much, given that we're both keen on music popular thirty years ago and movies even older than that. Sometimes, though, it hit home. Back when I was in school, we were lucky if there was a single interactive bot for the entire class to share. And it didn't make noises—it flashed messages on its readout. Fast-forward ten years and they're passing out walking, squawking, expensive-as-Faberge eggs to every damn kid in the class.

"The telly will keep them from greening out for a day or two," Corey said, "but then it gets wise to the fact that most people don't talk in well-timed sound bites punctuated by commercials. You probably got away with an extra day by parking it in front of one great big commercial, but it can still tell TV voices from real ones."

"Annoying."

"Yep. A chip off the old block." He picked up the egg with his meatworks hand, but cradled it in the crook of his prosthetic arm. The robo-hand curled to protect it with baffling gentleness while I tried to imagine how Corey had possibly put together a series of fine gestures that the sensors could interpret as that precise movement. "Are you emotionally scarred, kiddo? Yes you are, oh yes you are." He planted himself on the couch, detected an errant spring with his ass, then shifted to the right and dropped into one of my pre-worn sinkholes. "You and me both."

Though not scarred enough to keep him from stopping over. Even so, I couldn't be cocky about his presence. His Sea-Monkey guilt would only get me so far, and my asshole nature could easily screw up this tenuous chance at reconciling. He was likely to fling the egg at the wall and storm out if I didn't manage to smooth everything over, and I was well aware of how hard he could throw with either arm.

Mixing up the new Sea-Monkeys was pretty anticlimactic, since it doesn't really look like anything much for at least a couple of days, so I mixed us up a couple of vodka cranberries to try and lubricate the conversation. Although I'd perfected my pinch well enough to grab a pair of pliers off the floor, I didn't trust myself to walk a drink out to the living room in that hand without dumping it on Corey's lap. I handed the first drink to him, then went back for mine. Normally, his would be half gone by the time I joined him. Not this time. He sat with the glass on his knee, staring into the rosy cocktail like he was reading tea leaves. Hopefully our future wasn't mapped out in the subtle marbling of alcohol that swirled through the juice. I've given up on expecting anything to end well. It's better that way. Maybe I do know things will crash and burn, but at least I can focus on enjoying the ride.

I dropped down beside him, ignored the spring, and rubbed my knee against his. "Drink up," I said. "Better vodka than you'll get in an Allentown well drink, and less mixer."

Obediently, he took a sip, but just one. He set the drink on the coffee table and picked up the Parent-Egg box instead. I was torn between watching him work his prosthetic and studying his profile for clues about what was going on in his head. Both of those things were mysteries to me.

"Exact same egg we had in Health Class," Corey said. "I've heard some of the newer models have a diaper button, too."

"Just what the world needs. Robotic shit."

He turned the box around a few times with stunningly delicate movements. I'd always known his meat and metal were perfectly synchronized, but I hadn't fully appreciated the extent of his ability. Not until I'd drilled myself practicing the arm for a whole week and come up with nothing better than a wimpy pinch. "I need your help," I said. It wasn't easy, but as it came out of my mouth, it occurred to me that maybe asking for gimp lessons wouldn't insult him at all. Corey got off on helping people, kind of like Jim. And without even planning it, I now found myself pushing another one of his buttons.

Except it didn't really register. He'd pulled a brochure out of the box and flipped it open, more stunningly lifelike gestures punctuated with the subtlest actuator whirs. "What's this about?" he asked. I leaned against him and read. *WAYSIDE SERVICES - Providing opportunities for homeless men to achieve self-determined goals and affordable, stable housing.* "Seriously?" he said. "That dried-up twat gave you a side order of homeless shelter with your omelet? Manipulative bitch."

"It wasn't in the...I mean, I was the one who put it in the box, not her." Since my one hand was busy carrying my robotic arm, I'd needed to consolidate as much as possible.

"Are you defending her? What is this, Stockholm syndrome?"

"No—hell, no. I was just thinking maybe she can help me. Eventually. After she gets through all the lame steps that she's been trained to follow. Looking at coffeemakers and thinking about automatic doors, stupid shit like that. Once she says I can wear my arm again."

"But you're wearing your arm now."

He had a point.

"Your assignment's due when?" he asked.

"Monday."

He sighed. "Yeah, I'll help you. Hopefully a weekend of quality nurturing will even out whatever trauma you've inflicted on Junior so far."

While parenting the Fucking Egg wasn't really the place where I'd been looking for help, I decided to take it where I could get it. Corey answering my calls, talking to me, sipping a drink on my ancient davenport? More than I had any business to hope for. I took a nice gulp of my drink, set it down, slid my meat arm around his shoulders and cozied up against him. He didn't stiffen, exactly, but he didn't sag against me like he used to, back when we'd spent that week on his pull-out bed. I nuzzled the side of his head with the top of mine, and said, "You smell good."

"I should've known you'd try and seduce me."

"Is it working?"

"Look, I don't want to turn into one of those assholes always going on about their feelings...." He shifted uncomfortably and toyed with his drink. "But there's something I need to figure out."

I forced myself not to tense up—because a question about Jim was coming, and how the hell could I answer it when I was probably the last person in the world who understood how I felt about Jim? I hated him for being a self-righteous prick. And yet I wanted him so bad it ached inside, even more intensely than the phantom pain beyond the end of my stump. I pined for what we used to have, the thing I'd never appreciated when I'd had it. In so many ways, we'd sucked together. Hell, maybe our incompatibility was the main reason I was drawn to him, the fact that we were cut from different cloths. It tickled the contrarian in me to try and stitch us together.

And what about Corey? I wanted him too. Just as much, I was surprised to realize. Thing was, I stood an actual chance at having Corey. Why torture the poor kid by talking about Jim? There had never been a good time to tell him I had a history with Jim, but now that it was out in the open, I could at least try to apologize for that failure. I was figuring out how to word it when Corey said, "You know your calls have been coming to my place."

Shit. I guess hoping I'd had no phone calls to answer for would've been too much to ask. Had Jim been trying to follow up after he dropped off the book? He must have. Because Jim Murphy never forgets to dot his I's and cross his T's. And he'd ended up talking to Corey, and...goddamn....

"Why was Ken Roman calling you?" Corey asked.

Relief—with a sinking feeling right on its heels. I'd forgotten about the leering guy with the tattered prosthetic, and here he'd been calling me all along? "I dunno. Did you talk to him?"

"No. Hell, no. But he left four messages inviting you to some flea market."

"I scored a ride off him once," I said, "and now he thinks we're tight."

That explanation was spontaneous and sincere enough to pierce Corey's reserve. He did lean in to me then, finally. "That guy's not hot for you, is he? I didn't think he was a fag."

"He said he wasn't," and really, how often is a straight man interested enough to need to clarify that point? "But he seems to want *something*."

"Too bad I'm banned from support group." Corey ran a fingertip around the wet rim of his glass. "I'd snag his paperwork from Pam's drawer and we could figure out his dealie-o."

When his eyes cut to the clock, I realized he wasn't just speaking in general terms. Gimp Group started in a couple of hours. And talking about Ken Roman gave Corey and me a place to create a bond, some fragile thread of revulsion to shudder over together. It wasn't the first place I personally would begin rebuilding what I'd nearly pissed away, but the momentum was already there. "What's she gonna do if you show up to your own brother's house? Throw you out?"

Corey smirked. "If you think she wouldn't…then you don't know Pam."

CHAPTER 18

"Feels pretty stealth to drop you off at Hugh's house without going in myself." He dug a pack of gum out of his pocket. "If Pammie smells booze on your breath, she'll report you."

Was there anything I *couldn't* be reported for? Made me wonder how anyone managed to get any kind of government assistance at all. Maybe all those lowlifes and bottom-feeders were a lot more virtuous than I'd ever realized. Or maybe I was just nowhere near as crafty as I'd always thought.

Or maybe I was just under the microscope thanks to my involvement with both her brother-in-law, and with Jim.

I took the pack in my meat hand and smacked it with my metal when I attempted to open it. Smooth move. But once I got it stabilized in the wimpy pinch, I could pull out the gum with my left hand and open the foil sleeve with my thumb. Corey didn't comment, though I'm sure he noticed. I jammed the gum in my mouth and dropped the foil wrapper on the floor. "Minty fresh," I said. "How about a kiss? For luck."

Corey raised an eyebrow and looked pointedly at the base of my throat, where the padlock still hung.

"C'mon. Don't be that way." I used my most sincere voice. "You're reading too much into it. I lost the key. That's all."

He looked doubtful. But he also looked like he could be persuaded.

"Listen," I said. "First thing tomorrow, we'll find a locksmith and see how much they'll charge to pop it. Okay?" An arm and a leg, no doubt. I should have dealt with the damn thing when I'd had a chance. But if I played my cards right, I could plant the key and "discover" it before any money needed to change hands. Hell, if he was willing to come back to my place, maybe Corey could even find it himself.

He looked from the lock, to my mouth, to the lock again, then echoed, "First thing. No matter how hung over we are."

I leaned toward him and said, "First thing." And when I fit my mouth to his, he let me.

As I marched down the block, up the drive and across the porch to ring the doorbell, I tried to imagine what I'd tell good ol' Pam Steiner, who would be the opposite of "delighted" to see me. I was reminding myself to call it *Support* Group when the door opened. Not Pam. Corey's big brother, Hugh.

The face that was so like Corey's (yet, not) registered a dozen shades of surprise at the sight of me. But finally he said, "My brother's not here."

"I know. I'm here for Gim—uh, Support Group."

"Oh." The handsome not-Corey face screwed up in confusion. He wasn't very fast on the uptake, this one—unlike Corey, who never missed a beat. "You're really early. You sure you don't want to run an errand and come back in an hour?"

"No wheels. By the time I grabbed a bus, I'd need to turn right around and come back. You've got stuff to do, I get it, but don't worry about me. Just park me in a corner and I'll keep myself amused." Like Ken Roman always did. The realization that I'd be stuck visiting with him shortly was none too welcome. Corey and I had planned my arrival so I'd get there well before the professor, but we hadn't really focused on the span of time where two of us, me and the creepy professor, would be early-birding together. That was probably for the best. Faced with the prospect of being alone with that guy and his knowing eyes would've made me bail on the whole expedition.

I'd worn sneakers this time so I could toe them off in the hallway without making a big production out of it. Although Hugh was hovering, I didn't get the impression he was worried I might mark up his hardwood floors. No, something about me spooked him. I was so busy wondering what that might be, I almost forgot to scan in. It takes a hell of a lot to make me forget that I need to stick my hand into a housebot, believe you me. But those guilty hangdog looks rolling off Hugh nearly triggered my convenient amnesia. Getting my calls back to my own damn house was a high priority, though. Scanning in to the Steiner's would route them away from Corey's, and scanning out would default them back to my botless hovel.

"Pam's not here," Hugh blurted out. "I forgot to buy dip, she says we can't have group without it. She probably went to Wegman's. The parking lot's brutal, especially on a Friday night. It'll take her half an hour just to get to the door."

I checked the digital clock on the housebot's readout. "S'okay. She's got plenty of time."

"Right." His eyes flicked to the time, and then he took a deep breath as if he'd made a decision. "Uh...do you want a beer?"

"I thought there was no drinking allowed in group."

"Shoot, you're right. I'm sorry. God, I'm so stupid—I'm sorry."

Had I ever met anyone less like Corey? Despite the similarity in facial features, I was beginning to doubt they'd been extruded from the same womb. "I'd take a Pepsi."

"Sure. Pop—we do have pop. C'mon in."

Back when I was a two-handed bastard, I made the sheep of the population nervous by skulking around in my badass facial hardware and projecting the fact that I didn't give a shit. I guess they figured I might carjack them, or rape them, or both. Now the attitude is long gone, but most people see the robotics and they freak out just the same. Hugh should've been used to dealing with gimps, though. In fact, he hadn't thought anything of baby bro rooting around in the party mix with a prosthetic. So whatever it was about me that raised Hugh's alarms, it wasn't my fake hand.

Try to put him at ease, or make him even more uncomfortable? Hard to say which tactic would be more likely to leave me alone with his wife's files. He handed me the pop, in a can. Unopened. Good thing I didn't have my heart set on getting chummy. What followed was uncomfortable for both of us. I clamped it to my stomach awkwardly with my robotics and struggled to open it myself left-handed. Meanwhile, he hovered, unsure whether to take it back and do it for me, or leave me to my humiliating independence. All that effort, and we weren't even out of the kitchen yet—but it did give me an idea.

The Steiner's house has stuff on the walls, and by "stuff," I don't mean dried ejaculate. Cutsey sayings burned on precious wooden plaques, embroidered flowers, framed drawings, all of it competed for attention with dozens and dozens of photographs. If you ever want to know what Pam Steiner looked like at her wedding, just take a gander at any vertical surface in her home. You'll undoubtedly find some cheesy photo featuring her and Hugh, ten pounds thinner, looking glazed and awkward on their big, expensive day.

Looking at pictures gave me a pretty innocent reason to snoop. I'd scoped out a good chunk of the first floor by the time I spotted him: a slightly awkward dark-eyed teenager rocking a tux at the Steiners' wedding. First thing my eyes went to was his left hand. There it was, pretty much like you'd expect, a mirror image of the right. I hated that I couldn't help but look, but I supposed I just needed to get it over with. Once I was past it, checking out that long-gone limb, I could consider what hadn't really changed. That naughty smile. The insolent tilt to the head. How old, sixteen, seventeen? At that age, he knew his way around the block already, you could see it in his eyes. Changed? Sure, his neck had filled out and his skin was clear now. But the essence of him was still there. The conveyor belt hadn't managed to tear off enough to destroy his Corey-ness.

I was so fascinated by the sight of teen Corey that I didn't notice Hugh watching me until he spoke. "Corey was just about to start his senior year when I got married." I grunted. My senior snapshots showed all the kids trying to pass for Kurt Cobain or a chick he might screw. Corey's was from the current era, only a few years past, nothing much changed but the obvious physical transition from teendom—that, and the robotics. "Those are our parents, and our Nana. There's Pam's two sisters and her dad. And then in the front row...."

One thing Ken Roman had been right about: Hugh Steiner was phenomenally easy to tune out. While he named all the groomsmen and the bridesmaids, I lost myself in Corey's sparkling eyes. Self-confident. Even at that age where most kids are awkward, hormonal sacks of Emo angst. I tried to imagine him cutting his arms and writing bad poetry, but I came up blank.

"There's a better picture of Corey at the reception," Hugh said.

For the first time in my life, I found myself eager to look at some yuppie douchebag's family photos.

Hugh led me to the living room, the place where I'd first met him, first laid eyes on Corey. He hauled a massive white album out from a slot in the coffee table, and damn if that thing wasn't so heavy he needed to lift it two-handed. It was so full of doodads and dingdongs it couldn't even fully close. Printed napkins, pressed flowers and bits of lavender lace plumped out the pages, and among the memorabilia was photographic evidence of the Steiners cavorting with Pam's family of origin in a rented hall filled with balloons and Chinese lanterns.

With all the groomsmen in matching tuxes, it was harder than you'd think to pick out Corey as Hugh flipped through. I did catch a couple of glimpses, mainly by focusing on the eyes. Hugh seemed to know where this particular pic was that he wanted to show me, though, as he found it with a minimum of page turning.

My breath caught in my throat before he even said the words, "This one's my favorite."

It was a closeup shot—rare enough among all the group pictures that attempted to make sure no family member got away unrecorded. But it was also dynamic and real in a way the other photos couldn't possibly match. Sweat glistened from teenaged Corey's upper lip, his back was arched, his tie was askew and his cheeks puffed out like a set of bellows. In his two meatworks hands gleamed a bright brass tenor sax.

That notion of Corey being in any way awkward—even at that precarious age—evaporated. Corey Steiner owned that fucking saxophone like he owned my sorry ass. In that event where everything was fancy and formal and unbearably upper middle class, he'd owned that moment, too.

I asked Hugh what the song was, some Kenny G thing, and I knew in the pit of my balls that Corey had rocked that godawful tune. Maybe it wasn't his style, maybe he'd rather be cranking out some rudeboy Ska, but in his capable hands, even some sappy, crappy wedding song had shone.

"He was good," Hugh said quietly, in that magical way he had for stating the obvious. It pissed me off, because of course Corey was good. I didn't even need to hear him to know it.

And I didn't need to ask to be utterly sure he hadn't picked up that sax since his accident.

Hugh tried to turn the page and show me...heck, I don't know what. Didn't matter. I brushed his hand away and stared even harder at the sax picture, following the contour and learning all the lights and darks, as if by committing that single image to my booze-pickled brain I might understand something about Corey, something deep, something important. Something he'd lost that I never realized he'd even had.

I asked, "Was he in a band?"

"Marching band?" Corey's brother couldn't have been older than thirty. What the hell kind of twenty-something dumbass presumes you mean a *marching* band and not a rock band? But before I could even scoff, he said, "Not just any band, state champions. He won more Golden Dinkles than anyone else—uh, that's a special award for the best performer. Sounds funny but it was a big deal."

No doubt Corey would shrug off parades and Golden Dinkels as some embarrassing part of his nerdily misspent youth, but only as much as punk rock etiquette demanded. I would also see a gleam of cynical pride there, if he'd chosen to share this much of his past with me. Maybe someday he planned to. Then again, judging by the recent photo on the mantle where he stood shoulder to shoulder with his brother, left arm angled away from the camera and the cocky light in his eyes dimmed, maybe not.

The silence had stretched between us longer than I'd realized when Hugh said quietly, "He quit before the accident. Sometimes I wonder if he regrets it, or if it's more of a blessing, having less to lose."

Maybe that explained why he was poised to take me back. He already knew what sort of disappointments he was setting himself up for, so when I screwed up, there wouldn't be as far to fall. "So why'd he give it up?"

"When it came time for college, he figured he'd get a big scholarship. His guidance counselor always thought so. I dunno, maybe she shouldn't have encouraged him like she did. Made him think he'd have his pick, when colleges don't really value music like they do sports or academics. He only applied for two schools—and he did get in. To both. My parents would have paid for him to go wherever he wanted, but it wasn't about the money. Most people would be worried about getting in, especially kids with grades like his, and lousy test scores. It wasn't his fault, it was the ADD."

I didn't know much about attention deficit disorder other than the fact that my old man told a middle school teacher to go screw herself when she suggested I be screened for it. "He doesn't seem all that hyper."

"No, he wasn't one of those kids always bouncing off the walls. Impulsivity, that's what they call it. No internal censor, and the drugs didn't help, they just made him weird. So he did whatever he wanted, which didn't include schoolwork. The only thing that ever held his attention was music. He knew he was good—his room was so full of trophies and awards he had to stick the older ones up in the attic—and maybe that was part of the problem. He was convinced he'd get a full ride—but instead there was only one small scholarship. Five hundred dollars a semester, a token, really." Hugh shut the wedding album and sighed. "When he got that letter, he tore it up, threw it on the floor and peed on it."

Now, that sounded like the Corey I knew.

Maybe Corey had flaunted his geek flag in marching band, but that wasn't the only place he got his sax on. More photo albums came out. Corey rocked out at a family gathering with Hugh accompanying him on guitar. Even though Hugh was older by a good handful of years, everyone's eyes were on Corey. And in later pictures he'd even found a few fellow rudeboys to jam with, down in a basement surrounded by cobwebs and hockey gear. I imagine some of those cronies were supportive right after the accident, until the permanence of Corey's situation sank in. Sympathy wore thin, the gaps between phone calls and invitations broadened, and pretty soon almost no one was willing to give him the time of day.

Or maybe that was just my story. But I'd spent a week with the kid and didn't notice any guys in skinny ties or pork pie hats knocking down his door, so I'd bet a round of drinks it was his story, too. The last thing he needed was someone who wasn't one hundred percent invested in him, and if I wasn't willing to be that guy, than I was even more of a moron than I thought. Even now, even broken, Corey had way more potential to be somebody than I ever did. Not only did I regret lying to him about the padlock, but I regretted that I hadn't sprung it then and there when I saw the key.

As I realized all the ways in which I could easily fuck up my chances with Corey, I lingered over a particularly striking shot of his teenage self looking directly at the camera. His grin was beyond cocky, with that one crooked eyetooth displayed like a badge, and his grip on his horn seemed particularly intimate. The veins on the back of his hands formed a shape like a creek flowing through a patch of woods. I was following the sensual curve up his forearm when the front door opened and shut, the housebot blipped, and the ceiling fans powered on. "Hugh?" Pam called out. "Come help me with this. I bought a throw to put over that chair where Ken always sits. That way we don't need to keep smelling him on the upholstery afterward."

Before Pam could blurt out any more secret opinions, Hugh bolted out of the living room like a dog in fireworks. "Uh, hon? It's... we're...there's someone here."

Pam Steiner paused in the doorway and gave me a dirty look. It didn't quite soften when she saw I'd been browsing through their family photos, but it might've become a shade less annoyed. "I didn't see your car," she said.

"I didn't drive."

She shoved a massive shopping bag into Hugh's arms and he scurried away to the safety of the kitchen. "You're not on my list," she said. "I wasn't expecting you tonight."

"Oh." Quick. What's a plausible excuse? "I started with a new shrink and thought it would help me make better progress with my desensitization."

"Desensitization? To what?"

Crap. Why was she so hung up on the details? "Robotic prosthetics.

Where else are you gonna find such a wealth of metal all in one place? But if you don't have room...." I ended with a shrug, since clearly she had plenty of space, and let it hang there between us that she'd be guilty of impeding my progress if she turned me away.

Luckily, it's not just Corey's buttons I was capable of pushing. Pam gave a resigned sigh. "No. Go ahead and stay. I'll write you in. But you need to scan in to the housebot."

"Already done."

My compliance annoyed her, which in turn amused me. I quelled the urge to smirk. Pam spun on her heel and stalked off to handle the paperwork. The last laugh was at me, though. It turned out I'd been a few yards away from my goal the whole time. All I'd needed to do was dump my pop on the floor, and Hugh would have darted off to the kitchen for paper towels, leaving me in spitting distance of the prize: Pam's unlocked desk. I'd allowed myself to be distracted by photo albums, though, and now I had two wardens to get out of my hair instead of one.

CHAPTER 19

I tried dumping my pop anyway, but that only resulted in an urgent Hugh-summons, plus a big dose of stinkeye from Pam. While it was amusing that Hugh actually apologized to *me* for the spill, I couldn't really enjoy the moment. The irony was marred by the arrival of Ken Roman.

The fat professor stood in the archway in his stocking feet, eyes on me. "Mr. Poole, what a pleasant surprise."

I aimed for casual. "How's it hangin'?"

He answered with a knowing smile. Maybe he was presuming I'd spent the last week at Corey's, since that's where his calls to me had routed, and maybe he enjoyed knowing that Pam would be appalled to know it too. Maybe he actually knew something I didn't. Or maybe that supercilious smirk was simply his default expression, in the same way Perma-Bitchface belonged to Pam Steiner. He waded his way through the Steiners' immaculate living room with ease. Watching him approach his throne was like seeing clips of swimming hippopotamus herds on the nature channel. Surprisingly graceful. As he lowered himself into the chair, I realized that my unscheduled visit caused Pam to neglect to break out her new furniture throw... and I wondered what Ken Roman smelled like. Hard to say from where I sat, across the room, and especially with my senses dulled by Marlboro Reds.

"You missed a particularly fruitful day at the flea market," Ken said, once his bulk was ensconced. "Old Time Harry had an exquisite set of Victorian dentures. Female." You'd think that with all the speculating I'd been doing about which way Ken swung, I'd be pleased to discern a note of longing in his voice when he said they were a *chick's choppers*...but instead I experienced a major case of the heebie jeebies. "The hinge-work in the jaw was absolutely stunning. The spring mechanism was stiff—what would you expect, over a century later—but what a treat to see it with all its original parts."

Unlike Hugh Steiner, Ken Roman was impossible to tune out as he regaled me with stories about the things he'd seen on his latest flea market adventure: walkers and canes, orthopedic shoes, and an embroidered eyepatch that was an "absolute steal" at a mere hundred dollars. By the time Hugh laid out the spread that included the precious dip, my fellow amputees started showing up. Gimp Group was officially underway, and it was actually a relief to hear the fingerless teenager gag his way through the timeline of his last fateful encounter with fireworks.

At one point, Pam asked for clarification on a part of the poor kid's story. "You were where? On the train tracks?" At least, she'd framed it as a clarification. It sounded more like an accusation to me, though. *What the hell were you doing out there, fucking around and blowing things up?* That's what I heard. That's how people like Pam Steiner usually talked to me, anyway.

People like Pam generally didn't get the allure of train tracks and viaducts and abandoned riverfront warehouses. While north side snobs like her went to prom, Riverside scumbags like me were drinking Molsons when we could get someone to buy for us, and huffing airplane cement when we couldn't. Knocking up tenth-graders—or, in my case, on my knees in the mud with some skeevy kid who would've graduated three, four years before me if he hadn't jumped the gun and dropped out. Where? Not in rented limos like the fancy brats. Hell, no. Our limos were the train tracks, the viaducts, and the bellies of the abandoned warehouses. And they didn't last only that single night. I lived the glory that whole summer.

It would've been a perfect time to haul out my old nickname, but by then we'd all taken a turn at upchucking over the guard rails. One kid actually nailed an old Pontiac right as it passed beneath the viaduct. When it came out the other side with its windshield wipers flailing, the rest of us laughed so fucking hard we literally pissed ourselves. Then I had to turn away from the sight of Biggie with that dark stain spreading down the inseam of his jeans. I was eighteen, and could pop a boner by thinking of an underwear ad. I've never gone in for watersports, but the shape of that patch of moisture is etched into my brain like it was burned in by a flash of lightning. Raw intimacy…something I wasn't supposed to see, but there it was. And I was far enough gone that I actually considered running my hand up that hot, moist stretch of thigh just to see what would happen.

Biggie would've killed me on the spot, of course. Not a year later I heard about how he put "some faggot" in traction, him and his revolving group of thugs. I wasn't hanging with him much at that point, so I'd been spared the dilemma of whether I'd need to join in the beating to preserve my secret. By then I'd started banging some married foreman I met at work, and it took a lot of time getting to Niagara Falls and back when we wanted to hook up, which seemed like every other day. That lasted through the spring, and by the time I was spared the forty-minute round trip back and forth across Grand Island, the Crowley Ave Boys had relocated their party to some other bridge, or warehouse, or viaduct. I checked all the old haunts, but the tagging had been painted over, and nothing was left of my old cohorts but some vodka bottles, a spent lighter, and a few dented empties of Molson.

* * *

"Well?" Corey asked as I slid into his passenger seat. "Did you score?"

I'd found out plenty of things at Gimp Group. Unfortunately, the dirt on Ken Roman wasn't one of them. "Thought I was in the clear since Pam wasn't home, but then…." The photo albums were on the tip of my tongue, but then I decided that the last thing Corey wanted from me was my pity. The basement full of hockey equipment in the Ska band picture popped into my head, and I said, "Your brother—big Sabres fan, I take it."

"Such a jock. If everyone had as big a hard-on for the Stanley

Cup as Hugh, Viagra would go out of business." We looped around Delaware park and approached the bleak grunginess of Black Rock, where an abandoned car with smashed out windows marked the perimeter between Yuppieville and Tweakerland. "Too bad we hadn't planned on the possibility of a No-Pam zone. My brother's pretty cool when his ball and chain's not around. I'll bet you could've just asked him to let you take a peek."

I told Corey about the dentures and the eye patch, and we gave a simultaneous shiver. "Fetishist," Corey decided. "Ken wouldn't be the first one I've met." So I gathered, from things Corey'd alluded to in the sack. "Better guard your virtue, Des-mond. That guy's gotta outweigh you by a hundred pounds. If he gets grabby, duck and run."

Even thoughts of Ken Roman grasping for me with his tattered prosthetic couldn't taint the elation I felt over Corey saying my name like he used to, with that saucy lilt. When we pulled up in front of my place, I leaned across the front seat and laid one on him...and he let me. More than just let me. There was a hitch in his breath as I tongued his mouth open, and the need to be with him flooded through me, stronger now for having stewed in his history while I tuned out the rest of the group and pondered those pictures. I would've reached over and cupped his crotch while I kissed him, but my meat arm was trapped between us and I had no desire to accidentally punch him in the nuts with a hunk of robotics.

While I wanted nothing more than to drag Corey upstairs and nail him, what I really wanted was for him to come back for more once the heat of the moment had cooled and the fluids dried. It seemed like I'd have a better chance at building something solid if I made an effort for the two of us to do something together—something other than drinking or fucking or watching TV. And definitely something other than speculating about the creep in the picked-apart arm.

I let him up for air, and he scanned out from his Servo so the car powered down. I got out and waited for him on the sidewalk. When he stepped up beside me, I turned away from my butchered Colonial and led him instead toward old Mrs. Zelko's garage. He paused, then shrugged and followed.

It would've made for a dramatic reveal if I'd replaced the tarp on my Gray Lady before so I could sweep it off now in a grand ta-da. Unfortunately, I hadn't. With my wimpy pinch, screwing around with the canvas would've been too much effort. Despite my poor planning, once I hauled open the garage door and the over-bright yard lighting hit the Gremlin's front bumper, I presented the car with a proud sweep of my left arm.

Corey laughed. "So your neighbor owns an ugly old car?"

"First of all, it's a classic. It held its own in any drag race, and that was before these fucking robo-cars, when people could actually floor it. Nowadays it's the fastest thing you'll find on the road." I took a deep breath. "And second, it's not my neighbor's car, it's mine."

Corey gave a low whistle. "If there was ever any doubt as to that robophobia diagnosis...."

"Look at it this way. You can go to any dealership and get a robo-car, no problem. But you've gotta go that extra mile to keep a real car on the road."

"Sure. If it doesn't die on you before you reach that extra mile."

I ran my meatworks fingertips along the hood. "Things break. No denying that. But pre-robotic cars make sense. There's cause and effect: when you step on the gas pedal, the throttle valves open. Not robo-cars. They mimic real cars, but when you step on those pedals, what you're really doing is asking some bot's permission to get rolling."

"If you say so."

"Just you wait. When you feel the rumble of the engine and the wind in your hair, you'll understand."

Corey wasn't anywhere near as impressed as I would have been. Mostly, he looked like he was still waiting for the punchline. "Does it run?"

"Of course it runs. Well, it did, before I put it in storage." Technically, it had been Jim who'd stashed her while I was busy not-doing my physical therapy. "I changed the coolant, and the belts look good. A little more work and I can take you on a ride you'll never forget."

Corey gave a snort.

"C'mon." I slipped an arm around him and eased him up to the car. "Have a seat." The driver side door gave a metallic squawk when

I opened it. Corey climbed in and rested his meatworks hand on the gearshift. "You gotta admit," I said, "that don't feel nothing like a robo-car."

"That's for sure. I don't even know how to work one of these things."

"Driving stick's no big deal." I leaned in the open door and did my best to sound fuckable. "I'll bet you're a natural."

"I've never really been into cars."

"I could show you."

"I'm sure you could show me plenty of things...naked things, for instance. That'd be a lot more fun than arsing around with this old car."

Figured. His idea of a tune-up was marching around in a high school band. "Fine. Then all you gotta do is sit back and enjoy the ride...once I get 'er back on the road."

"Okay. When you get it running, I'll go for a spin." He slipped out of the car and put an arm around my waist. His prosthetic arm. Reach, gesture, pressure, all of it was exactly right. When he brought his face up to mine for the kiss I expected, he paused and searched my eyes, from one to the other and back, then said, "So what's really going on? You feeling nostalgic tonight, or what?"

He was nowhere near as interested in the car as I'd hoped. I would need to press the help-button. "A couple of the spark plugs are shot."

"Not much I can do about it." He brushed a kiss over my jaw. "I'm no gearhead. Maybe I screw around with my arm, but tweaking robotics is kid-stuff. You can do that with an eyeglass repair kit. This heavy mechanical shit is way out of my league."

"You don't need to know squat—I can fix it. You just have to hold up the plug socket for me." He chewed the inside of his cheek, considering. I twisted the screws a quarter-turn. "A job like this, I can't use power tools. Push too hard and the plug breaks off, and then it's a bitch and a half. C'mon, it's bad enough I gotta do it left-handed, where I don't have a good feel for it. Don't leave me to struggle with my fucking metal, too."

He sighed, mostly for show, then came up with a flimsy objection—but only so he didn't seem too eager. "I just got this shirt." He plucked casually at his new Specials T-shirt with his prosthetic in an eerily lifelike gesture. "I don't want to fuck it up."

"So hang it up over there and take one of mine."

He gave a beleaguered sigh, though he did pull off the shirt, which he twirled a few times like a stripper and then hung off a rake propped in the corner. I passed him my flannel. He rolled his eyes and said, "How butch." Another sigh. "Okay, mister mechanic. *Use me.*"

I angled a work light toward the car and popped the hood while Corey went through the tool boxes, absently, like I might flip through a trashy magazine in a checkout line without actually seeing what was between the covers. When I asked him to hand me something, he didn't know the difference between an adjustable wrench and a bolt-cutter—which he tried to pass to me at least half a dozen times. He'd never even had shop class, probably. Not in some ritzy prep school where all he cared about was how many Golden Ding-Dongs he could take home from marching band. I'm not sure whether he was learning something in that garage or just biding his time until we could call it quits, but I kept my cool and explained everything to him, even the steps that seemed like plain common sense to me.

Unplugging the coil packs was easy enough. I used the robotic hand to stabilize the pack while I did all the work with my meat hand, and tried not to think too hard about Corey seeing how useless I was with the prosthetic. Once the plugs were accessible, I stood the socket in the hole and then transferred the holding duty to Corey. You'd be amazed at how much it can flop around while you're trying to fit the wrench on...especially left-handed. "Nice and straight," I told him. It wasn't rocket science. "There you go."

Corey watched me extract the plug without even making a snide remark about the word *straight*. "So will you need to replace all your tools with special left-handers, or are they ambidextrous?"

"Depends which tool."

He held up the bolt-cutters he'd mistaken for a wrench. "This one."

"That'll work either way."

I steel-brushed some debris from the threads and moved on to the next plug. We worked our way through the set. One was stubborn, but the rest weren't bad. I might be as negligent as they come, but I'd always kept my Gremlin a hell of a lot cleaner than any other thing in my possession. Corey seemed antsy, and I began to doubt the wisdom of trying to force an ADD kid to work on a project that didn't spark his interest. Here I thought I'd gleaned some extra insight into his brain from my big chat with his brother, but maybe not. By the tenth time he handed me the bolt-cutters, I stopped trying to explain things and focused on getting the job done so we could get back to our TV and Stoli.

Finally, the new set was in place, tightened down just so, not too loose and not too hard. I looked up at Corey, expecting to bond over our self-satisfaction at a job well done. He looked sour. "You don't still need me," he said, "do you?"

"Course I do."

He gestured at the engine. "But you can put the rest of it back together yourself."

"Maybe so." I backed him up against the car. "But I still need you."

I tried for a kiss. He turned his head to the side, gave me a push and slipped out from under me.

"What?" I asked. "Where ya going?"

"This was a mistake," he said as he strode out of the garage.

"Hey, look, I thought it would be something to do, working on the car. It's no big deal—we've been out here less than an hour. I didn't think you were serious about not wanting to do it, you seemed like you were just yanking my chain. If you had that big a problem with helping me in the garage, you should have said something."

I'd never seen his mood tank so fast over something so small. One minute he was ready to go upstairs with me, and the next he was storming out the door. He kept on walking with me right on his heels, but he wouldn't stop and have it out. When someone stays and fights, at least there's a chance to patch things up. It's when they ditch you that the battle's well and truly lost.

"Corey—"

He opened his car door, pulled the Fucking Egg out from the back seat, and handed it to me. It was red and whimpering. "Feed it.

Or not. Since you don't give a shit what anyone wants but you."

"Whoa, hold on." I pressed the food button and the egg shut up. "I'm sorry. I'll never ask you to work on the car again. Okay?"

Corey went very still, and searched my eyes again under the harsh gleam of the streetlights. "Is that what you think this is about? The car?" He shook his head in disgust. "It's about choices, Des. It's about you figuring out what you want. And me being sick of hoping you'll make up your mind."

I couldn't stop him from taking off, not without laying down in front of the car—and given his thing with impulsivity, I couldn't say for sure he wouldn't drive that Servo right over my sorry ass. I watched his tail lights round the corner, and I wondered how his mood had sunk so low while I was digging around under the hood. In the crook of my meat arm, the egg pulsed. I looked down. Now it was glowing faintly green.

"I'm sure you'd rather be with him," I murmured. Can't say I blamed it. "Sorry, kid." The egg went dark. Satisfied, for now. No doubt I'd screw it up before the night was over, because somehow I managed to fuck up everything I touched, like this dumb idea of changing the spark plugs. I'd only been trying to connect on a deeper level. Corey'd been ready to come upstairs with me when I pulled my lame attempt at bonding, and now he was on his way back home...or back to one of the Allentown hipster bars to get his cork popped by someone other than me.

CHAPTER 20

By the time I shook off the spins the next morning and managed to keep down some dry toast, morning was technically afternoon. The Fucking Egg was flashing a few different colors, but it shut up quick enough when I jiggled it and fed it and asked it whether I should consider walking in front of a bus. Although Jim might think different, I'm not actually suicidal. If I were to make a grand asshole gesture, I'd be more likely to rob a bank. If I succeeded in carrying out a heist, I'd get to stop worrying about my monthly check. And if not, at least I'd land somewhere with a roof, a bed, three squares a day, and scads of potential fuck buddies. But since vodka was scarce in prison, I figured I should just keep on keeping on, and get the damn Gremlin on the road.

Too bad my robo-arm wouldn't cooperate. Feeding some gas into the carburetor and turning it over is as easy as pouring a cocktail. Until you try to do it left-handed, anyway. While the egg could lend a sympathetic ear, it couldn't steady the line while I tipped the gas can. For that I'd need help, actual help, from a physical person.

I did briefly consider asking Corey. Then I imagined trying to replace the windshield one-handed after he expressed his displeasure with a brick, and I shifted to plan B. The gin mill.

According to some useless ordinance, you can't smoke in bars or restaurants anymore, or really, much of anywhere. Even so, the inside of Schmidt's still smelled like a tarry filter. Decades of smoke had seeped into the fibers of the upholstery and the pores of the wood. It had dulled the barback mirrors and coated the metal fixtures with a fine, stubborn film. It tinted the linoleum yellow.

Homey place.

I almost wondered what had compelled me to stop coming…until I went to grab a barstool, right-left, and the reason hit me. For a second, it seemed like the barbot had shone a spotlight on me like I was an underage drinker dumb enough to scan in. But I hadn't scanned in, and in fact, no one had even given me a second glance. What would be the point? I was just another sorry old rummy, exactly the same as everyone else hunched over their drinks at three in the afternoon.

Since my gut was still roiling from last night's Stoli, I ordered a beer and braced myself to be cool when someone I half-remembered mentioned my accident and asked how I was doing. Except, nobody did. Nobody even looked up from his own drink. Even the bartender had nothing to say as he set my fresh-pulled beer on the sticky bar, but I reminded myself his silence was nothing new. The stooped old Polack with a face like a carp was never one to chat. He did his job—kept the booze coming—so what more could you want?

The TV overhead played some all-day cable news station, but since I doubted there were any other B-movie fans in the joint, my preferences wouldn't have been enough to make the barbot flip the channel. No sense scanning in. It surprised me that I'd even considered it.

Since there was nothing to watch and nothing to smoke, the beer went down fast. Nobody said jack, not to me, not to each other, and I didn't remember anyone well enough to break the ice and beg some help in my borrowed garage. I went to take a leak before my long walk home. The bathroom was the same, fluorescent bright and filled with the overpowering stink of urinal cakes and piss, and that sameness was disconcerting. It felt like cramming my residual arm into the cuff after the meat had shifted, though as far as I could tell, it was the same old Schmidt's. Somehow, I no longer fit.

If the gin mill was the same, then I'd been the one to change. No big surprise, I guess. Losing a hand'll do that to a guy.

It was disappointing that I hadn't spotted anyone I knew on a first-name basis, but I reminded myself that I hadn't invested anything more than a few bucks and a half-hour hike. That's what I was thinking when I walked out of the can and nearly headbutted Georgie Argusto. "Desmond!" He looked like he'd seen a ghost. "How come you ain't working down at Digi-tech no more?"

Save the fingers.

No way was I about to let him in on my little *episode*. "Some shit with Social Services," I said with a casual shrug, which made my right pinkie jut out sideways. It took a few shoulder rolls to straighten that out, but once I did, I offered to buy good old Georgie a beer.

One beer turned into five, but at Schmidt's, I could afford it. With our mutual hatred of Social Services, Georgie and me had plenty to talk about. And once that subject ran dry, I picked his brain about installing custom gardenbots, and the two of us came up with some pie-in-the-sky scheme of offering a kickback to a landscape designer for recommending us to do the installation, not that either of us knew anyone with such a fancy job. That's what the Yellow Pages are for.

That afternoon, Georgie and me said more to each other than we had in the entire decade we'd known each other, so when I told him about the Gremlin and asked him for ten minutes of help in the garage, he was happy to oblige. He even gave me a ride, mostly on the correct side of the road, too.

"Whoa—wouldja look at that?" he said when I rolled up the garage door. He circled the Gremlin, touching her on the hood, and roof, and hatchback. "AMC...why don't they make 'em no more? My cousin Paulie had an old Hornet when I was a kid. Fast fucking car. Not like these goddamn fucking robo-fucks."

"Fuckin'-A."

We managed to feed the carburetor a few sips of gas without getting too much on ourselves, and when I turned over the engine, it roared to life. Georgie and me roared right along with it, while old Mrs. Zelko's next-door neighbor yelled at us to shut the fuck up and we yelled back for her to go fuck herself. We were having a grand old time, but the mood soured when I tried to take the car out of neutral with my right hand, and realized I didn't have anywhere near enough control. It wasn't a lack of fine gesture, either. Theoretically I could make a cupped shape with my robo-hand, lock it, and control the stick with that. But I was so unaccustomed to doing anything with my right arm anymore that I didn't trust it to stay on the shift without winding them together in duct tape first.

Of course, Georgie offered to drive, but he understood when I told him it should be me at the helm when I took the Gremlin back out on the road. That was good. Drunks tend to get belligerent when you question their ability to drive, but without the cushion of robotic sensors, I didn't trust him not to sideswipe every parked car on the block. I offered him a drink instead, so we tucked the Gray Lady in for the night and wended our way up to my apartment...where the Fucking Egg on the couch was bleating, and flashing all three colors.

"What the hell is that?"

"The world's most irritating bot." The sound of our voices made the green drop out of the mix. A quick press of the feeding button took care of the red. A few jiggles and the room went quiet. "The Social Services shrink thinks I need to babysit."

"Give it here," Georgie said, but I pretended not to hear him. "C'mon, lemme see."

"Not now." Quick, what's a good excuse? "I gotta put it in the box to finish the cycle."

Luckily I only put things away once the piles reach a certain threat level. The box was right there between the ash tray and the broken remote. Georgie watched longingly as I boxed up the egg, wishing he could take it apart, or wondering what would happen if he ran it under the faucet, or maybe anticipating how it would feel to chuck it off the side of a bridge. Once I sloshed together a drink and shoved it into his hand, the egg was entirely forgotten. Bullet dodged.

Georgie finished his first drink and I followed it up quick with a second. I was nursing mine along, but he was too loaded to notice. Normally I'd match him drink for drink—but it occurred to me, in my warm-bellied state of moderate drunkenness, that if I ever wanted to ask about Biggie, this was the perfect time to go for it. Georgie wasn't exactly the most observant set of eyes, but if he'd been there, he could tell me something. Anything.

Back at Digi-Tech he'd given me the rundown of everybody else I didn't give a rat's ass about, so I couldn't lead in by asking how "everyone" was. Maybe it didn't matter. Maybe Georgie was soused enough that I could be direct. Casual, but direct. "So, Georgie, I been meaning to ask. How's Biggie?"

Georgie shrugged. "Ain't seen him lately."

Sonofa.... Talk about the least satisfying answer he could have come up with. "When was the last time you did see him?"

"Dunno." He'd picked up the colorful Sea-Monkey box Corey'd left behind, scanning it, head cocked like a dog trying to figure out calculus. I wondered if he knew how to read, or if he'd disrupted his way into the principal's office enough times to avoid that particular burden.

"So when *did* you see him last?" I prompted.

"Who?"

"Biggie."

Another shrug.

Shit. I should've been patient and let the vodka do its work. Now Georgie knew how curious I was, and he'd only be more stubborn about avoiding the topic. I tried to make like I didn't care. Switched on the TV and manually turned it to some true-crime forensics show that we could watch without watching, and poured him another drink. Stiff. And when he finished that, another. By the time he got up to use the can, his shoulders brushed either side of the living room's arched doorway as he wove his way through.

How could I word it? *Did Biggie ever say anything about that night—about me?* Maybe Georgie was finally drunk enough to answer. Or he would be after a couple more drinks.

Biggie had been there that night, ducking in from the rain, rolling hard. *Fire it up, Desmond. We'll crank the tunes.* Turning over that massive workbot so we could plug in our boombox was a hell of a lot of work, too damn much like my day job for me to even consider tinkering with it when I'd rather enjoy being monged out and stupid. I wouldn't have done it for just anyone. Biggie, though, he'd given me that lingering look, that secret smile he always gave me, with the twinkle in his eye...and I got to work. Since when had I ever said no to Biggie?

I heard the toilet flush, and then I heard Georgie, loud enough to drown out the TV from the other end of the apartment. "What the *fuck?*"

Something had spooked him good. Served him right for pawing through the gimp stuff. Me, I was used to it by now, the wrappings and powders and lotions with their helpful diagrams all over the package, like you're too stupid to figure out how to wrangle it onto your own stump. But Georgie'd never seen any of that shit, and he was so blotto it probably looked twice as bad in his double vision. The last thing I wanted was to freak out my guest, especially when I was so close to getting the scoop on Biggie. Best to pull the poor drunk out of there before he discovered the compression bandage in the back of the medicine cabinet, the one with all the graphic photos on its box.

I was so sure I'd find Georgie handling the stump powder—plus I was none too sober myself—that it took me a second to comprehend that he'd glimpsed graphic photos of an entirely different nature. The thing in his hand, the item that had caused him such alarm, was a well-worn copy of Colt Men.

"Gimme that." I snatched right-handed and ended up slapping it out of his grasp with my prosthetic. The magazine hit the toilet rim, flapped around, and landed on the floor open to the spread of a big, hairy brute of a guy who looked something like Jim, minus the septum piercing and the stretched-out tattoos.

"Everyone callin' you a faggot—that's for real?"

I squinted into Georgie's bleary eyes and tried to figure out if he was seriously unaware that I liked dick. He'd never been too swift on the uptake, and me, I guess I'd learned to ignore the way the old gang tossed around the word "faggot." In their lingo, it could mean anything from a suburbanite, to a college graduate, to anyone with a sweet set of wheels that *they* should have been driving instead. "I thought you knew." I thought everybody knew.

"Is that why you brought me over here? You're gay for me?"

"Fucking hell, Argusto, don't flatter yourself. I needed help with my car."

"Yeaaah?" he slurred. "Then why'd you get me so wasted?"

A reply didn't immediately spring to mind, but I was spared from scrambling for a believable excuse. Drunk as he was, Georgie still had full use of his dominant hand. He clocked me so hard I barely knew what hit me. And once I was down, he called me a disgusting fucking perv and gave me a good kick to the kidneys to remember him by, then staggered out my door.

CHAPTER 21

"I'm not hot for that dumbass Georgie Argusto." I paused in my jiggling of the Fucking Egg and took a sip of Stoli. The bot hadn't been whining or flashing or anything. But since the stupid hunk of plastic and circuitry did sorta hear me, I felt slightly less pathetic for baring my soul to it than I would talking to my fridge or coffee pot. "He looks okay. Not bad, actually. But he doesn't swing that way, y'know? And the connection you get with someone, when you see 'em looking at you and they're thinking, *yeah, I'd tap that*. The look is the thing that gets me."

It was the look that Jim had slid my way the first time I saw him at a dilapidated tavern at the foot of Hertel, when he caught me sneaking a glance at his junk as he was taking a piss...a look that ended with me backed against a busted crapper and him on his knees between my Doc Martens in a filthy toilet stall. It was the look that Corey had lavished on me in his brother's living room before he floored me with the story of how he lost his arm. And it was the look that Tony Bigliani had been giving me—I shit you not—since we were ten years old.

Back then, I didn't even know what it meant. Why Biggie understood is a mystery. I guess some boys are born knowing their dicks are more than just the punchline of a bawdy joke that other kids will intuitively laugh along with, whether they get it or not. Even early on, Biggie knew.

In those days, before all the businesses moved out, there was a five-and-dime on T-Street that sold every kind of crap you could think of, but they kept the good stuff behind the counter. While we could sneak smokes a few at a time from our parents, sometimes an entire pack if the old man was loaded enough, the lighters at the store were beyond our grubby little reach. Sure, we could fire up using matches. But obviously that wasn't half as cool as flicking a Bic.

When Biggie lured the clerk down to the end of the aisle to ask her a half-dozen questions about the difference between one cheap perfume and another, supposedly for his grandma's birthday, the other kids stole jawbreakers and novelty erasers and fake tattoos off the shelves. I was the one who pocketed every last sleek plastic lighter from behind the counter. Looking back, I can see it wasn't exactly the crime of the century. Security consisted of a couple of fisheye mirrors and the shell of a surveillance camera that wasn't even hooked up. Back then, though, I was so proud of myself, you'd think I'd cleaned out Fort Knox.

The rush I got from stealing those lighters was amazing. But it was nothing compared to the way I felt after Biggie gave me the *look*—a look I replayed over and over and over, laying in bed that night and staring up at the ceiling while heady pangs I couldn't name churned through my gut.

Biggie didn't toss that look around lightly. I didn't see it again until I was twelve, maybe thirteen. It was the summer between seventh and eighth grade, our last big-shot year before starting all over again at the bottom of the totem pole at Riverside High, where freshman initiation sent two of our gang to the hospital and nearly cost me a tooth. The summer of my big, shining moment. These were the days before scanners, when pay phones and vending machines and video games took coins. Not only had I discovered a working pay phone at an abandoned gas station down by the river, but I'd filed down a metal slug just right so it could trip a credit and buy us a phone call, then bypass the chute and fall through the coin return, primed for our next victim. Biggie's voice had dropped by then—thanks to one hell of a growth spurt, he'd grown into his nickname. When he pranked someone with that new voice of his, he didn't sound like some kid random-dialing the phone. He sounded like a grown man.

The premise of the crank calls wasn't exactly genius. Biggie would speak some made-up foreign language, and he'd babble at the sap on the other end of the line to see how they'd react. Most of 'em hung up. But some (you'd be surprised how many) hung in there to try and make sense of the call. Some of 'em were good Samaritans who encouraged the poor "immigrant" on the other end of the line to go call the cops. And sometimes, as Biggie's twisted pig-latin pleas grew more frantic, more intense, the sorrier schmoes would get so worked up, we'd have them in tears, at least until one of us couldn't contain our glee over making an adult cry. Once our stifled giggles told them they'd been duped, they'd slam down their receiver in disgust, usually before Biggie could sing out his *coup de grâce*, "Psych!"

The other kids had grown tired of the prank, probably because no more than two people could successfully share that handset between them—and since I'd found the phone, and I'd filed the slug, I was the man of the hour. It was late. Everyone else had trickled away to find a viaduct or a parking lot or a bridge, but Biggie and me, we stayed and crank-called well into the night. Long after the sun went down and the clammy, fish-reeking wind blowing off the river raised goosebumps on our skin, we stayed.

Summer sunsets stretch long into the night, and once they're gone, street lights flicker on to take their place—at least in spots the city thinks deterrents to criminal activity are needed. The old lot was lit up so bright I almost didn't notice the headlights. The distance, the pitch, the intensity, I'm not sure what exactly tipped me off. But even a block away, it was uncanny how quick I could spot the headlights on a police cruiser. Once in a while I was wrong, and it turned out to be nothing more than a civilian Crown Vic with a little old lady behind the wheel. More often than not, though, once I was far enough out of the headlight glare to see the rest of the car, I'd spy those telltale strobes up top.

Biggie was deep into his distressed-foreigner schtick, so I yanked him away from that pay phone so hard, you'd think I was saving him from a grenade. "What the fu—?"

I clamped my hand over his mouth as I mashed him into the gritty cinderblock wall. "Quiet—pigs."

You might think the closeness would overwhelm me, but no, I was still too young to think anything of it. Mostly I was worried that I'd been wrong, and the car would turn out to have a geriatric driver on a late-night cat food run. Lucky for me, it didn't. We both held our breath as the Interceptor idled past, slow and menacing. We'd gone so rigid, it felt like we were playing freeze tag. Even as the cop car drifted to the end of the block, around the corner, and out of sight, we held our positions for several more keyed-up heartbeats, until I came back to myself and realized I'd been pressing Biggie up against the wall with my hand clamped over his face for God knows how long. I backed off and gave an uneasy laugh, hoping he wasn't going to pound me, and said, "That was close."

He stared at me for a second, expression totally unreadable, then turned and peered deeper into the shadows. "Check it out. Back door's busted."

Talk about a lucky break. I was on a streak.

If I knew then what I know now, I would've been more concerned about stumbling into a den of crackhead child-molester cannibals, or at least stepping on a needle crawling with AIDS. Kids, though...they might think they know the score, but until they've been through the school of hard knocks, they're clueless.

Doors don't bust themselves. Someone had been inside that derelict gas station before us—lots of someones, judging by the nests of stained fabric and piles of trash we navigated by the light of our stolen Bics. Biggie found the stump of a candle cemented to a workbench with melted wax. I pried it free with a rusty screwdriver, and he took it up, lit the wick, and led the way deeper into the bowels of the building. It wasn't a huge place, only three rooms. The garage had a single repair station with a lift, and beyond that was the office and a john. In the stifling humidity of the night, though, it felt like we could get lost in that dank cinderblock building, take a wrong turn and never find our way out again.

The garage was the spot the crackheads had congregated, judging by the mounds of junk all around, and the broken glass pipe that crunched under my sneaker. Although I was already a dedicated scavenger at that age, those filthy piles of junk couldn't tempt even me. The office, though...maybe there was something left in the office, some stash that the druggies had been too tweaked out to discover, the type of goodies that might fill the now-empty racks where the cash register used to sit. A box of candy or gum, maybe. A stash of lighters. Some well-hidden cartons of cigarettes that magically wouldn't be stale.

Unsurprisingly, if anything of value actually was left behind when the station closed, it had been picked clean ages ago. There was nothing worth taking unless you were in the market for some rat turds or a chewed ballpoint pen. Biggie assessed the lack of salvageable goods much quicker than I did. He was already making off with the lit candle before I was convinced there were no hidden catches or secret compartments to be found. I tried my lighter, but before long the striker wheel was too hot to hold. "Wait up," I called, but of course, Biggie never let anyone tell him what to do.

There was only one room left to explore—the can, where the resident crackheads had been shitting and pissing in the broken toilet. Funny, how that tendency is more universal than you'd think. I'm not sure if I actually remember that smell, or if I'm just thinking of the stink from the warehouse that ground off my right hand two decades later, and fleshing out my old memories with new detail. Whether or not the stench was the same, I do remember that it felt close. Stifling. Something was brewing in that dark, reeking hole. Like the summer heat had been trapped deep within the layers of cinderblock and moldy drywall, fermenting through the long, humid days despite the night chill outside.

It started so innocent. Biggie laughing, pointing out a decaying porn mag in the sink. "Tits."

I craned my neck for a better look. The only reason tits interested me at all was because I knew they were taboo, so yeah, I was curious. I struggled to make sense of the image by the guttering candlelight. Tits, easy enough to spot, two pair. The rest of the picture had me stumped, though. I'm not sure if the chick getting blown was a she-male or if she was wearing a strap-on. Back then, I didn't know jack about any of that. All I knew was the chick somehow had a dick, and she looked pretty damn pleased to be shoving it down the other chick's throat. Before I'd seen that perplexing image, *suck my dick* was just one of many dick-references we all threw around. Suddenly it meant something else entirely.

"Bet that feels awesome," Biggie said.

Gross was more like it. Plus, what if the chick decided to take a bite out of you? What then?

More revisionist history here, because logically, it must've been too dark to see. But when I replayed the scene now, I pictured Biggie giving me that *look* with the full force of his larger-than-life personality behind it. Why else would I have been dumb enough to do what I did? When Biggie said, "Let's try it," did I do what any normal kid would have done? Did I sneer at him and call him a faggot? Did I laugh and tell him to fuck off?

Nope. Me, there in the dark, hunched against Biggie in my pathetic, gullible state of confusion, I took a deep breath, I gathered my nerve...and I knelt.

"Psych!"

He cuffed me across the top of the head. Just a glancing blow, but it must've knocked some sense into me. Before I knew which end was up, he'd darted from the bathroom, laughing, candle in hand, leaving me behind in that reeking black pit. Lucky for me, Biggie never said another thing about it. Maybe he didn't need to. Those *looks* of his held a wealth of meaning, and after that night at the gas station, I'd cracked enough of the Rosetta Stone to get the gist.

Sometimes I wonder why I never brought it up again, especially once I'd hit my growth spurt and matched his height, or once we were done with school and embarking on a life of dead-end jobs or.... I dunno. Maybe there was no good time. Whenever I plucked up the courage, I'd remember another look: the look in my old man's eyes that night when I slunk back home at half past midnight. As usual, he was so plastered he could hardly hold up his own head. "Get in here," he slurred from his recliner, loud and insistent enough that I figured it was safer to obey than to sneak upstairs and hope he would forget about whatever was eating him by morning.

Since there wasn't any booze on my breath and it was no big secret I was already smoking half a pack a day—and since any idea of me having a curfew was a joke—there wasn't any reason for him to be pissed off. That's what I thought...until he gave me a long, slow, rheumy look, and drawled, "What the fuck happened to your knees?"

I looked down and saw two oily dirt-crusted stains on my jeans in the shape of my kneecaps, with a wad of gum stuck to one, plasticky pink and studded with broken glass that sparkled like cheap rhinestones. The dark paneling in the living room sucked the light out of the air so bad, you could hardly see anything in that damn cave but the glow of the TV tube. Yet somehow, even in that shitty light, and even through his double vision, my father had managed to zero directly in on the evidence of what I'd almost done.

"I fell," I said—or at least, I tried to. Before the words were out, he'd uncoiled from the recliner and backhanded me so hard, I did a perfect one-eighty. Although I hadn't seen it coming, I had the presence of mind to use the blow's momentum to run upstairs, shut myself in my room and drag my dresser over to block the door. Looking back, I imagine that pathetic old rummy could've easily shoved his way in anyhow by simply stumbling against the door.

Guess I'm lucky that pursuing my sorry ass was just too much effort.

So, the gas station incident. That must've been the reason Biggie wasn't particularly shocked to find me tumbling out of a bathroom stall a few years later with the notoriously gay owner of a dive bar, the one where all the indie bands gigged. I must've been legal at that point, since this dump actually carded, but barely. Biggie didn't say a single word to me about it. But with the way everyone began treating me like a leper after that, I had no doubt that each and every member of his crew knew which way *I* swung.

CHAPTER 22

Wearing a robotic limb wasn't my idea of a good time, but as I tried to squeeze onto the Niagara bus carrying my bus pass, the prosthetic and the Fucking Egg, I was surprised how desperately I wanted something more than the gaping sleeve of a leather jacket at the end of my right arm—even if that thing was made of silicone, alloys and graphine robofilament.

"Today'll be the day," I murmured to the egg. It had to be. No way would any government shrink drag out the process any more than they absolutely had to, and this would be my third meeting with phobia chick.

Apparently the morning was full of surprises. Not only had I thought fondly of my robo-arm, but I found myself hesitant to give the Fucking Egg back to Dr. Ivery. She'd seen the box, though, so it was too late to tell her I'd lost it. Plus I wasn't $400-worth of hesitant.

So I surrendered that little pain-in-the-ass of a bot, and stood by anxiously while Ivery plucked it from its box, keyed open a compartment, and plugged it into a cord on her desk console. Data scrolled by. Ivery read. I held my breath. Her expression was so unreadable, though, that after a minute or two, I broke. "There was, y'know, a learning curve. But once I got the hang of it, the F...uh...egg was hardly lighting up at all. It even made this cool chirping sound, eventually. Sometimes."

Ivery scrolled to the end of the data. "The numbers are adequate."

Not only was I sad to lose the Fucking Egg, I was disappointed in my final grade. Surprise, surprise. What was I expecting, a Golden Dingaling?

"So I can start using my prosthetic again?"

Ivery's face was stony. She didn't say the word *no*, but her expression told me I was unlikely to hear anything good. "Let's go over your form."

"My form?"

"The daily form where you charted your relaxation and visualization exercises."

Oh. That thing. I hadn't even thought about it since our last meeting. In fact, the cassette tape that went with it was still in my pocket. Shrink-wrapped. I made a show of pawing through the plastic grocery bag I'd used for toting around my robotics. "Sorry, it must've... look, I can tell you from memory. The exercise worked great. The three and four anxiety scores that I started with are mostly ones now that I did the breathing and stuff."

Ivery's expression hadn't softened.

"I really think I'm making great progress," I said helpfully.

"Mr. Poole, give me your prosthetic."

What, could she plug it in and glean my secrets from those robotics too? Traditional machines are one thing. I understand how they work—I've had a grasp on them since I took apart and reassembled my Karate-Action GI Joe. But robotics are so far beyond me they might as well have been an alien technology. I hesitated, and Ivery said more firmly, "Give it to me now, or this session is over."

I don't spook easily—I've seen too much—and I've certainly never been scared of a skeletal chick in a pink cardigan. But as I handed my arm to Dr. Ivery, my better judgment was telling me to cut my losses, take my robotics and run. I was relieved when she didn't pop open some secret port and download data from my prosthetic...but that relief curdled when she tucked the whole thing away beneath her desk.

"What is this?" I asked. "Some kind of exercise?"

"You've been wearing the prosthetic when I expressly instructed you not to."

She got that from the egg? Impossible. The bot had sensors, but nothing that could've known what I was or wasn't wearing. Someone had been tattling, but who? Not Georgie, too dumb. Definitely not Corey, who hated authority even more than I did. Ken Roman, annoyed that I hadn't joined him in his antiquing? It didn't seem like his style. I went through every person I'd encountered in the past week, casting around for someone to blame while I tried to sell Ivery on my worthiness. "But I really am trying. I even racked up an extra visit with the support...group."

The support group. Pam Steiner. That goddamn sanctimonious yuppie bitch. "Whoever's been talking shit about me, it's a lie. I've been going without, just like you said."

"I find that very hard to believe. You've resisted every attempt at desensitizing you to the robotics."

"That's not true. I was good enough with the Fucking Egg, you said so yourself."

"I don't care for your language or your tone. Step away from my desk and lower your voice, or I'm calling security."

I staggered back, confused and alarmed. "It wasn't a tone—it's just—what're you doing with my arm?"

"How would you rate your anxiety, on a scale of one to ten?"

My brain scrambled to provide her with the answer she wanted to hear. "Eight...no, three...no, five...."

"Sit down and we'll do an exercise. Mr. Poole? Mr. Poole, sit."

Numbly, I sat.

"Close your eyes and we'll begin the relaxation."

I closed my eyes, all right, though I was anything but relaxed. She went through the body parts, ordering me to clench and relax, clench and relax, while I racked my brain trying to figure out if she could actually take my arm away for good. Unfortunately, I didn't have enough understanding of the twisted hierarchy of Social Service's bureaucracy to even guess. For all I knew, the limb might not even belong to me technically, since it's not as if I paid for it out of my own pocket. Holy fuck, what if she had the authority to seize it?

Ivery restarted the relaxation process at my toes, so I followed along, half-listening, just enough to convince her I was doing her damn exercise. "Think back to your first bot," she said, once she was through making me clench my whole body again. "How old were you then? You must have been in high school. Picture it in your mind. Was it the Closet Valet? Or the Personal DJ?"

Not that it mattered, but I really did remember the first graphine bot I ever owned. It was a DayStart Alarm System, and it was the size of a fucking toaster oven. It didn't have a scanner on it—that technology was still a few years away. Instead, you were supposed to use a clumsy keypad to log in your sleeping and waking patterns for a good month so it could begin waking you at its best approximation of an appropriate time. Which was wrong just as often as it was right.

"Think about how advanced it seemed. And how lucky you felt to own one."

I didn't. I'd never asked for the thing to begin with—it was my old man's idea. He was infamous for the occasional grand gesture of buying something no one asked for, something he couldn't afford, in an attempt to convince himself that he was the Father of the Year. In the end I suppose it worked out well enough for both of us, since it spared us from having our typical morning conversation from there on out, the one that went, *Get outta bed, you worthless shit—Oh yeah? Fuck you.* Even if I was late for homeroom at least once a week.

"Now I'd like you to think about something more recent. Recall the last time a housebot made an adjustment for you that you noticed. Maybe it dimmed the lights after you came home from a long day at work." I managed to stop from scoffing at that idea. Probably because I was in panic mode over the thought of her stealing my arm. "Maybe it warmed your bedroom on a chilly night. Maybe it got your coffee just right."

Like the coffeebot at Corey's place.

"Remember to breathe." Now there's something you don't usually forget. "Inhale. Hold it. Now exhale gently."

My breath hitched on the way out.

"Thinking about your interaction with that piece of robotics, on a scale of one to ten, how would you rate your anxiety?"

"Five? No, not five. Not then. Maybe now, now that I think about it.

Because for everything I noticed coming out of the bot, I'll bet it was doing ten more things that were too subtle for me to see. The movies, the TV, the coffee. But what else? I've seen the guts of a housebot. There's stuff like humidity and white noise that even the base models can control, and the advanced ones? I wouldn't put it past 'em to be zapping subliminal messages into our heads. Makes you wonder if you can trust your gut at all anymore, or if the course of your life is just based on the housebot's latest upgrade."

"So you're saying the housebot was...manipulating you?"

Was it?

Or was I just trying to come up with some excuse as to why I'd actually been happy again, despite my stump, when I spent that week at Corey's?

"I think I fucked up." My voice had gone all wobbly. "I almost had something good going, and somehow I fucked it all up."

"And your anxiety level now?"

"Eight? Ten?" I knuckled away the sting of waterworks. "The fuck if I know. We were having a good time, working on the car, and then he says I don't know what I want and he takes off." When my nose started to run, I couldn't exactly deny the fact that I'd let the maudlin overtake me...and me not even drunk yet. I cracked an eye open to cast around for some tissues. When I grabbed at the box with my right hand, I found a gaping sleeve where my robo-arm should have been. Quickly, I snatched up a tissue with my left hand and blew my nose.

The whole time, Ivery was writing in my file. Intently. Hoping she hadn't noticed me blubbering, I took a deep breath and went on. "Is he jealous of the Gremlin? Is that it? It's just a car. Fuck, if it's the car, I'll get rid of it. It's gone. I haven't driven since there was snow on the ground, so it's not like I can't live without it."

Embarrassing as my outburst had been, I couldn't exactly take it back, so I figured I might as well get some use out of the headshrinker. "What do you think? If I sold my car, would he give me another chance?"

Ivery stopped writing, and paged back through the surprisingly large amount of notes in my file. "This was the non-robotic car?"

"Right. A '78 Gremlin. Like I said."

"Then it won't impact your treatment one way or the other."

She told me to think about things like stereos and sliding doors, and when she asked me about my anxiety I gave her random numbers. She was the professional—she *had* to know what it would take to win Corey over—but she was holding out on me. I was wondering how best to sweet talk the answer out of her when she said, "That's time." She handed me a piece of paper: a third copy of the blank chart waiting to be filled with numbers. "Continue with the relaxation tape, but focusing specifically on housebots when you rate your anxiety. Next week, I'll expect you to bring the actual form, not just recite the progress you think you remember. And also put a tick mark in the margin whenever you feel as if a housebot is manipulating you."

I folded the note one-handed, shoved it in my pocket, and waited.

"Same time next week," she said. It sounded like a dismissal.

"Aren't you forgetting something?"

"I don't think so."

She wanted me to beg? Fine. "My arm."

"Don't worry. I'll take good care of it. The locks in this building are state of the art and the officebots run flawlessly."

"You're kidding," I said, though judging by the look on her face, she wasn't. "Listen, your scare tactics—they worked. Totally. So give me back my arm and I'll be on my way."

Ivery continued writing in my file, unhurried. I stood there watching her looping cursive fill yet another page, then finally she stopped writing, looked me in the eye and said, "You claimed you haven't been wearing your robotics."

"I haven't."

"Then it makes no difference if I keep it here. Does it?"

* * *

Contrary to popular belief, I really had put effort into going armless to desensitize myself from my robotic limb. I'd gone several days without getting laid when Corey couldn't stand the sight of me rocking a compression bandage. No, it wasn't as if I'd gone without for weeks. But it sure did feel like it. And hell, maybe that period of separation, however long it had actually been, was enough to do the trick.

'Cause now I missed my arm something fierce. And I couldn't think of a damn thing that would get it back anytime soon.

I hunkered down in my apartment for a few days, and I hid. That worked fine until I ran out of booze. With nothing better to do and no desire to be seen in public with an empty armhole flapping around, I decided to break out the cassette tape and give it a listen. It was warped so the volume rose and fell, though it still played well enough for me to get the gist in five minutes. Relax this and that and who the fuck cared? I wanted my life back. I wanted my arm. I wanted Corey.

To make sure I didn't forget my homework again, I filled out the form ahead of time in three different pens, starting with mid-to-high anxiety ratings then dropping them down to ones and twos. That comment about marking down how often I felt manipulated? I ignored it. Most likely it was some sort of trap, a punishment for being honest enough to speak my mind. Manipulation is a way of life, and not just in robotics. Everyone's a manipulator and everyone gets manipulated—that's what really makes the world go 'round. It's just impolite to come right out and admit it.

Pre-doing my homework just pissed me off, so I decided to swallow my pride, buck up and walk to the liquor store. It wasn't as if I needed two arms to buy booze. And it wasn't as if the nicotine-leathered old man behind the counter would even notice, anyway.

Too bad I'd wasted so much time deciding which numbers to fill in the stupid chart. By the time I got there, it was closed.

I stood there staring at the locked security grate, as if maybe by the force of my longing, the grating would spring open and yield up a bottle of Stoli.

No such luck.

That's the problem you get when you deal with these little mom-and-pop joints. Mom and Pop don't like to work more than twelve hours a day if they can help it. Plus the prices are high and the selection sucks. Used to be, I only shopped there when I was too drunk to drive to a real liquor store. But since the accident, it had become my regular place.

I stared hard at the red security light blinking, blinking, blinking, somewhere beyond the bars and the bulletproof glass and the years of smoke and grime, and I thought about what a pain in the ass it would be to bus it to Liquor Land. For all I knew, it wasn't even in business anymore. With a car, I'd be there in ten minutes.

I did have a car. She even started.

While I didn't think I'd stand a ghost of a chance taking a driver's test, getting myself to the liquor store was doable. Turning the key left-handed? Reaching across my body to shift into first? No fun, not by a long shot. But doable. I kept it in first the entire way, and the experience of driving again—the insane rush of freedom—was intense enough to keep me from feeling like an old lady on her way to church, even though I only topped twenty when I was rolling downhill. Parking was a bitch. The reach-across was harder when I was busy worrying about putting the Gremlin through the store's plate glass window. If I'd thought things through better, I would've fastened the sleeve of my leather to the stick so I could work it right-handed...or right-armed, as the case may be.

If I'd thought things through better, I wouldn't have lost that hand to begin with. The meatworks, or the prosthetic.

I didn't wallow long in my regret. Seven months ago, Liquor Land was only a stop on my way home from work. Now it was more like a mirage greeting me from the corner of a battered strip mall, a glorious mystical land that promised ample cigarettes, reasonable booze, and more lottery tickets than you could shake a stick at, though I wouldn't go so far as to say I felt lucky. My old ritual of grab-and-pay was replaced by actual shopping. Had there always been this many varieties of mid-priced vodka? As I gathered bottles, I debated hooking a shopping basket into my right elbow to allow me to carry more booze. But then I realized, what's the rush? I had a car. And I could come back anytime I damn well pleased.

Between my left hand and the crook of my right arm, I wrangled three bottles of Stoli up to the front. The clerk was a bored-looking black guy I didn't recognize, but that was no surprise. I hadn't been on a first-name basis with anyone at Liquor Land before the accident. Maybe it was for the best that I didn't get a "Welcome Back" party on my big return. I asked for two packs of Reds...no, make that three, and I waited for the damage.

Instead of stating my total, the bored clerk said, "Scan in."

"What?"

He nodded toward a hand scanner set beside the lotto machine. "Scan in."

That was new. I'd remember if it wasn't. "Since when do I have to scan in at a *store*?"

"New statute." His eyes were on my empty right sleeve. He looked slightly more interested. "Supposed to curb underage drinking."

Great. Now I couldn't even score my fucking alcohol without being scanned. Not unless I shopped at the mom-and-pop in Riverside...which was currently closed. Plus, even the small shops would be forced to abide by the scanner rules at some point too. And then they'd raise their already outrageous prices to compensate for the cost of the machinery.

"If it's easier," the clerk offered, "I could key in your license."

Which I didn't have. I considered telling him to forget it, and swinging by the gin mill instead. But Georgie might be waiting there to take another crack at me, maybe with a whole group of pissed-off deigos. Plus, how would I get home after that? I had a hard enough time driving one-handed when I was sober. "Nah. It's fine." It's not as if I'm robophobic or anything. "Fucking politicians, nothing better to do than make things harder for everyone else."

The clerk gave a harrumph of agreement and began wrapping my glass bottles in old newspaper once I scanned my left hand. My anxiety level? Maybe a four, maybe a three...or maybe not even that, because I couldn't say for sure that the twisting feeling in my gut would be labeled as anxiety. Maybe it just pissed me off that if I wanted a drink, I was now required to scan in. What came next, begging a robot's approval to take a shit?

I chewed on my anger as I made my way back to Mrs. Zelko's garage. The night could've been worse. I could've lost some Stoli to breakage if the clerk hadn't gone that extra step to stop them from clanking together. Some pigs could've found me driving with a suspended license and expired plates, but my drive had been fine. I could've had to deal with one-handed parallel parking if I hadn't rented the garage. But even the fact that my little expedition was relatively successful, my booze was intact and my Gremlin ran like a champ, it still seemed like robots were taking over the world. Not box-shaped robots from 1950's sci-fi flicks, either—small, subtle bots that ran the doors and the phones and the coffee pots. If I couldn't figure out how to adapt, I might as well bend over and steel myself to be nailed with a giant robotic dick.

What's worse, I couldn't even practice with my own robotic limb, because currently it was downtown, hidden beneath a candle-covered desk.

CHAPTER 23

While the shopping channel babbled to me about a robotic juicer I couldn't live without, I pondered my catch-22 over a cocktail. To acclimate myself to robotics, I'd need to master my arm. But my arm had been taken away to cure me of my supposed phobia.

I wanted my arm back, and I wanted it now. But short of breaking in to Ivery's building, it wasn't going to happen. Chances of her seeing me early were slim. It was obvious she wasn't any fonder of me than I was of her, so she had no reason to do me any favors. Even so, I had to try...but when I called to leave a message, her voicemail let me know she wouldn't even be there again before Monday. Not only weren't there any earlier appointments to snag, but showing up in person and trying to squeeze my way in between other patients would be futile.

As my cranberry juice ran dry, the level in my Stoli bottle dipped lower and lower at an accelerated rate. I yearned for my arm, mostly on principle. But what I really wanted was my car. Even rolling along in first gear, I'd felt more alive in my Gray Lady than I had since before I lost my meatworks. More than likely I was just waxing nostalgic, but it was also clear that sometimes you don't know what you've got 'til it's gone.

I drank myself to sleep and woke up on the couch with a sandpaper tongue and a sick throbbing in my skull. When I cast around to assess the situation, I found the first Stoli was nearly empty. More juice next time. Less vodka. I turned my attention to a wrinkled newspaper on the coffee table. It was the page that'd been wrapped around my liquor bottles, now opened flat, clumsily smoothed. I scanned it to see whatever it was that I'd been bored enough to read, and determine whether or not I remembered reading it. No comics. Not even articles. Had I been desperate enough to peruse the classifieds—and if so, what had I been hoping to find? An arm? A life? A sliver of hope?

None of the ads rang a bell. But then I noticed a few numbers scribbled in the margin in my spidery left-handed writing, and the last few conscious minutes of my night clicked into place. Maybe my phone call to Ivery had been fruitless, but the subsequent call I'd made to the Department of Motor Vehicles hadn't. Their robots were there 24/7, and one of them had been helpful enough to make me an appointment for a road test.

Fuck. Leave it to me to drunk-dial the DMV.

The thought of waiting for my road test to roll around with me not being able to practice for it was unbearable. My initial impulse was to go crying to Jim. He'd know which strings to pull to get my arm back. But whatever atrophied sense of pride I possessed simply wouldn't allow me to ask him to do me any more favors. Not this time. I could try Corey, since he had a hard-on for helping me and he'd be eager to prove to himself that he could handle the sight of my stump. But even I could tell that idea was a sure plan for disaster. My eyes were roaming the classifieds as I cast around for inspiration, and on the second or third pass, I paused on a tiny display ad for a flea market.

According to Ken Roman, the flea market was positively bristling with prosthetic limbs. And if I could drive the Gremlin (albeit poorly) with only a stump, with some kind of hand-shaped thing to help me shift, I could pass a road test whether or not Ivery gave up my robo-arm. I whiled away my day in Mrs. Zelko's garage waiting for Saturday to roll around, convincing myself that the perfect limb would be waiting there at the flea market just for me. Meanwhile, I focused on planning to get myself to a part of town where the buses didn't run. When I took a more experimental approach to shifting, I discovered that if I splinted my jacket sleeve with a few paint stirrers and duct-taped the end over the gearshift, I was golden. I had no illusions I'd pass a road test that way, but my makeshift solution would be enough to get me to the flea market.

The American shores of the Niagara River are rife with hulking, half-rotted factories, docks and silos where trade thrived, maybe a hundred years ago. As tire plants and steel mills closed, the population dwindled, and so did business. You would think there'd be real estate potential for the robotics industry to flourish in Buffalo, but it never did. All the prime parts are manufactured overseas.

The flea market was easy enough to spot, since nothing else was going on within a three-mile radius of the abandoned riverfront lot, unless you counted the hobby fishermen bobbing around a quarter-mile out in their dinghy. Plans to renovate the lakefront surfaced every few years around election day, but once it came time to make good on the promises, the money always evaporated. Now industrious folks with stuff to unload had set up shop, at least for the day.

There was a lot of crap. A lot. Faded Christmas decorations, beat up furniture, half-used cologne. I was just about to wonder aloud who bought this stuff when I saw a middle-aged guy clutching a manual typewriter to his chest like he'd just struck gold, and I figured I'd be better off keeping my mouth shut.

The flea market sprawled wide, and sifting through the flotsam in the punishing October wind driving in from the water was more mind-numbing than I'd bargained for. Hours passed with no luck. Hopelessness began to creep over me, until among a spill of kitchen utensils and wall ornaments and old toys, I spotted something jarringly familiar.

A remote control.

I reached for it, right-left, and hefted it in my hand. "Make me an offer," the seller called without looking up from the National Enquirer he was reading. Shit, who could put a price on the ability to work the volume again, and change the channel without crossing the room?

Who could put a price on a second chance?

"Ten bucks?" I said.

"I can go fifteen."

Sure. And if I'd offered five, I could've had it for seven. "I'll give you ten," I repeated.

The seller shrugged and said, "It's an antique."

An antique buried in a pile of junk. I wasn't cut out for bargaining, but I gave it another shot. "I don't even know if it works."

"No corrosion around the batteries...no reason why it shouldn't."

A low voice behind me purred, "Might I suggest you revisit your negotiation in an hour." I nearly gave myself whiplash turning to find Ken Roman lurking there behind me. "The closer it is to the end of the day, the less precious their dubious wares become. There's a unique hand-carved walking stick two rows down, walnut, I believe, but I wouldn't give her half of what she's asking. I'll circle back around and see if she changes her tune. Usually, they do."

I forgot all about the remote control. God only knows why Roman spooked me more than even Georgie Argusto. It's not as if the old freak had ever so much as laid a finger on me. Hell, he'd even bought me a bagel. But the sight of him put me on high alert, regardless. "How long have you been here?"

"Long enough." He glanced at my empty sleeve. "I take it you haven't found what you're looking for."

Although my impulse was to deny it, I realized that if anyone could find a prosthetic needle in the haystack, it was him. "Not even close."

"No." He nodded sagely. "You wouldn't have. It's tucked out of the way to preserve the masses' delicate sensibilities. Come—I'll take you to Old Time Harry."

Roman strolled through the flea market with the surety of a sonar-guided submarine. It was a different route than I'd originally taken, yet I began to see a sameness in the junk that was being offered. Battered sporting goods and vinyl records and comic books and tools. Stuff upon stuff upon stuff, all of it forming a field of visual noise, a field that Roman waded through like a patch of daisies. We came to the outer corner of the sprawl, by the far end of the parking lot filled with sellers' trucks and vans. When I expected him to tell me the dealer must've gone home, he stepped around a sawhorse at the perimeter and kept going.

If it weren't for Roman heading directly for the old delivery truck, I wouldn't have thought much of it. A rusty beater with a couple of guys leaning against it, having a conversation. But as it grew clear that this truck was our destination, suddenly everything seemed sinister, from the dented sides to the rusted muffler to the overly-casual manner of the people who knew what it actually held. By the time we strolled up, I had myself convinced I'd be able to score anything from kiddie porn to stolen kidneys, if I was willing to pay the price.

Roman greeted the guys with, "Gentlemen." Maybe they were shifty-eyed, or maybe I was projecting. Either way, Roman didn't introduce us. Maybe real names were a liability. One of them nodded, dropped his cigarette to the gravel, then circled to the back of the truck and heaved it open without ceremony.

Anticlimactic. Behind the door was yet another pile of junk.

But then I looked closer...no Christmas decorations here. More like Halloween, a scare-your-pants-off slasher flick of a Halloween. Handcuffs. Brass knuckles. A canister—of what? Tear gas? Agent orange? My skin crawled at the sight of the collection, and the more I saw, the more creeped-out I felt. The jumble of stuff became a sinister field of camouflage, where God-knows-what was lurking in wait.

Not for Roman. He was a big, hairy, overgrown kid in a fucking candy store. "Ah...very nice, very nice indeed." He plucked a dusty jar from the dross and held it up with his meatworks hand to admire. A glass eye rattled to a stop inside, staring, cockeyed, at a point somewhere over my shoulder. "Hand-blown—quite a difficult art to master." He set the jar to one side and continued to browse, while I shifted to ensure I didn't make eye contact with the thing. Still, I could feel it staring in my general direction.

He drew a wooden foot from the pile, sighed, and said, "Shoe form, for cobblers. Another fading art. Easy to confuse with a prosthetic." Imagine that. I found it plenty creepy as it was.

I looked from item to item, unseeing. The dread in me had hijacked my ability to make sense of anything. Or maybe I was busy watching Roman, and trying to figure out why he had such a hard-on for the stuff. And when it finally came, this wordless exclamation, I felt myself shudder. It really did sound like he'd creamed his shorts.

"Here it is. Just look at that articulation." From the shifting, clattering pile of tarnished metal and dusty wood, he drew out a wooden arm with a skeletal whalebone hand. I would have flinched away when he held it up to my empty sleeve if I hadn't been frozen in place. "Is this what you were looking for?"

No way. Not at all—not like *that*. I shook my head rapidly.

"The buckles are intact. Original leather on the cuff. It's brittle, but with a bit of care, a bit of saddlesoap...at least try it on."

He shoved the thing toward me and I fell back a couple of steps. "Get that hunk of junk away from me. I'm not looking to join a freak show—I just want to pass my road test."

"I see." With a longing look, he placed the skeleton arm back on the pile. "Something less decorative, more utilitarian, more modern. Mid-century, yes. I could see how that would better suit your personal style, with the leather and the chain. A hook would be just the ticket. Surprisingly useful, once you get the hang of it. Not a single hook, but dual hooks set at an angle, and the vee between them is where all the...here. Here's a worthy specimen."

Sure. If you were hoping to hit a costume party dressed as Blackbeard.

I was on the verge of cutting my losses and bailing when Roman snagged the top of a bottle in the angle joint of the two hooks and manipulated it like a stick shift. "Indeed. With practice...."

I watched, numb with dread, and tried to see myself wearing a fucking garden tool on the end of my stump. But it was either that or the duct tape, at least until I got my robo-arm back. And the duct tape method was a serious pain in the ass. "How much?" I asked the guy who might or might not be Harry.

"Thirty."

Way too much for something to get me by until my next appointment with Ivery—in which I'd damn well reclaim my arm, I was sure of it now. I wasn't leaving that goddamn candle-filled office without it, even if I had to sucker-punch her to pry it out of her bony hands.

"A veritable steal. I'd be happy to buy it for you, if only to see it go to the right home." Roman handed me the metal claw. "Try it on."

No. Every fiber of my being screamed, *no*. But he'd just shown me how easy it would be to drive a stick with it. I'd come all that way. I might as well try.

Glad at least that my leather jacket covered the area where the dirty deed would take place, I checked that nothing was nesting in the resin socket, found it clear, and slipped it into my sleeve. If my gut had been balking at the sight of the antique prosthetics before, it was nothing compared to the stance it took when my naked stump touched the socket. It felt powerfully wrong, a sickening reverse-rape. Prosthetics aren't one-size-fits-all. They're formed on careful casts of the residual limb. Slipping my arm into my own prosthetic is like shrugging into the leather jacket I've been wearing since high school. But cramming myself into this antique arm was viscerally repulsive. I threw it back onto the pile and said, "It doesn't fit."

Roman grabbed it back up. "Of course, adjustments would need to be made."

"You don't get it. This isn't permanent. It makes no sense to wait a week for the prosthetist to do his thing. By then I won't need a fucking hook, 'cause I'll have my old arm back in a few days."

He was appalled. "I would never suggest you take a historic piece like this to a prosthetist."

"Then what the fuck are we even talking about?" I was about to repeat his words back to him when I realized he hadn't said the *prosthetic* had to be adjusted—only that adjustments would need to be made. Bile filled my throat. "You can't—you wouldn't—"

He took my measure in a leisurely glance, then said, "Denial is such a fascinating thing."

"You're the one who's got yourself convinced that whatever freakish crap you can find at the bottom of a trash heap is some kind of fucking treasure. If anyone's in denial, it's you."

"That's not denial, Mr. Poole. It's a healthy outlet. We're the same, you and I—"

"The hell we are."

"Neither of us can bear the thought of being strapped to some travesty of a prosthesis. Oh yes, I knew the moment I saw you that you loathed your robotic limb as much as I did mine."

Did I?

"You hadn't mastered even the simplest of gestures. No, you did everything left-handed instead, and bore your loathsome machine like the burden it clearly is. Whether or not this is something you've chosen consciously, the fact remains, you're taking a stand against this violation to your person. And if that's the case, which would you rather be? Victimized, or empowered?"

"And your idea of being empowered is getting chopped up so you can fit into a fucking hook?" I backed away. "I'm not like you. Hear me? I am *nothing* like you."

CHAPTER 24

I could tell Jim was home not only because his beater station wagon was there, but because a bass riff vibrated the floorboards of his porch and the windowpanes on the door were rattling. I pounded on the door for a good five minutes in my panicky daze before I remembered that the doorbell was wired in to the housebot. When I pressed it, the music paused and a flat buzz sounded through the speaker system. Despite the music, I must've been expecting Jim the social worker to answer the door in a thrift store tie and a polyester blend shirt with strained buttons. That's how he'd looked the last few times I saw him.

The Jim who pulled open the door was a different Jim entirely—the badass Jim I'd picked up in a crusty bathroom stall in a crappy bar at the foot of Hertel. He filled the doorway. Metal glinted from his earlobes and septum. His short hair was in spikes. The sleeves of his Motorhead T-shirt were cut off to show his wrist-to-shoulder ink, the crotch of his old jeans was worn thin in the shape of his package, and the whole of his body pulsed with a barely-tamed energy. His expression was leery. *Who the fuck's that,* he must've thought, since he couldn't have been expecting me. Then his expression shifted—from annoyance, to recognition, to confusion, and finally, to resignation. Until his gaze fell to my empty sleeve, and the annoyance returned. "What happened to your arm?"

"Fuck my arm." I shouldered my way in and planted myself in the middle of the room so he couldn't slam his door in my face. Simba was stretched across the back of the couch. She opened her eyes, gave me one slow blink, then closed them again. Familiarity flooded in, and it gave me the strength to find out what I needed to know. "Ken Roman, the professor. His case belonged to you. Right?"

Jim stared at me like I'd lobbed something at him straight out of left field. "What of it?"

"You dropped him. Why'd you drop him?"

Eyes narrowed, Jim looked me up and down, gears turning, then came to some kind of decision. His broad shoulders slumped. "You come over here all jacked up, looking like you haven't slept in a week, with duct tape hanging off your empty sleeve, demanding to know about Ken Roman. Fucking hell, do I even wanna know why?"

"I need to know." I steeled myself and repeated, "Why did you drop him?"

Somehow, I'd managed to hit a sore spot. That shouldn't have surprised me. Prodding Jim's wounds was one of my best tricks. Jim shook his head. "How could I advocate for that guy? I could barely stand the sight of him. I tried—I really tried. But then...."

When his explanation petered out, I took it upon myself to finish. "But then you saw first-hand how futile it was to deal with a robophobic gimp, and you decided he was a lost cause, so why keep fighting for it?"

Jim looked at me, really looked at me, and I could tell that what I'd just said was churning through the wrinkles of his brain. He went to his bookshelf as if to choose a reference to corroborate whatever he was about to say, but must have decided that there were no printed words that would do it justice. "I've got nothing to back it up, but I don't think he was actually robophobic. I think he was just good at pretending to be."

I wanted to argue and ask why anyone could possibly want to come off as robophobic if they weren't, but my gut was already agreeing with Jim.

He sat at one end of his couch, still chewing on his thoughts, and numbly, I sat at the other. He said, "You know how many times I had to put in to replace the silicone sleeve on his prosthetic? Too many. Social Services wouldn't pay to refurbish it anymore—it came out of his paycheck, and that shit's not cheap—and even so, the arm was in the shop just as much as it was out. You're right about one thing. Watching you struggle to get used to your hardware made me wonder how Ken could deal with all the back-and-forth, and that's when I started to dig deeper."

I sagged into the couch. Simba set a paw on my head and began to knead my scalp with gentle, rhythmic pinpricks.

"That blowhard Hewitt fought me all the way in finding out anything," Jim said. "Big surprise. But because so much unusual paperwork had been generated on the case with all the requests for modifications and refurbs, eventually the officebot routed the non-confidential pieces of his file to me. Chunks of his history were missing. Huge gaps. But there was a photo of him where he's maybe eight years old, posing in front of the Christmas tree with the plastic hook from a pirate costume on his hand. And the look on his face... Des, they might have kept whatever notes went with that picture from me. But when I saw that look in his eye, I knew. He'd done it to himself."

In some sense, hadn't we all? Hadn't the kid who'd blown off his fingers been asking for it by playing with fireworks? Hadn't Corey worn himself into a state of reckless ennui by giving up his dream and settling for a dead-end job? Hadn't I put the cherry on top of the stupidity sundae by cramming my hand into a workbot while I was loaded?

"Look at me, Des." Jim grabbed me by the elbow of my empty sleeve. "I'm not just saying he brought it on. Ken did it to himself."

That blanked-out feeling I'd experienced back at Digi-tech began creeping up. I teetered on the verge of being able to understand what Jim was telling me, with the tiny prick of Simba's claws as my wisp-thin tether to the living room, to reality. "He hardly seems like the kind of guy who can work a power tool." Although I imagine Old Time Harry might've helped him, for the right price.

"From piecing together the paperwork, here's the way I figure it went. He tried to have his left arm surgically removed, but no real doctor's gonna do that. Not without losing their license."

I sucked in a breath. Then I wondered how long I'd been sitting there without breathing.

"But Ken's a pretty smart guy," he said. "Fucked-up, but smart. And he figured if they wouldn't take off a healthy limb, they couldn't deny treatment if he had frostbite. So he went to the science lab and got himself some dry ice...."

I pulled away from Simba with a groan, sat forward, and cupped my face in my left hand.

"You gonna hurl?"

I shook my head.

A moment of silence stretched, long. I had nothing to fill it with. Finally Jim said, "God, I wish I'd.... It was on a bus line. It was far enough away from any bars or liquor stores that you wouldn't drink yourself to death the second you walked out the door. And now...fuck. You wouldn't have even met that nutcase if it wasn't for the support group I picked out."

"Wait a minute." I took a long look at him. Tats and muscles and trying to curl into himself. He'd mirrored my posture, except he had two hands to bury his face in. "You think this is on you?"

He turned toward the kitchen so I couldn't read his expression. "Who else set you up at the Steiners' house?"

"It's not on you, Jim." I grabbed him by the wrist and gave him a shake. "You've always been there for me. Putting up with my shit and bailing me out. Above and beyond what I ever deserved. None of this is on you. It never was."

For all that Jim had been trying to style himself into a man of words to replace the "punch now, ask questions later" derelict he used to be, he sucked at talking about what was going on inside him as much as I did. He stood and tried to shake off the conversation with forced brusqueness. "So now you know. If you got what you came for, I'll drive you home."

"Yeah. About that."

I didn't get a lecture when Jim found the Gremlin parked across the street, though he did glance down at my empty sleeve as if the duct tape suddenly made a hell of a lot more sense. I told him about

Ivery taking my arm, but I was careful not to incite him to try and get it back since he'd done way too much for me already. I played the whole thing up as part of my therapy. Hell, maybe it even was therapeutic. It'd lit some kind of fire under me, that's for sure. I tossed him my keys. He opened the passenger door for me before he walked around to the driver side. Just like he'd always lit my cigarettes.

We buckled ourselves in and he turned over the engine. A piece of plastic on the dash buzzed from the blower fan. I fumbled with my cigarette pack in an attempt to tear off a piece of stiff paper to shim it with, but I couldn't manage with one hand. I resolved to do it later, though I knew I'd probably just forget. Meanwhile, Jim ran his fingertips along the flaking chrome-like paint and said, "I missed this car."

No kidding. I missed seeing him in it. You'd think I would take issue with someone else driving my Gray Lady. But I'd always respected her enough to know that at the end of the night, with me drinking all the vodka I could stomach and Jim clocking in at only a few beers, he should be the one getting us home.

When Jim slipped his arm across the passenger seat to do a head-check—around my shoulders—the realization of how much I'd actually lost punched me right in the gut. Maybe we'd stopped fucking like horny kids after the first couple of months, but he was still good in the sack. Besides, sex was only one piece of the puzzle. I suddenly missed things that no one in their right mind should have missed, like our trips to the home center that always ended with me helping him unload something heavy or awkward or smelly from the back of the station wagon. I missed the contentious pizza debates we'd have in the frozen aisle at Tops. I even missed the way he'd bitch about work, like him and his overtaxed co-workers were the last bastion of justice standing against the collapse of society as we knew it. I missed being involved with someone who actually gave a fuck about something—from the state of his lawn to the state of the world. Caring was a luxury I'd never indulged in, myself. It took too much fucking courage to care as intensely as Jim did, and I was a coward. Not Jim. He cared enough for both of us.

And I'd thrown it all away. Why?

The short answer: I'm an asshole. That's a given—but I sensed I was on the verge of understanding the deeper reason. "Can we make a quick stop on our way?" I asked.

Jim agreed, of course he did. When had James fucking Murphy ever failed to step up to the plate? I directed him through a few turns. When he saw we were heading downtown, he tensed up as he realized where I was taking us. He didn't say anything, though, and he didn't turn the car around. Maybe he thought this excursion was part of my therapy too. And maybe it was.

Although I was wrapped up in my internal melodrama, Jim didn't need any more directions. He took the last few turns on his own, rolled into the patchy gravel lot, and cranked the parking brake. I stared at the graffiti-covered shell of a factory for such a long time that eventually Jim felt the need to say something to kill the silence. "How much do you remember, really?"

"Some." I'd learned that much at Gimp Group. *The sound of rain. The smell of wet asphalt. The laughter of a bunch of wasted guys.* Enough to know that whatever I'd buried was still doing its damage whether I could recall it or not.

Jim would've hung back in the car if I'd let him. When I extended my hand to him, it wasn't because I needed someone to lean on. It was because I thought that if anyone deserved to know what the hell had been going through my mind that night, it was him.

I expected the shit smell of the toilets to hit me like they had way back when, but all I could smell was dirt, old brick and fresh wood since the innards of the factory were blocked off now with sturdy new construction. Liability. Not that I'd thought to sue whoever owned the place, since it wasn't as if the owner had put a gun to my head and forced me to stick my hand in that slot. The lobby was still open, though, since shoring up that crumbling outer wall would've involved a lot more than just blocking off a doorway. And since the voracious workbot that ate my hand was long gone.

Laughter. A knowing smile. I considered the slot. It was as empty as my sleeve. *Fire it up, Desmond. We'll crank the tunes.*

My voice was rough when I said to Jim, "I wasn't fucking Biggie, you know."

Jim grunted noncommittally.

Fire it up, Desmond. No, I wasn't fucking him. But I was so desperate for his approval, I might as well have been. I knew damn well what kind of damage a revolving-shift workbot could do. I knew the chumps who lived there had vandalized every square inch of the place, even if it meant breaking all the windows, then patching up the frames with cardboard when they realized they were getting rained on. Even rolling, I knew the job required a long shielded screwdriver and not a pocket knife. But Biggie gave me that look—the look that was bursting with unspoken promises of the kind I'd grown to fully understand—and I did what I'd always done.

I tried to please him. Whatever it took.

Standing in the very spot where I'd made the decision that tipped my life in an irrevocable direction, I strained to recall more detail. But all that came to me were the fleeting snatches I already remembered. The smell. The rain. The promises Biggie was using to manipulate me—promises he never intended to keep. Here I'd had Jim, a better man than I ever deserved, and I treated him like shit. But I bent over backwards to please Biggie.

I'm sorry didn't cut it, but it was better than nothing. I was turning to apologize to Jim when I caught a glimpse of graffiti on the wall, a Crowley Ave tag in spattered red spray paint, and memory flooded in.

Fire it up, Desmond. We'll crank the tunes.

With what? My magic wand?

A pocket knife pressed into my hand.

Juice. One of the lines still had juice—the line that powered the exit lights. None too easy to tap in the dark. But me, I knew my stuff. A clever splice and the PA system crackled to life...unfortunately, so did the cold, dead workbot.

The pain was indescribable, but it wasn't the pain I'd blocked out. Worse was that sick moment of knowledge that finally, I'd horribly, irrevocably fucked up. I staggered as I relived that piercing glimpse of my own stupidity when I saw how my repair was gonna all play out.

I gasped and turned away. Jim hovered, not knowing whether to give me space or comfort me.

The pain of my hand being crushed, even though the deed was already done and there was nothing there to hurt anymore, even though I could see as I sank to the ground that the workbot still had it, the whole fucking thing, all the way up past the wrist.

Get out of here, Biggie says. Go.

We gotta find a phone, someone says. We gotta call an ambulance.

With a wheeze, I knelt. Jim was repeating my name but it sounded really far away. Because feeling that pain and watching myself fall away from my hand was brutal...but that wasn't the thing I'd been so busy trying to hide from myself. That precious gem came back just as clear as if Biggie was with me again, right there, saying it all over again.

Don't bother.

I'd known Biggie since I was nine years old...I'd maimed myself trying to please him. I'm not sure what I expected to find in his gaze as he looked down at me. Panic? Sadness? Concern? None of those emotions were there. Nothing at all. The look on Biggie's face when he saw the wreck of me was utterly cold and flat.

I got no use for this faggot. If he can't jack the wiring, what good is he?

I'm surprised I didn't bleed out. One of the guys who'd been squatting there must've realized that having a corpse turn up in his flophouse would attract the kind of attention that might get somebody arrested. That's the best the cops can figure. Whoever called never took any credit for it, in fact, they didn't bother to wait for the ambulance. When the paramedics got there, they found me lying in a pool of blood, alone.

CHAPTER 25

The drive home wasn't awkward. I was too wiped out to feel awkward. The aftershocks of what I now remembered hurt like the hangover of a week-long bender. Jim didn't ask. I was glad. I didn't have the strength to explain.

He pulled into Mrs. Zelko's garage. Georgie Argusto was the last person I'd been there with—and I still had the remnants of a bruise under my stubble where he'd clocked me in the jaw. Maybe I should thank him. Could be his homophobic outburst that helped shake my stuck memory loose. Or maybe I should pay him a visit once I got my prosthetic back and return the love tap. Phobias are curable, evidently. And I'd be happy to provide the treatment.

Jim set the parking brake. "So what's going on with your license?"

"Road test is Friday."

"Not a good idea to practice alone. You'll get pulled over. It's just a matter of time."

"You're probably right, with my luck." Besides, I needed to get my arm back first. And then I needed someone to take me. Seeing Jim behind the wheel, watching him coax the Gray Lady out of a looming stall and enjoying the way he'd handled the turns made him the obvious choice. "So...would they give you a day off to drive me there?"

Jim got out of the car. I did the same. I'd figured he was mentally reviewing his schedule, seeing if there was anything he couldn't miss, anything he'd need to juggle. Maybe a day was too much. Maybe I should have only asked for a morning. But then I realized he wasn't working through the logistics at all. He was staring point blank at the Specials T-shirt hanging off the rake in the corner. He turned to me, nostrils flaring around the gunmetal post, and said, "Why doesn't that trust fund brat take you? Can't bear to miss his soap operas?"

"Forget about Corey." We were yelling again. Already. "And don't be so hard on him. You two have something in common—he can't stand the sight of me either."

Jim turned his glare toward the garage door. "So that's really why you tracked me down? You're on the outs with the new kid?"

Was that a trick question? Yes. No. Maybe, deep down inside, maybe. Goddammit. If Corey fought like a chick, Jim fought like a fucking shrink. "What do you want me to say?"

"Nothing—I want you to shut up. I'm not going to get back together with you, Desmond. I just...can't."

"I wasn't asking."

"You didn't have to." Jim pulled out a cigarette and lit it. Not only did he fail to light a smoke for me, he didn't even offer me one. He took a drag, exhaled through his nose like a bull pawing the ground, and said, "You're still wearing the padlock."

Fuck.

My heart sank, no, everything in me sank, and my eyes dropped immediately to the tool chest. Corey'd damn well known the difference between an adjustable wrench and a bolt-cutter. His latest temper tantrum really did have nothing to do with the car. Not a thing. And I was lucky he hadn't brained me with that goddamn tool.

Jim was halfway to the driveway when I reached for him, but there was nothing there to grab him with but an empty sleeve. "Jim," I called. "Wait."

He paused at the curb, but he didn't turn.

"I'm sorry. That's not good enough, I know. But I am."

Without another word, he strode off into the night.

※ ※ ※

On Monday morning the bus to Ivery's was packed, standing room only, but somehow I'd managed to exude enough menace to clear a barrier around myself a foot wide in every direction. My clothes were filthy, I reeked of half-metabolized vodka, and I'd gouged a deep cut along the side of my jaw when I discovered that my bolt-cutters were not ambidextrous after all. The fucking key was no better. With only a stump to hold the chain steady, I was useless. The padlock crawled around my neck like a living thing as I tried to unlock it. A couple of times, after hours of struggling in the mirror, I'd managed to fit the key in. Both times, it slipped right back out when I tried to turn it.

The result? I was hungover. I was frustrated. And I was mad enough to spit nails.

The entire ride, I seethed with the anticipation of grabbing that quack by her scrawny neck and shaking her 'til she surrendered my arm. By the time I got there, I could practically feel the sinews crunching in my grasp. I stormed up to her office full of piss and vinegar, and knocked so hard the doorframe shook. She must not have been expecting anything less. She looked at me steely-eyed and unflappable, and asked to see my worksheet. I panicked momentarily, then realized it was in my pocket, filled out with three different pens and everything. I dug it out and slapped it down on her desk with great satisfaction. She scanned it, shook her head, and said, "You filled this out in the same sitting without doing the exercise a single time."

Panic resurged. "The fuck I did."

"Further, I will not tolerate your tone. It's inappropriate, it's abusive, and it's threatening."

I'll show you threatening...that's what I meant to say. That's what anyone who'd fantasized about strangling her for the length of an hour-long bus ride would say. But now that I was faced with the probability of her refusing to cough up my arm, my bravado was gone like smoke in the wind. Instead I was throwing myself on that cold-hearted bitch's mercy. "Okay. You've got hoops you need to jump through. I get it. But I don't have time for cassette tapes and charts and robotic toys. I need my arm back."

Because without my arm, there'd be no road test. And without my road test, my car would rot in Mrs. Zelko's garage. By the off chance that I could convince Corey to give this boyfriend thing another shot, if I couldn't drive, eventually he would end up carting me around to my various penances—just like Jim had. And I had no intention of losing another decent man by turning him into some kind of fucking caregiver.

"It's not a matter of *jumping through hoops,* Mr. Poole. Systematic desensitization is a proven technique."

"So when can I have my arm back?"

"I'll return your arm once you do the exercises—actually do them—so I can assess your progress."

"I did the exercises," I said, though from the look she gave me it was clear she didn't buy it. "Listen to me, I can't wait another week."

"This treatment isn't about your short-term convenience—"

"And you're not about to waste resources on someone who won't get with the program. Okay. Fine. That's the way it is. But here's the thing." I jumped up and headed toward the office door. "The treatment won't do shit 'cause I'm not even robophobic." I jammed my hand into the officebot. It bleeped.

"Mr. Poole—"

"Maybe you can keep my prosthetic, but you can't keep me away from scanners, can you? Those fucking things are everywhere." I thrust my hand in again and it scanned out. And again, scan in. Bleep, bleep, bleep. "I'm not afraid of scanners. I just hate them. I hate the thought that anyone who knows how to tap into the system can figure out where I've been all week, where I am right now. I don't think anyone has the right to know what I choose to watch or listen to or eat. And I don't want my calls following me all over town, either. Not because I'm afraid, but because I only want to talk to somebody if I damn well feel like it."

To drive my point home, I stopped with my hand deep inside the scanner and held it there. The officebot scanned me out, but when I didn't clear the scanning mechanism, it flashed red a few times, then gave off a couple of blips, followed by something that sounded like a pre-robotic phone that'd been knocked off the hook. Was my anxiety at a zero? Hell, no. I now remembered getting my hand crushed in a scanner—in excruciating detail. Of course I was anxious. But I had a point to prove, and I would damn well prove it.

I waited for Ivery to argue with me, but she didn't. It was as if she'd frozen mid-word, mouth partially open, collarbones jutting at either side of her skinny neck, stretching toward a bit of understanding that was just out of reach. The officebot announced it had put a call in for repair, then shut itself down. The room was silent, except for my ragged breathing.

I allowed my meatworks hand to slide from the scanner. Ivery nodded slowly, then began to write in my file. I stood there, unable to argue if she refused to participate. She'd made some sort of decision, that much was plain from her focus on my file. So much for demanding my arm back. What was plan B, begging? Fine. If I had to beg, if I had to grovel on the floor for just half a chance at keeping Corey, I'd beg.

"Please...."

Ivery's head snapped up. Briskly, she said, "Mr. Poole, I've done all I can for you. It's my opinion that if you were ever robophobic, it's no longer the case." She pulled a familiar prosthetic-sized box out from behind her desk and set it on the far edge of the desktop with exaggerated care. "Since I'm not qualified to deal with your negativistic personality disorder, there's no need to make another appointment. Please show yourself out. I'll need the remainder of our time today to finish my notes."

CHAPTER 26

Since I'd managed to sway Dr. Ivery, I was hoping my powers of persuasion would extend to Corey. I could tell him that I missed him. He seemed like he would like that—though my chest started to ache when I said the words to myself. And when I looked at my empty couch and my empty bed and my empty life, and I compared it to the memory of watching Plan 9 from Outer Space on his big-screen TV together in our underwear with a belly full of cheese popcorn and Bloody Marys, I missed him even more.

I held my thumb over the 2-button to ring my call through, and I steeled myself to say, "Let's start this conversation over—just hear me out."

Instead of a ring tone there was a chime, but not the same chime as before, I realized. I'd been prepared for the phonebot to tell me I was calling the last location I'd scanned in. And instead it said, "This user's phone is unplugged. Goodbye."

Great. Now he was letting the phonebot do his dirty work.

I could hop on a bus and go see him. And he could tell me to piss off and slam his door in my face. Or he could refuse to buzz me in at all. The thought of both of those things made me feel even emptier than I already did. But then I spotted my uncle's old Polaroid Instamatic sitting on the bookshelf, and I decided that snubbed phone calls and spurned visits weren't my only two options.

Between the photo and the walk to the mailbox, it took less than half an hour to enact my grand scheme to get Corey back. It took three long days for me to get a response. I wasn't sure if that meant he needed time to think about it, or he didn't check his mailbox every day if he wasn't expecting his benefit check, or if it took the letter a day longer to go a few miles than I would have thought. I also wasn't sure if I should expect a phone call or a letter-bomb in return. What I got, though, was a visit. In person. Unannounced. Just my style.

My speaker-prodding stick made a good substitute gear shift. I was busy practice-shifting into second gear with my robo-arm when my intercom buzzed. "Can I come up?" Corey said. No lilting "Des-mond Poole." But hopefully it would be a start.

I opened my front door and waited for him to make his way up the stairs and down the hall. He was dressed to the nines in red plaid pants and a black bomber. And he had a Polaroid in his meatworks hand, tapping it against his robotic hand natural as you please. He paused in my doorway, looked down at the picture, then up at me, and said, "You wrote it in permanent marker?"

"I needed to make sure you saw it."

He tilted his head and studied my bare neck—which was a weird shade of gray-green where the nickel of the old hardware chain had rested against the skin all these years. Funny, how I hadn't realized how bad it was until I popped the lock and watched the chain slide off. It probably wasn't a permanent stain, but only time would tell.

"You're lucky I could even read it." He licked his thumb, then scrubbed at the corner of the message I'd laboriously printed across my own throat in thick black letters.

"In my defense, I did it in a mirror, left-handed."

"Thought so. The S's are backward." He held up the photo.

It wasn't the most flattering shot of me. It was out of focus and overexposed, and the top half of my head was out of frame. But the *I MISS YOU* that now lived in the spot where my chain and padlock used to be was loud and clear. Backwards S's and all. "By the time I realized I'd screwed up, I couldn't exactly go back and do it over."

He tucked the photo into his pocket. "Arguing with that would be the pot calling the kettle black. I've been known to go off half-cocked now and then myself." We stood there, anxious and awkward, both of us worried about saying or doing something that would break our fragile truce.

"So..." I said stupidly.

Corey shuffled his feet. "Aren't you gonna ask me in?"

"You don't need my permission." I stood to the side and he came in. I nudged the door shut with my foot, then followed close enough to catch a tantalizing whiff of vanilla.

We didn't quite make it to the living room. He turned and flung his arms around my neck while I caught him by the hips and backed him against the empty slot where our new Sea-Monkeys were cavorting around in their deluxe habitat like tiny bits of silt. We kissed with our entire bodies, grinding and panting, short of breath and ready to roll in no time flat. I was dizzy with wanting him—and me stone cold sober. Even though one of the hands raking through my hair was covered in unpleasantly grippy silicone, I didn't care. This was Corey. And I'd never known him any different.

His mouth skittered off mine. "Shit, I knew this would...look, before we get too carried away...."

I buried my face in his neck and breathed in his sweet candy scent, then released the breath in a bone-deep shudder.

"Hey, I mean it." He took my hair in both hands and angled my head so I couldn't help but meet his eyes. "I need to know. If I do this—then you and me, we're exclusive. Right?"

"Absolutely."

I dove back in for a taste of his neck while he let his breath out in a dreamy sigh. I'd thought maybe we were good to go, but he wasn't done negotiating. "It isn't just a matter of not fucking other people. In your heart, Des. Only me."

Obviously I wasn't going to get anywhere with Corey until we hashed this whole thing out. And frankly, it was long overdue. I planted my meatworks hand on one side of his head, and after a few clumsy, deliberate shrugs, mirrored the gesture with my prosthetic. "Here's the deal, Corey. There is no one but you. But if you want to be with me, keep this in mind: I'm no good. I'm drunk and lazy. I'm an asshole, always was, and on top of that, now I'm a gimp."

"And here I thought you hit support groups for the snacks."

"So you still want to sign on for this?"

He frowned. "If that's the song you've gotta sing, then yeah, I'm angling to hitch myself to the drunken asshole gimp. Just for the record, though, that's not how it is." It was killing me to keep eye contact, but the kid was so damn sincere, I couldn't bring myself to turn away. "When I look at you, what I see is a guy who always makes things ten times harder than they've gotta be. You need to struggle? Fine. Swim upstream if you have to...but not when it comes to us. We're amazing together, you and me. So stop fucking things up."

I could hardly promise something that wasn't under my conscious control, but having him there pressed up against me after I'd figured I lost him for good, I resolved to give it my best shot. "Okay. No more fuck-ups."

The look in his eyes said *I'll believe it when I see it*. But then his gaze dropped to my neck, and he scanned the clumsy lettering, *I MISS YOU*, half-assed backwards and slightly faded. The set of his jaw softened and his dark eyes got a little dewy.

"I did miss you," I insisted. "Something fierce."

He considered me for a moment, then nailed me with some killer eye contact and said, "Oh yeah?" He tipped me away from him with the gentle push of a single robotic index finger, then hitched up the front of his T-shirt. Right across his treasure trail, he'd penned the words *PROVE IT*.

Easy. While it was doubtful I'd win any Golden Dinguses for Boyfriend of the Year, I was an old pro at giving head. I dropped to my knees and got to work on undoing his waistband. I went at it left-handed, mostly. But I'd been practicing a tight-fingered scoop shape for my driving test, and I flicked into that gesture to wedge my prosthetic fingertips between waistband and stomach, allowing more play for my other hand. Corey gave a small gasp and I glanced up, worried I'd somehow managed to mangle the message. He was watching me hard, staring at my right hand. "I think you just blew my mind."

"Then I'm way off. I was aiming for your dick."

My attempt at lightening the mood fell flat. He didn't laugh.

Instead he dropped his meatworks hand to my head and cradled it gently, bracing me for a look of tenderness so intense it should have killed me on the spot. I survived the burden of his sympathy, somehow. And somehow I managed to get his fly open, but pulling down those skin-tight pants was another matter. For all that Corey usually got off on helping me, at that moment, he didn't. Or wouldn't. He watched and he waited, and somehow my determined struggling was amplifying the desperation in us both. Once I'd peeled those tight plaid pants down to his thighs, the seal was broken, and I shoved them down to his ankles with a whuff of triumph.

I ran my fingers up both of his thighs. While I couldn't feel that touch with one of those hands, Corey could. I went slow, and even though I was being careful, I felt a jolt of panic when I thought I'd bruised him. But no, it was just a glimpse of his ink, tattooed music notes hugging the curve of his thigh. He stroked my hair as I kissed my way up the scale. I lingered at his hip, swirling my tongue over the last note, and wondered if the thing I wanted to ask him was crazy. And then I figured that given the amount of head-shrinking I seemed to require, it probably was. I said it anyway. "You should play for me sometime."

He shook his head with a sad smile.

"Is it that you can't?" I asked. "Or you won't?"

"Neither. I don't want to." No doubt Dr. Ivery would have a bunch of conclusions to scribble about that response. "I'm through with all of that. Makes no sense to keep reminding myself about something I almost had."

But what was that "something," exactly? I couldn't imagine he'd been hoping to march in parades for the rest of his life. Had he been aiming for a seat in an orchestra, or something more fun, like a regular touring band? He didn't need a college degree for any of that, so the only thing in his way was the robo-hand.

Back when I'd first met Corey and I'd seen him pick a single peanut out of the snack bowl, his accuracy with his limb looked like nothing short of voodoo. I had no doubt he was capable of the fine gestures it would take to play again. They wouldn't be the same gestures he was accustomed to making, though. The brain didn't talk to the new limb in exactly the same way it communicated with a real arm. All those moves needed to be relearned. While Corey was perfectly willing to erase the old meatworks programming for all those mundane gestures that didn't really matter, he couldn't bring himself to override the moves that mattered to him most.

None of that made any real difference, since his talent didn't come from his hands...but I doubted he felt that way now that he'd lost one.

"Doesn't have to be the sax. Any band would be crazy not to grab you. You'd make a great frontman—you'd look awesome behind a mic."

"And you'd look awesome with my dick in your mouth."

That was all bravado. I let it slide. If anyone knows what it's like to be unable to face your own demons, it's me.

A few good licks was all it took to get him hard, and then I went deep. I had a brief flash of disorientation when he pushed into my throat, met resistance, and went deeper. For a moment, I was back in Ivery's office, unboxing my arm so I could jam my stump in. Despite the compression bandage I'd kept on it all week, there was some shift in the residual arm. The socket felt familiar and strange, all at once. And here, now, I was the socket.

I braced myself and welcomed his meat.

Nothing else mattered, the sound of actuators whirring in my right ear where he held my head in his hands, or the phantom-limb feeling I had that told me I was grabbing him by both hips. We were stuck with our robotics, nothing could change that. What mattered was the point where our meatworks met.

I put everything I had into sucking him off, my fear and apprehension and need, my whole heart and soul—and by the time he spilled down my throat, he was practically sobbing. We fit together, Corey and me. Yeah, we were broken, and maybe it wasn't always pretty, but together the two of us could be whole.

CHAPTER 27

November rain dotted the Gremlin's windshield. I was watching it, lulled by the patter, when something hit the glass with a gentle tap. Snow. Not a real snowfall, but the hard-pellet type of snow that scatters in the wind like BBs. From his spot in the driver seat, Corey found the wipers without me having to remind him where they were. No surprise—Corey's a fast learner. He even got his m-class license before I did. Scored the damn thing while I was waiting to take yet another road test. Turned out the titanium arm was the least of my problems. I should've been more worried about my lead foot.

More snow, gathering along the wiper blades. They'd need replacing before a big snowfall came. The car always needed patching up, but in the end it kept on running. Kind of like Corey and me. I suppose keeping my Gray Lady on the road gave me something to do, what with me being an unemployed gimp, at least until springtime when the custom gardenbot biz started picking up.

I wasn't the type of guy that potential buyers would trust with thousands of dollars. Too rough. Too shifty. Too likely to scoop up their deposit and never be seen again. Good thing Luis had a trustworthy face. Despite being burdened with two robotic arms, he did the scouting, the selling and even the majority of the work. Since I had the license, he called me in to hook up the wiring. It was nowhere near as lucrative as running my own custom gardenbot business, but that was probably for the best. If I ran a legitimate business, I'd have to pay legitimate taxes, and I was just as happy having Luis slip me a few hundred under the table for an hour of my time. My needs weren't much. Rent is crazy cheap in Riverside.

Maybe that wouldn't be the case forever. Every so often, someone got a notion in his head that riverfront property was valuable—never mind the rotting silos and warehouses a couple miles down the road—and they'd convince investors to throw money into reviving a local business. The tavern at the foot of Hertel was like that. I only went there once in a blue moon since their booze was overpriced and their jukebox sucked. Their wings weren't half bad, though, and on ten-cent wing night, you could eat your fill for a couple of bucks. Too bad the wing night poster was gone now. Just like the old façade. And the torn awning. And the yellowed Schlitz sign.

"You told me this place was a dive," Corey said. "Looks pretty ritzy to me."

"Well, we're here. Might as well see what's what."

"I'm not dressed to eat somewhere nice." No, probably not. Corey required at least another hour of primping before he felt he was presentable enough to get hot sauce all over his face. "Go see if they'll do takeout."

I gave him a sarcastic bow with an exaggerated flourish, then headed into the refurbished tavern to scope out the possibility of dinner. If it was a bust, no big deal. You can't walk ten paces in Buffalo without tripping over a chicken wing; at least ten other pizzerias and bars within a stone's throw could use the business. It turned out takeout was available, though prices had risen just as steeply as you'd imagine. I put in an order anyway. Whatever we might blow on overpriced wings, we'd save by having our drinks at home. While I was waiting for the food, I tried to dredge up more details from my memory of the tavern. Dark wood paneling was gone, exposed brick was in. A broken down pool table had been laid to rest, and a small dance floor was now in its place. Flickering neon beer signs had been supplanted by local "art." I fidgeted. I glanced at the clock. I squirmed around some more. And finally my bladder made a decision for me, a decision I'd been so pointedly trying not to make.

The john was different.

Of course it was different. One look at the old men's room would guarantee any new clientele would high tail it out and never return. There was no crusty tile, no reeking urinal, no cracked mirror. But the bones of it were the same. I planted my feet in the spot where I'd first laid eyes on James fucking Murphy, and I allowed myself to remember that fateful night. I stood there for quite a while, just thinking. When the creak of the door announced another customer was about to intrude on my reverie, I headed for a stall. *The* stall. But then our eyes met in the new mirror, and recognition rocked me to my core.

Jim filled the doorway, filled his leather jacket, filled the space. The new bathroom lighting glinted off his facial hardware. His head was shaved, and his eyes looked all the more striking with no hair to distract from them. To see if it really was him, or if my brain was just playing tricks on me by dredging up a figment from my past, I said out loud, "You still come here?"

"My cousin tends bar."

I vaguely remembered that. Okay, not really. "I'm just waiting for my food."

"Alone?"

"Corey's in the car."

I expected some sneering remark about whether he was old enough to drive, so I was shocked when instead Jim said, "I've been thinking about all the shit I gave you over Steiner. Don't get me wrong, that kid gets on my very last nerve. But you and him…maybe you really are perfect for each other."

"But you—"

"Listen to me, Des. I met someone." He said it all in a rush, like he was worried he might not have the guts to tell me—and him the courageous one. I felt a pang in response, a sharper pang than I might have imagined. But also a sense of relief. "It made me realize it was never fair for me to be pissed at you for dating again. I was mad at you, no sense in denying it. Corey's got a lot of growing up to do. But maybe for you to know someone who's actually good with a robotic arm—seeing that someone with a prosthetic can still be young and hot, with their whole life still ahead of them, a life where good things might even start to come their way again...maybe it's exactly what you needed. Hope."

Most times I took things like hope for granted. But not now, not in the face of Jim. He reached out for me and cupped my jaw, and I leaned into his big, strong hand. He tilted his head and gave me a sad smile—and, I think, there was actually pity there, the pity he'd never once given me when he was massaging my sore shoulder after physical therapy or dabbing antibiotic ointment on my scabs. "You're better off after a couple of months with Corey than you ever were with me."

No, it wasn't pity, it was sadness, or maybe regret. What the hell did he have to be sorry for when he'd done everything right, and it was me who'd pissed it all away? I would have protested, but he leaned in and shut me up with a kiss. Two years with Jim came flooding back to me—and nine months without. And the realization that I'd been missing something a lot more in those past nine months than I'd been missing my right hand. I'd been missing Jim's body putting a dent in my mattress, and Jim's hard stubble chafing my cheek like coarse-grit sandpaper. Jim's tender acceptance of me, not just some image of me in a leather jacket and an attitude, but the real me, stripped naked, in all my vulnerable uselessness.

His lips were parted when his mouth crashed down on mine. Mine were too, mostly with shock. I expected him to hold back, but he didn't. He seized my lower lip in his, sucked it, then filled my mouth with that powerful tongue of his—and more memories came flooding back, like the way he would only kiss me when, and if, he absolutely meant it.

I felt brittle under the force of his kiss, like the shell of a rusted tailpipe left over after too many hard winters, ready to crumble from the next pothole hit—because I knew that this kiss meant goodbye. "I wish...."

He turned away and I grabbed for him with no hope of actually stopping him. Jim is a force of nature, and I'd be just as likely to stop storm clouds from rolling in once the barometer falls as I would be to keep him once he'd made his mind up to leave. Except a funny thing happened before either of us realized it. I did manage to catch him—with my right hand. Which did indeed stop him.

He stared down at my prosthetic with undisguised wonder. The fingers were curled around his forearm just like human fingers. "Every last doubt I had about Corey...it's gone now."

"That's one of the easier gestures," I admitted. "Once you get your head right."

A flick of my right shoulder, and my hand released Jim with a gentle whir of the activators. He took back his arm and ran his fingertips over it as if to test whether what had just happened was real. I wanted to tell him I was sorry, that I'd been a shitty excuse for a boyfriend, and in fact I was never good enough for him, when he beat me to the punch by saying, "I'm glad that's working out for you. You deserve to be happy."

After all I'd put Jim through? Probably not. But I knew better than to piss away this last chance at happiness.

I don't normally think of Corey as being young, but when I slid into my passenger seat and saw him there behind the Gray Lady's wheel instead of Jim, I couldn't help but notice it was true. He was young. And lean, and graceful, and striking. His dark eyes had a twinkle to them even when he wasn't smiling, though when he turned to me, more often than not, that infectious smile did appear.

"Hope you didn't forget the extra blue cheese," he said.

"Perish the thought." Though if I'd run into Jim before I ordered, I probably wouldn't have been able to articulate my own name, let alone remember what we wanted to eat. We rode home in silence. Corey needed a lot more focus for the road than he did in his Servo. Normally I razz him about riding the clutch, but he got some peace and quiet since I was still shaking off the cling of memory. When we pulled into Mrs. Zelko's garage and Corey cut the engine, he lingered an extra moment in the car. I was halfway out when I realized he was still just sitting there, so I paused with one foot on the concrete pad and looked at him expectantly.

"So," he said. "I was thinking. I'm glad we're staying in."

Had he come inside the tavern while I was ordering?

Had he seen Jim?

Shit.

I swallowed cautiously and waited, and after searching for his words, he went on. "Out there in the parking lot, on one of the telephone poles, there was a flier for a band I was in. Before. In high school. Guess they're doing all right now. Headlining, even. And I thought some more about what you said a couple weeks ago, about me playing again." He raked his hair back from his forehead with his robo-arm. The gesture was effortless, and chillingly accurate. "I'm through with the sax. It was supposed to be my ticket out of the rust belt. It was gonna take me somewhere big, New York or LA or London, y'know? And it let me down."

The sax is just an inanimate object, like a prosthetic—but without the fancy graphite circuitry or the grippy silicone sheath. The sax wasn't at fault in Corey's failure any more than my prosthetic was in mine. It was Corey who'd let himself down, and Corey who felt the need to keep punishing himself for it.

I was trying to figure out how to tell him so without sounding like a Jim Murphy when he added, "I don't think I'm cut out for being a frontman either. I don't really care too much about lyrics. Plus, when you front a band, you need to have half your head with the band and half with the audience—except, really, you need your whole brain for either. I worry if I landed that gig, my priorities would shift. If my job was to make the crowd love me, I'd get so wrapped up in the performance aspect of playing that eventually the music would suffer."

Just yesterday, I'd needed to explain to him that South America was a continent but South Africa was a country. What the hell happened, did he re-engage his brain when I wasn't looking? He'd taken the conversation so far over my head, I had nothing whatsoever to add.

"So if I did play again, it would need to be something else."

I dropped my meatworks hand to his knee and gave it a squeeze. He thought a moment more, then said, "Drums. I want to play the drums."

"You'll kick ass." I had no doubt.

We locked up the garage and headed toward my botless apartment arm in arm. The takeout bag swung securely from my prosthetic, while Corey lit a cigarette with his. I had to release him to unlock the vestibule door, where I proceeded to ignore the corner of a yellow envelope peeking out from my overstuffed mailbox. At the sight of those four mailboxes, though, I thought of my neighbors, one of whom works third shift and gets really pissy over the volume of the TV. "You got room in your apartment for a drum set?" I asked.

"Hell, no. But that's the beauty part." We tumbled into my apartment and he flattened me against the wall. As he explored my mouth, I wondered if he'd taste Jim on me. It was unlikely. He's a pretty heavy smoker. When he drew back to look at me, he had that impish twinkle in his eye, and I felt my guts relax. Corey and me—we were good. He nuzzled my cheek and said, "My folks would spring for the kit, and I'd practice over at Hugh's house."

"Hah. That's fucking brilliant. Pam's gonna shit a brick."

"No doubt about it, I'm the man with the plan."

I dragged the ghost of a kiss across his lower lip, and murmured, "That's what I love about you."

ABOUT THE AUTHOR

Though Jordan Castillo Price has made some ridiculous prank calls, she never stole a lighter. She was a bookish kid who spent long hours of her tweendom at the Riverside Public Library, drawing comics and crushing on a librarian.

jordancastilloprice.com

ACKNOWLEDGMENTS

Special thanks to all my early readers and helpers. Without their contributions, I wouldn't have finished this challenging project. In the most formative parts of the writing, prosthetist Honkeytonk Fil was generous with his anecdotes and advice. Without his help, I wouldn't have even known where to begin my research. At the other end of the process, Andy Slayde not only cleaned up the manuscript, she surprised me by pointing out various places in which she found Desmond Poole relatable! Aniko Laczko and Elizabeth Zinkham also helped me immensely by giving the novel a final spit-polish.

During the writing phase, my Madison critique group was invaluable. I'm grateful to romance writer L.C. Giroux for reading out of her comfort zone, and I'm pleased she was compelled to know what happened to Desmond even though she wanted to kill him. Fantasy author Mercy Loomis gave valuable guidance on handling the Social Services aspect of Desmond's conundrum, and a wonderful big-picture view of the flow of the story. Our resident scientist, Mark Anderson, helped me figure out what the robotic stuff might feasibly be made of, along with the gratifying observation, "This is not a gentle read." Reviewer Joe Alfano's incisive comments on the way he saw the characters' motivations shaping their actions was a great barometer for me to see if their internal logic was playing out realistically. And Jesi Lea Ryan, YA author, somehow managed to see a deep vulnerability in Desmond that she could empathize with, which gave me hope that maybe other readers could connect with that facet of him too.

As for completing the darn novel, I needed my online writing partners to take me by the arms and help me limp across the finish line when I thought my will to keep writing was tapped out. Piper Vaughn read the story at various stages of completion, multiple times, to help me determine if and how it might fit in the m/m genre. Meanwhile, Dev Bentham gave me steadfast daily (sometimes hourly) support and encouragement when I was at the bleakest middle-phase of the project.

I couldn't have done it alone. Thank you all.

Made in United States
Orlando, FL
22 February 2025